DON PENDLETON'S

STONY

AMERICA'S ULTRA-COVERT INTELLIGENCE AGENCY

MAN®

EXTERMINATION

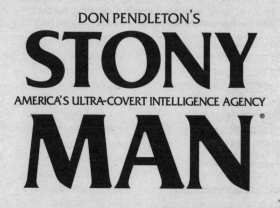

D0057552

A GOLD EAGLE BOOK FROM

W⊕RLDWIDE®

TORONTO • NEW YORK • LONDON
AMSTERDAM • PARIS • SYDNEY • HAMBURG
STOCKHOLM • ATHENS • TOKYO • MILAN
MADRID • WARSAW • BUDAPEST • AUCKLAND

Recycling programs
for this product may
not exist in your area.

First edition October 2011

ISBN-13: 978-0-373-61999-3

EXTERMINATION

Special thanks and acknowledgment to
Doug Wojtowicz for his contribution to this work.

"KEEP THIS QUIET OR NO PART OF YOUR NATION WILL BE SPARED THE WRATH OF GREENWAR."

"You must bid higher than your opponent. The opening bid is one-fifth of your nation's population. Those willing to sacrifice the most people will survive total extinction. Those willing to resist will be completely exterminated."

Bezoar smiled, though there was no mirth or warmth in it. "Have a nice day, sir."

The video ended.

Brognola felt as if he had to scrub himself down. He'd only been watching for ten minutes, but the horror carried the weight of hours. He set down the small smartphone, plucked out a handkerchief and mopped his brow.

"They either have someone inside Homeland Security or they have good spies. Given the aerial footage…" the President began. He rested a hand on Brognola's shoulder. "Stony Man is our only option. Bezoar is insane, asking for me to kill one in five people."

The smartphone beeped. The two men looked at it.

It was a text message.

"France has a bid to kill one of every two of its citizens. Make up your mind quickly."

The Oval Office fell silent as the specter of doom hung over the big Fed and the leader of the free world.

EXTERMINATION

CHAPTER ONE

One of the things that Trooper Eugene Robespierre liked about the state he'd sworn to protect was that all of Iowa felt like a small town. He was one of less than four hundred state troopers who saw to the safety of the roads and supplemented local law enforcement. His Ford Crown Victoria was fifty miles out of Lansing, the end of Iowa Highway 9 and this current leg of his patrol. In Lansing he'd spell himself for the night before returning to the District 10 barracks back on Oelwein. This was a once-a-month roll for Robespierre, mainly because this corner of Iowa was quiet. The road twisted and bent to find the path of least resistance between the rippling hills and strips of farmland.

"Unit 327, Unit 327, call in," his radio chirped.

Robespierre picked up the receiver. "I'm here, Janice. What's going on?"

"We've got a call from the Allamakee Sheriff's Department about a problem in the town of Albion," the dispatcher, Janice Clayton, told him.

"Problem?" Robespierre asked.

"It seems like there's a riot in Albion," Clayton said.

Robespierre had never been near Albion, a quiet little stretch of farmland that had never boasted more than six hundred souls. The town had been so peaceful, the only reason he knew anything about it was that his best friend had been born and raised there, and railed about how absolutely boring the place had been.

"Riot," he repeated. He was already turning back to the west. The computer beside him in the squad car was already determining the best route to Albion by GPS. From what Robespierre remembered, Albion was a place where everyone was well fed. It wasn't in the cornfields of central Iowa, but this area still had pockets of farmland between rows of trees and the rolling hills. Some were conventional crop fields, but a few orchards were sprinkled here and there. Even as he gunned the engine, racing toward Albion, he noticed that something akin to a tornado had landed by the roadside.

He stomped on the brakes, skidding to a halt beside a fruit stand that had been assaulted. Broken, half-eaten fruit was scattered everywhere, and there were bodies littered among the mushy remains. Robespierre pulled his radio.

"Dispatch, we've got eight casualties at roadside, by marker 12," the trooper called. He hit the dash computer, transmitting his GPS position to the barracks.

"We're aware of them. All were announced DOA by the local sheriffs' deputies," Clayton replied.

"He left the bodies out here?" Robespierre asked, sliding out from behind the wheel to get a closer look. It might have been a trick of the light, or smears of mashed fruit, but a couple of the corpses on the ground looked as if bites had been taken out of them. Another body lay just outside the carnage of twisted corpses and pulped food. The man had been wearing flannel, the front of his shirt hanging in ragged strips where it had been torn by the unmistakable violence of a twelve-gauge shotgun. Unlike some of the others lying amid the ruins and carcasses, his face was fully visible. There was no apparent reason as to why he had been shot, except for the fact that his belly was distended to the point where shirt buttons around his stomach had popped off.

"The hell?" Robespierre muttered, hoping someone was out there who could give him an answer.

"Robey, you need to get to town," Clayton replied. "The deputies are in deep shit. They need backup now!"

Robespierre turned back, but he had seen more that was unusual among the dead.

One of them, a young woman, had apparently asphyxiated trying to swallow gulps of squash. Her belly was distended, too, recalling the images of horror from Ethiopian and Somali droughts. The woman's mouth and cheeks were stuffed with a choking mass of pulp, her crazed eyes wide with terror.

She'd literally eaten herself to death, and Robespierre looked to see half-eaten fruit scattered in a trail leading back to Albion. "How many deputies are on scene?"

"Three of them, but they're running out of ammunition," Clayton answered. "I've also diverted more troopers, but you might want to make sure you have easy access to your rifle."

"Running out of ammo," Robespierre repeated. "Are they in a restaurant or a grocery store?"

"Uh…no. A delivery truck, refrigerated, for produce," Clayton said. "How did you know the call-in was about a food riot?"

"Because I saw the damage done at a roadside fruit stand," Robespierre told her. "I don't get it. There's all kinds of food around, and these people are scrambling to down so much that they choke on it?"

He'd reached the rise of a hill and looked down on the small town of Albion. Bodies were strewed in the road running through the center of town, and fires had broken out in different corners of the little burg. Robespierre looked at the Smith & Wesson Military and Police 15 rifle locked into its dashboard rack. The weapon was one of the latest M-16 clones built by various companies foreign and domestic, but the M&P was the same "brand" as the .40-caliber pistol on his hip, so the Iowa state troopers had received a deal on both sidearms and patrol rifles. Robespierre had enjoyed shooting the MP-15; it was accurate and wasn't prone to jamming like other M-16 knockoffs, but this would be the first time he'd have to utilize it in an actual fight.

Gunfire crackled in the distance, and from the sound of things, it was more than just a few deputies firing. This was a back-and-forth gunfight; no surprise here since rural communities and guns went hand-in-hand. Almost every household had a gun rack of some sort, and more than a couple had full-size safes. But these were sporting arms, legally purchased and owned, not the stolen outlaw arms that were smuggled into cities with weapons bans that only ended up disarming law-abiding citizens. Raging gun battles just didn't happen in small, friendly communities where everyone had jobs and the means to support themselves.

But now, that had all changed, Robespierre realized.

People were starving so badly that they risked shot-gun blasts or gorged until their throats swelled and suffocated themselves. Now they were taking any means necessary to find a way to fill their starving gullets. That meant that someone between them and their food would have to die. Hunting rifles and shotguns might have been far too much for handgun-equipped deputies to deal with, unless starvation had been severely detrimental to their marksmanship.

Robespierre didn't know what to expect, but he saw the refrigerated truck, bodies sprawled around in a battlefield of pure carnage. His Zeiss binoculars were sharp enough to give him a crystal clear view of the siege. Sweeping the scene, he saw one of the county deputy cars peppered with bullet holes. The fender hung off it like fluttering, ragged wallpaper, it had been blasted so ferociously. Deer-hunter rifles and 12-gauge buckshot were devastating against body armor, and even the fiberglass and metal of a squad car could be weakened so drastically with perforations that it fluttered like a tattered flag.

"Clayton, can you put me through to the deputies?" Robespierre asked as he adjusted the collapsible stock on his MP-15. His rifle was sighted in for point-blank at 100 yards, but the distance he looked at now was closer to 250. Immediately, he recalled his training class. The M-16's classic 5.56 mm NATO round was lighter and much flatter shooting than the rifles Robespierre had grown up with. He'd have to trust the micrometer flip-up sights to not undershoot at the gunmen harrying his fellow lawmen. While he'd heard that abbreviated M-16s in the Gulf and Afghanistan had proved to be less than fully effective at long distances, the Iowa DPS had assured him that those failures were with rifles with barrels two inches shorter, and utilizing standard military ball ammunition. None of the alleged shortcomings were apparent in the hands of marksmen who placed their shots well.

"You're hooked up now, Robey," Clayton said over the radio.

"How many troopers we have here?" a deputy asked.

"Just one," Robespierre said. "But backup's on the way. What's the situation down there?"

"I've got one officer down and bleeding badly," came the response. "And there's six crazies with guns still active around us. I'm on my last five shots."

Robespierre hoped that his sights were tuned correctly as he pulled the trigger on the MP-15, spitting a single projectile out of the barrel. The 5.56 mm bullet struck the metal of a railing 250 yards away, sparks flying and causing one of the food-caked gunmen only inches from the point of impact to flinch, rifle slipping from his hands. Robespierre's heart hammered as he realized that he'd taken a shot at another human being. As a lawman, his job was to save and protect lives, not take them, and shooting someone in the back was something he hadn't anticipated.

This wasn't a wild canine stalking a chicken coop or an injured farm animal that had been mortally wounded by a car; this was a fellow American citizen. Robespierre pulled the trigger again, nerves getting to him as his finger jerked hard, pulling the weapon off target.

The second shot made another of the marauding rifle-men stumble, and he realized that it was a teenage boy, his face smeared with crusted food. His shirt buttons had popped around his belly, exposing livid red welts where the skin and tissue had split from where his belly had expanded. The kid collapsed to the ground with enough force that his overstretched stomach burst, coils of stuffed intestine rolling out of splits in the skin.

Robespierre recoiled mentally from the horror of what had happened to the kid he'd just shot.

"Christ, not another popper," the deputy groaned.

"Another?" Robespierre asked.

"These guys are crammed full of shit that's been sitting in their guts for days. None of it's digested," the deputy explained. "Look out, they're heading up toward you."

"Then get out of there," Robespierre said. "I've got their attention."

"You can handle this?" the deputy asked.

Robespierre tried to tame the butterflies that whirled in his stomach, but managed the strength to lie. "I got this."

The windshield of his Crown Vic suddenly violently shuddered, a fist-size hole punched through it. One of the remaining gunmen had cut loose with his bolt-action rifle, a powerful .30-caliber deer-hunting round easily penetrating the squad-car-quality safety glass. Another bullet made a loud crunch against the grille of the car, steam suddenly spitting out of the cracks between the hood and the fenders. Robespierre, even crouched behind the door of his car, had to recoil from the sudden wave of heat blowing over him. Other guns boomed downrange, but nothing came close. They were either pistol-caliber carbines or they were shotguns, unable to reach all the way up to the squad car.

It was a small consolation. Robespierre was half blinded by steam and he was in no mood to go up against a group of people who might as well have just been more victims than madmen.

Suddenly, the world seemed to go silent around Robespierre. A weight built up in the trooper's chest, an oppressive force that seemed to crush his ribs and threatened to burst his lungs and heart. He glanced down at his chest and saw that his uniform blouse was darkening, growing slick against his chest. The squad car's door had smoke curling through a hole that hadn't been there before and Robespierre toppled helplessly away from the squad car, gasping and trying to fill his lungs.

He'd worn his vest, but the bullet, after cutting through sheet metal and the car's interior wall, had gone through his side, only clipping the edge of his Kevlar. The overwhelming trauma of the impact was not an indication of the lethality of the hit, thankfully. The .30-caliber slug had shattered a rib and entered Robespierre's thoracic cavity, but it had miraculously avoided brachial arteries, coming to a stop as it deformed against the man's shoulder blade. With the scapula and rib broken, Robespierre felt as if he were being crushed by a python. The effects would be lethal if the internal bleeding wasn't stopped.

He wasn't dead, though his mind was completely out of the fight. He'd taken the hit, and like most human beings, he equated severe injury from a gunshot wound with the end. Finally, he sucked in a breath, and it felt like heaven, his senses starting to clear.

Blurry-eyed, he rolled his head, looking under the car door. There was movement downhill, and through the fog between his ears, he could finally hear the chatter of gunfire. He wanted to speak up, to continue shooting and fighting back, helping the deputies on hand.

"Get up," he croaked to himself, reaching out to the door handle for leverage. "Your brothers need help."

With that and the strength of his uninjured left arm, Robespierre was able to haul himself off the asphalt, the car door creaking under the unnatural pressure put upon it by the wounded trooper.

"Statie? You still alive up there?" came a call over his radio.

"I'll have…back…you…that," Robespierre grunted out loud, each breath feeling like a dagger plunged into the right side of his chest. He could have sworn he'd sounded more eloquent, less bestial, when he was trying to revive himself. "You?"

"We're fine," the deputy replied. "You distracted them enough for us to put the last of the crazies down."

Robespierre rested his head against the padding under the window of his car door. "Got hit."

"Damn, why didn't you say something?"

"No chance," Robespierre replied. He could already hear Clayton's excited voice over the patrol car's dash radio, calling for medical assistance.

"Be fine," Robespierre added, hanging on for dear life. He wasn't having trouble breathing now, but he was starting to feel light-headed. The blood was dark, nonarterial, which was good news. If it was an artery, his chances of survival would be lessened considerably. Veinous and capillary blood wasn't what fed his body the vital reserves of oxygen it needed to keep going, though eventually blood loss was going to become a life-threatening factor. Most of his incapacitation was due to the nearly paralyzing pain of broken bones.

The deputies were fairly distant, but they were making good time racing up the incline toward his car. Robespierre also heard the distant whir of a propeller growing louder, cutting through the ringing in his ears from the brief gun battle he engaged in. Even outside, the MP-15 patrol rifle put out a considerable wave of pressure and sound that had funneled into the interior of the squad car and rebounded, making his right ear full of a pealing whine set to drive him nuts.

He turned his attention toward the approaching aircraft, wondering if the Iowa State Police had dispatched a helicopter. Robespierre didn't think it could happen this quickly, but he was glad for the arrival. The faster he got to a hospital, the faster his bleeding and broken bones could be taken care of.

He didn't see a helicopter, nor even a Cessna-style prop plane. The approaching craft looked akin to a torpedo with long, slender wings.

"'Zat?" Robespierre asked Clayton, slurring "what's that" into a single utterance.

"You have something in the air by you?" Clayton returned. "Nothing has been dispatched."

Through the fog of his traumatized mind, Robespierre recognized the odd object as it crawled slowly closer to him like a white, ramrod-straight maggot. He'd seen it on TV on a show about military weapons hosted by a bald guy who whispered dramatically to the point where he seemed more like a caricature than a soldier.

Global Hawk, the name came in a breathless, hushed tone pulled from the show. The wings seemed wrong, with cylinders nestled up beneath its pale belly.

This Hawk, came the host's voice again, *has talons.*

"No…it couldn't be," Robespierre said to himself, his internal dialogue indeed clearer.

"Robey?" Clayton called over the radio. "What did you croak about?"

"Global Hawk," Robespierre repeated, putting every ounce of strength into getting the name right.

"What?"

The unmanned drone soared over the squad car, and as it did so, two of the cylinders detached from the wing points. Robespierre tapped his sagging reserves of energy once again, hauling himself behind the dashboard of the car as he saw them release.

"Cover!" he bellowed into his radio.

He wondered if the warning was in time, then he heard a loud, powerful thump in the distance. The windshield suddenly cracked as if struck with a sledge-hammer, the glass turning white with fractures as the flexible polymer core sandwiched between the panes did its job, preventing razor-sharp shards from flying into the interior of the car. The squad car, being a hundred feet from the blast center, had absorbed the wave of three pounds per square inch of increased air pressure, the roll cage and safety glass absorbing the shock wave that proved powerful enough to fold the metal struts holding up traffic signs.

Robespierre remained safe and conscious for the fifteen minutes it took for backup and an ambulance to arrive at the quiet town of Albion. What the trooper hadn't noticed, thanks to the impact of a rifle bullet into his thoracic cavity, was a prior explosion at the fruit stand he'd paused at, where he'd seen the remnants of people who ate until their throats clogged or were maddened enough by hunger to charge a man holding a shotgun. The previous blast had turned the roadside attraction and the corpses around it into vapor, the combined force of two 500-pound laser-guided bombs more than sufficient to produce a thirty-meter-wide crater where any body parts found would have been made of ash or crumpled, blast-shattered bone.

The town had been rocked by more than just two of the canisters. Robespierre had been shell-shocked for the devastating explosion, missing the other two bombs that had been part of the MQ-9 Reaper's 3800-pound payload. The MQ-9 was far different from the jet-engine-powered Global Hawk RQ-4, precisely for the propeller wash that had convinced the trooper that an aircraft had been approaching. Its six 500-pound dumb bombs had been more than enough to turn Albion into a smoldering crater—actually, two huge butterfly-shaped craters easily thirty meters wide. Even though Iowa was in the dreaded tornado alley of the central United States, the construction of the town hadn't been sturdy enough to deal with the overpressure that flattened brick walls and turned wood to splinters.

Only Robespierre's distance from ground zero, and the bloody mess he'd been reduced to, had spared him as the Reaper's operator assumed he was likely mortally wounded. Had the trooper shown more signs of life than sagging against a car door, the drone's operator would have used one of the wing-mounted AGM Hellfire missiles on the squad car, turning it into a mass of twisted wreckage.

It was a bit of overconfidence and laziness on the drone crew's part. Not only did there exist a living witness to the carnage of Albion, but there was also dashcamera footage of a renegade, heavily armed unmanned aerial vehicle blowing a town on American soil to oblivion.

THE RINGING of a phone jarred Hermann "Gadgets" Schwarz from his sleep, and his head popped up from the pillow. In the dark hotel room's other bed, Schwarz's best friend, Rosario "Politician" Blancanales, continued to snore. According to the luminous dial on Schwarz's watch, it was a little after five in the afternoon.

Able Team, a three-man counterterrorism and anticrime squad, had been hunting leads from the shadows of evening past the crack of dawn.

This particular hunt had brought them to Chicago, and the search was on for the steering and laser guidance models that would turn a gravity-flung conventional bomb into a precision strike munition. Such a device—let alone a large shipment—in the hands of the wrong people would result in large death tolls. One well-placed warhead, even of the 250-pound variety, would be able to collapse a skyscraper in on itself as if it were made of precariously balanced playing cards. A crowded office building or a federal building would go from bustling workplace for thousands of people to a tomb for those teeming multitudes.

Schwarz let the phone stop ringing and pulled out his personal Combat PDA. The screen blipped to life, and Barbara Price was on the other end.

"What's going on?" Schwarz asked.

"We found a few of the laser guidance modules," Price said, her voice grim and eyes unwavering from the webcam she looked into. "Northeastern Iowa, near the Illinois border."

"How many killed?" Schwarz asked.

That bit of conversation prompted Blancanales to sit up, fully awake, turning on the bedside lamp. Schwarz grimaced at the pile of pizza boxes and junk food bags overflowing from the room's tiny garbage pail.

Though Blancanales's hair was whitened with age, his weathered face lined with wrinkles, the man's back and shoulders were tautly muscled, ropy coils of sinew flowing as he threw on his shoulder holster and then tugged on a sport shirt to conceal the carry rig.

"We can't tell. Official reports put the population of Albion at 250, but there's no finding most of their bodies," Price said. "But we have an eyewitness and dash-cam footage. Hal's doing everything to keep this squashed in the press, so you guys better get out there."

Schwarz nodded for his CPDA's webcam. "Something else is wrong?"

"The survivor and radio dispatch are telling us stories of strange activity *before* the bombs hit," Price answered. "Very strange activity that makes the laser-guided bombs now a secondary concern."

Schwarz frowned. "We'll head to the airport and have Mott take us in."

The CPDA connection clicked off, and Schwarz looked to his old buddy.

"Worse than laser-guided bombs?" Blancanales asked. "This is going to be another bad one."

"I took the call. You go wake Carl," Schwarz told him.

Blancanales, already dressed, nodded and acceded to his friend's request. Schwarz took the opportunity to get his gear prepared for the trip. There was a knock at the room door much quicker than he would have expected.

Schwarz kept his pistol hidden behind his leg, just in case there was trouble. It was Blancanales again.

"You didn't get Carl?" Schwarz asked.

Blancanales held up a note. "He taped this to our door."

Schwarz unfolded it. "'Picking up a loose end,'" he read out loud.

Blancanales nodded. "We'll find him quick enough if we follow the sounds of the explosions."

Schwarz sighed. "I'll call Mott and have him wait for us while we rein in the Ironman."

"If I know him, he's been out all day," Blancanales replied. "He might just be done already."

CHAPTER TWO

Chicago's late-afternoon weather was just perfect for Carl Lyons. It was neither too warm for the loose gun-concealing leather jacket he wore, nor was it so cold that he would risk being seen as out of place by leaving the jacket unzipped, thus making it quicker for him to reach for his defensive weapons.

Lyons was a former LAPD officer, and he generally wore a spine-numbing scowl that could unnerve even the toughest enemy. In a shoulder holster, Lyons wore the replacement for his old Colt Python, a Smith Wesson Model 686 Plus. It was a 7-shot .357 Magnum revolver with a six-inch barrel, giving the Able Team commander the option to engage enemies at up to 200 yards. The weapon had been refined in the Stony Man Farm armory, given a matte, nonreflective finish, Pachmayer Compact grips and a trigger job that made double-action shooting swift and instinctive. His backup for the mighty Mag-Plus was another Smith & Wesson, this time the polymer-framed MP-45, a sleek weapon that carried ten fat .45-caliber rounds in the magazine and another in the pipe. Lyons and the rest of the team had gone with the version that had the same thumb safety levers as on their single-action Colt 1911 autos, a lifesaving option if it came time to wrestle for the big .45, but not a hindrance to a locked and cocked .45 user as the levers worked identically to their Colt counterparts.

Kissinger, their armorer, had wanted to see how the same company's 1911 version would work, but Able Team had grown spoiled with high-capacity magazines, and the MP-45 had one that fit flush instead of sticking out, making concealment difficult. Kissinger modified these with extended, threaded barrels for suppressed work and a knurled knob that protected the threads when not wearing a silencer. Lyons's belt carried not only the .45, but also spare ammunition pouches for both pistols, a flashlight holder, a folding knife and his PDA/communicator, as well as a flat package of cable ties that could be deployed either as handcuffs, improvised door locks or tourniquets to prevent massive bleeding.

As a former beat cop, Lyons didn't mind the weight that hung around his hips, especially since it would give him an edge toward survival. Schwarz and Blancanales had often teased him about being a big Boy Scout, always being prepared. Lyons had never been in the Scouts, and he doubted that there was a merit badge for busting up bar fights or dropping a hostage taker with a single gunshot from across a parking lot. However, that preparedness was what had elevated the burly, blond ex-cop to become one of America's top nine fighting men, the people called upon when every other option was either used up or any other law enforcement or military response was simply too slow to save the day. Lyons's entire existence now was lived day-to-day, looking out for worst-case scenarios and maintaining the mental agility to solve those problems as they came to him.

Lyons slid into a tenement building and slipped his flashlight into his hand, palmed to conceal it. It was a four-inch-long, squat, fat pipe of knurled steel with a rubber cap at one end for the toggle switch. The lens at the other end was surrounded by an octagonal collar that had the density and strength to shatter glass or lay open a cheek down to the bone. Lyons hadn't needed the nine powerful LED bulbs for illumination, his eyes quickly adjusting to the shadows of the lobby, but the flashlight would prove to be an effective impact weapon against an attacker, and those LED lights would sear the vision of someone trying to attack him with a gun in the close quarters of the lobby.

That kind of thinking was how the man called Ironman had become Able Team's leader, commanding two Special Forces veterans when Lyons hadn't had traditional military or paramilitary experience. The big blond ex-cop had survived the rough streets of Los Angeles and had also survived for years working undercover against the mob, quite often teaming with Mack Bolan, the Executioner. It was surviving against mob hits and backing up Bolan in his one-man war that had earned Lyons the nickname Ironman, a legacy that had been forged even deeper in hell zones from the jungles of South America to the deserts of the Middle East.

That kind of edge and awareness had been born in the streets, though. The team had been on the hunt for a shipment of modules that were capable of turning unguided bombs packed with hundreds of pounds of high explosives into precision killing machines. The most dramatic instance of such a tool utilized in a city was when the Israeli Defense Force had fired one at a terrorist leader who had taken up residence in an apartment building ringed with bodyguards and the added "protection" of innocent Palestinian civilians living in the building. The whole complex had been taken out by a single one-ton bomb that killed fourteen and wounded fifty others. The building had been turned into a crater, and had the warhead been launched at any other time, the death toll would have been even greater. It wasn't the kind of move that Lyons would have preferred, but to only kill fifteen people with two thousand pounds of high explosives, launched from a supersonic strike fighter, was a sign of how deadly those modules could be.

That was the kind of firepower that a terrorist group, no matter how disciplined, could hardly keep secret. There would be bragging, an increase in veiled threats, something that broke loose into the whisper stream, rumors flying through the underground that someone would trade in on. Hundreds of the high-tech units could be combined with weapons no more refined than steel pipes stuffed with plastic explosives and rolled out of the back of a cargo plane. One of these could easily be dropped into a meeting of Congress, or an airport crowded with innocent travelers, causing death and devastation in a manner that terrorists loved.

The arms-dealer trail was their only lead. It was what had gotten them to Chicago, but nothing had gone further. The Farm's cybernetic crew had worked hard, pulling out the stops on suspected foreign and domestic terrorist groups who would have the money and coordination for such a theft under the opinion that perhaps one cell had been disciplined enough to hold their tongues.

But that wasn't how it appeared. From radical Islamic fundamentalists—the scourge who gave the Arab world a bad reputation—to Illinois neo-Nazis—a scourge who gave all humanity a worse reputation—no one seemed to be primed with confidence or assigning extra security to protect their illicit firepower.

The laser modules had moved on somewhere, and they had most likely gone to be stored with the bombs that they were destined to steer toward death and destruction.

Lyons knew that the trail had gone cold, and with that sudden chill came the realization that the next chance they'd have would be when fire fell from the sky upon American citizens.

The lobby was empty except for the cage where a security guard leaned back in his chair, idly watching black-and-white screens. Lyons only got a glimpse of the man as he'd passed, but the ex-cop had his senses tuned to suck in as much data as possible.

The guard was all wrong. Instead of a bored, inattentive washout with a slight roll, or an exhausted beat cop working a second job to feed his kids, this guy was fit and he was focused. He'd given Lyons the same eyeball treatment that he'd received, and his attention returned to the security screens. The gun in his holster was a customized Colt-style 1911 autopistol, carried locked and cocked in quality leather. Modern cops were the kind of people who preferred different arms, and in a city and environs like Chicago, the single-action sidearm was not approved, nor as inexpensive as the Glocks and other polymer-framed pistols that had risen in popularity. While the guy might have been SWAT, thus having the standard of training to have a police rig for the 1911, he still wasn't in "second job" mode. No radio played in the silence of the lobby, nor did the guy wear earbuds attached to a digital music player.

The laid-back approach was faked. That level of security awareness, plus the high-profile, skill-intensive sidearm, added up to the sum that Lyons sought. This was the place he was looking for, and he strolled with renewed confidence and energy. He didn't believe that he'd need Schwarz or Blancanales for this leg of the investigation. After all, this was only an organized crime transportation service, and while there would be a need for armed guards around the storehouse and loading docks, this was too much of a residential building to serve as either, though Lyons wouldn't put anything past the mob. Chicago had a significant Italian-American organized community still, much like New York and New Jersey, and the Mafia had remained resilient enough to resist being put to pasture by groups who had risen to power in other major metropolises. These low-income tenements were nothing like the monolithic, soul-draining prisons like Cabrini Green, which had been demolished after they'd become cesspools controlled by powerful drug gangs.

Still, this particular tenement was big enough to prove to be a good fortress while still being low profile.

"Hey, Blondie." The guard's voice rose. "I gotta buzz you in. Who're you here to see?"

Lyons was halfway to the elevators and stopped, looking over his shoulder. If this guard was as sharp as he'd assumed, there was no way that the security man would miss the arsenal he wore, no matter how loosely the leather jacket draped over it. "I'm here on business. Didn't Scalia tell you?"

It was a bluff. Lyons had spent a few moments on the phone with Chicago's org-crime unit, making use of his old contacts from when he was an undercover Fed, and he'd picked up a few names from the police that he could drop. Scalia was high enough that security wouldn't want to be caught questioning his orders, but not so important that he would seem out of the loop giving such orders.

"Scalia?" the uniformed guard asked. "Don't matter. You're walking in here armed. I wouldn't be surprised if you had a 25 mm turret in there."

Lyons smirked, then pulled his lapel aside. "Nah. Just a six-inch .357 Magnum."

"Damn, son," the guard said. "Not far from it."

"So what? I have to leave my heat here at the desk?" Lyons asked.

The guard shook his head. "I do have to pat you for wires, and I'd like to see your cell."

Lyons nodded, doffing his jacket. The guard made note of Lyons's body armor, and kept feeling. He was a professional, not minding having to mess with another man's junk to look for concealed electronics. A signal sweep might not work in case the device had remote activation.

The guard took Lyons's Combat PDA, the only phone he'd had with him. Luckily, the Able Team leader had switched it over to a new identity, locking off any history of calls to law enforcement, replacing it with a series of random names and numbers produced by an logarithm devised by Hermann Schwarz and Aaron "the Bear" Kurtzman to provide a clean identity. Only Lyons's thumbprint could return the device to its normal contact list and background data. Stony Man Farm was nothing if not efficient and well-prepared when providing its members with secure communications.

"You kinda Nordic-looking to be muscle for the outfit," the rent-a-cop said.

Lyons chuckled. "And you bleed marinara sauce?"

The guard smiled. "Welcome to the new thing. Diversity in operation."

"My phone?" Lyons asked.

"Stays here," the sentry returned. "Someone clones your signal and dials in, it's like you're wearing a mike anyway. The only phones past this lobby are landline."

Lyons nodded. "Scalia don't fuck around when it comes to OPSEC."

The guard's interest was piqued now. "Military?"

"Private contractor," Lyons answered with just enough disappointment to let the real veteran know that he was someone who hadn't been tolerated in a war zone by military brass, but had been in action and carried the same battle confidence that someone in the Sandbox would have.

"Well, just keep things private, Mr. Contractor," the guard replied. "I'm not the only one here you're gonna mess with. Two pistols and lightweight undercover Kevlar isn't going to mean much if you do decide to get nasty."

Lyons gave the guard a small salute, then got on the elevator. He'd have to get the CPDA back from the front desk on his way out. Hopefully, he wouldn't have to pick it out of rubble if that was the case.

CALVIN JAMES LIKED Paris, a truly multicultural center that had accepted and nurtured some of the finest black American expatriates into global superstars on the music, writing and acting scenes. On these streets resided a history of great artists who'd come here in self-imposed exile rather than buckle under to an age of racism that did its best to snuff out their creativity simply because of the color of their skin. James often wondered how he would have dealt with those times, and knew that any chance a black doctor would have had would have been thin and as ghettoized as every other segment of American society back in those days.

James loved America; there would never be any doubt about that. He had bled for her even before he had been recruited to Phoenix Force. And part of his love stemmed from how America could heal, improve and right the wrongs of the past.

The infiltration of a country's leadership by clever, predatory scum was not the country's or the government's fault. The greedy and corrupt would always find a way to positions of power, and nothing short of complete martial law and the revocation of liberty could ever quell such ambitions. As a soldier of freedom, he would never let that happen.

Here and now on the streets of Paris, the flight was not from injustice, but from those seeking to bring evildoers to justice. The target was Aasim Bezoar, a Syrian biochemist who had been traveling through Europe. Bezoar's schooling had been in Moscow, back in the era of the Cold War, and he had been one of the top men in Syria's chemical and biological weapons programming, helping to build an arsenal that would give Israel pause should they ever attempt reprisal for their interference in Lebanon. Bezoar's machinations had been part of the reason for the cold peace between Syria and Israel, but they had also been part of other, more dangerous problems that had only been barely contained thanks to the efforts of law enforcement and espionage across the world.

One of James's first missions with Phoenix Force had been an operation in Greece where hardline Soviets had invented an enzyme that would have destroyed the stomach lining of people it was exposed to, dooming them to malnutrition. That terrifying attack had been stopped cold, and James had cemented his position as one of the five pillars of Phoenix Force.

Bezoar had been involved in the research, but not the execution of the Proteus Enzyme, and as such, he had escaped the wrath of Stony Man Farm's operatives.

Now Bezoar had popped up on the radar in Paris. His ties with the Syrian government had been dissolved for some reason. The Syrians had claimed he'd died a year ago, but here he was, alive and well.

James and his comrades hadn't been the first ones to take notice of Bezoar. A team of operatives from Damascus had made the attempt to retrieve him. It was their corpses, floating in the Seine, that had alerted Interpol, and by extension, Stony Man, that the chemist was alive and in the City of Lights. When a supposedly dead biochemist attracted a force of assassins, Barbara Price knew Phoenix Force was meant to be involved.

David McCarter, the leader of Phoenix Force, walked beside James. A fox-faced man with hard, glinty eyes, McCarter was a British citizen, and more importantly, a veteran of Britain's storied Special Air Service before being recruited to the Sensitive Operations Group. His mastery of counterterrorist tactics was second to none, backed up by a wild man's energy disciplined by years of experience. Throwing in his knowledge of Arabic, German and French—as well as his ability to fly anything with wings or propellers—was the icing on a hardcase cake.

The members of Phoenix Force were picked because they could fight, but none of them was just pure brawn. Each of them knew at least three languages fluently, as well as possessing a gamut of knowledge ranging from deep sea diving, archaeology, structural engineering, medicine and chemistry.

Hundreds of lives were at risk, and Phoenix Force had the Syrian assassins to thank for it. Damascus was hardly a friend of the United States and the rest of the Western world, but when the Syrian government reacted to one of their own going rogue, the globe had to sit up and take notice.

"Anything, Cal?" McCarter asked.

James shook his head. "Still nothing. How much longer are we going to watch that hole in the wall?"

McCarter took a deep breath. James knew that before he'd been given leadership of the team, his impetuous and impulsive nature had him chomping at the bit to get into action. Anything that hinted of hesitation crawled under McCarter's skin like a burr. Since his promotion, however, even the appearance sitting idly was misleading. The Briton's mind was buzzing, a gleaming light shining behind his eyes indicating thoughts racing along as he plotted angles and strategies.

Being the boss didn't make things easier, but it alleviated any boredom he used to have.

"Until we're ready," McCarter said.

James shook his head again. "A few years ago, I'd ask who the hell you are and what you'd done with the real David."

McCarter looked at James and winked. "The real David's having fun working out the probabilities of my plans a dozen times over, looking for every single outcome. Before, I had to twiddle my thumbs, waiting to do my thing. Now I'm rolling plans in my head to make sure all you little chickadees return home to roost, not just because you're all my mates, but because Mama Hen Barb would turn me into a fryer if I fucked up."

"I'm so glad that our friendship is more important than your fear of reprisals, David," James said.

McCarter chuckled, then brought his radio to his lips. "Gary, luv. Still warm up there?"

"A Paris evening in November?" Gary Manning asked. "In Canada, this is T-shirt weather."

"Any change of security?" McCarter returned.

"Same patrol patterns. Bezoar has some tightly wound people watching him, and they're not fucking around," Manning answered. "They haven't noticed you two yet, but then, it takes me a minute to locate you."

"Good news," McCarter said. "T.J., how're you doing?"

"Aside from the hairy eyeballs I caught from security, I'm peachy," Hawkins told him. "They noticed me just walking on the sidewalk, so Bezoar has plenty of sharp eyes and ears on the scene."

"A visit from Damascus woke them up, likely," Rafael Encizo commented from his vantage point.

"Not this bunch," Hawkins countered. "This wasn't cockroach scrambling, this was lions watching a zebra. Not a nice feeling being the prey."

"Just about satisfied, David?" Encizo asked.

"Almost," McCarter responded.

James noticed a sudden perk of interest rise in the Phoenix Force commander. "Spot something?"

"A truck picking up trash," McCarter said, nodding toward the vehicle. "Gary, how many guns are on it?"

They waited for Manning for a couple of moments, then the Canadian spoke up. "Five. How'd you guess?"

"I've done stakeouts in this area of town before," McCarter answered. "Rubbish isn't picked up on this day of the week, and not two haulers off a truck at the same time."

"Amazing the amount of crap you remember," James muttered.

"I noticed," McCarter replied. "The Syrians sent in reinforcements."

"We move on them?" Encizo asked.

McCarter shook his head, then spoke up. "No. We let them start this party, then we slip around the back."

"Worked for Striker, might as well work for us," James said.

McCarter reached for his valise and opened it, scanning the Fabrique Nationale P-90 concealed within. The tiny chatterbox was stuffed with a 50-round magazine. "We want Bezoar alive, chickadees. Treat him with kid gloves. Anyone else, fuck 'em. Especially the party from Damascus."

The garbage truck rolled close to Bezoar's apartment building.

McCarter and his Phoenix Force teammates were in motion before the first pop of a submachine gun was barely audible in the distance.

CHAPTER THREE

Arno Scalia walked down the hall, mouth turned in a frown that was only amplified by the downward turn of his black mustache. The fluorescent lights shone off his shaved head as he fiddled with his key in the lock. He'd just left the most secure room in the building, a structure that had cost one hundred thousand dollars to build and had been designed to resist any manner of eavesdropping. The phone call that had come in over a shielded and encrypted landline had made him uncomfortable.

Last week he and the outfit had moved crates of military electronics. Nothing could be identified, as it was still in the packaging and the labels had been scraped off, but the order was "don't ask, don't tell." For the higher-ups to actually have to repeat that to Scalia, one of the most discreet of men in the entire family, it was a sign that there was no fooling around with this shipment. Nothing falls off the back of the truck, nobody looks inside a crate and for certain no one will ever speak of it again.

That kind of double-checking was indicative of two conditions. One was that the organization had received a boatload of money to keep this well under the radar. The other was that his bosses, some of the hardest gangsters in Chicago, were frightened of the consequences of a single error.

Scalia was a professional, one who wouldn't make such a mistake, and if his subordinates had screwed up under him, he'd take it out of their hides. The shit would continue to roll downhill, until someone paid for the amount of grief he'd caused, the level of punishment rising with each and every person the frustration had passed through. No one in the transport office would screw things up. It was just too well enforced internally.

Now, he'd just received a phone call regarding a trio of Feds who were asking questions in town. Scalia had to keep an eye out for them, and if there was anything out of the ordinary, he was to quash it at a moment's notice.

"A trio of Feds," he murmured, repeating the term. "Actually, they were called 'super-Feds.'"

Scalia had been in the Mafia long enough to know what that term meant. Some government agencies didn't have to work by a set of rules that allowed groups like his to operate in relative freedom. The mention of a trio of super-Feds had also popped up all over the country, often just preceding a blitz that was second only to the horrors inflicted upon them by a lone vigilante whose name was never spoken anymore. Scalia had been present in other towns where the local organized crime had received visits from mystery men waving around Justice Department credentials just before war exploded on the streets.

The vigilante might have gone legitimate, Scalia mused, and picked up some allies. It was always a rumor, a conspiracy theory among the families, chatter about how the greatest scourge of their professional careers engaged in one bloody weeklong endgame that had crippled their infrastructure, then disappeared. Some had called it a monopoly-breaking strategy. Sometimes people using his old strategies of urban warfare came back for a visit, leaving wreckage in their wakes.

Scalia stepped into his office and saw that his multiline phone had a blinking message. He felt the blood begin to drain from his face as he could only think that it was someone in his own service telling him about a mystery visit. He hit the message playback, fumbling with the drawer of his desk to get to the pistol inside.

"Boss, it's Dev at the desk. Some blond bastard by the name of Steele came by, telling me he was called in by you," the message said. "I have the rest of security keeping an eye on him, but I didn't want too much of a clusterfuck."

Scalia sneered and hit the button for the main desk. "Dev?"

"He bluffed his way past me, pretending that he knew you," came the answer from Lebron Devlin. "I got a look at his gear, and I'm scanning his cell for signals. All he has is two pistols, a big fuckin' hog and a Glock or somethin'."

Scalia sneered. "Get everybody to surround him and ready to move in. This guy is trouble!"

The door clicked and Scalia looked away from the phone for a brief moment. The doorway was filled with a broad, grim-looking bastard in a loose leather jacket, cold eyes glaring from under a brooding brow.

"No need to go all-out for me," the guy said. "I'm just here to talk, not to fight. If I were here to cause shit, Dev wouldn't be talking right now."

Scalia swallowed. "So…let's talk."

The blond hulk in the doorway smiled, took a step in, and the door clicked in the ominous silence.

CARL LYONS COULD SEE the look of realization on Arno Scalia's face when he opened the door. The Able Team leader knew that he wouldn't have a lot of time before attracting the attention, and potentially the wrath, of the organization's security. He was glad that he was able to continue his bluff, riding the wave of audacity and confusion among the mobsters all the way to the boss's office.

"So let's talk," Scalia had told him, and Lyons closed the door behind him. There was a pleasing quality to the mobster's uncomfortable silence that only added to his graveyard grin. Scalia wasn't a small man, and the .45 auto he'd drawn from his desk drawer could easily have caused him some trouble, even with his body armor.

However, Lyons knew the value of intimidation and also realized the strength of adapting personality to the conversation. When he had been in the lobby, he was simply one of the guys, blowing smoke up people's asses and getting accepted. Now, when he needed some questions answered, he had slipped into crazy-caveman mode. The grin he wore was pure cockiness, but the glint of determination in his eyes signaled a willingness to spill blood by the bucket.

Scalia picked up on that insanity, which, coupled with Lyons's thick, muscular form, was a warning beacon.

"You...know that I have to maintain some secrecy for my organization..." Scalia said. "Professional..."

"Yeah, right, whatever," Lyons cut him off. "If you know why I'm here and suspect who I learned my trade from, then you know that I'm not here to listen to you jack off at the mouth. I want answers or I'll take blood."

Scalia's lips tightened into a bloodless line, his eyes flicking to the phone on his desk.

"Sure, hit your panic button, Arno. That's not going to save your life," Lyons said.

Scalia returned his gaze to Lyons's face. "I'm sure I know why—"

"Then I don't have to ask you any fucking questions, Arno," Lyons snarled. "Don't stall."

Scalia nodded. "You're wondering about some military stuff that went through here."

Lyons nodded. His eyes burrowed into Scalia, who shifted uneasily in his seat and swallowing hard. Lyons knew that while there were ways to get information out of people—and he'd been forced to utilize torture at times for the sake of last-minute expedience—the best interrogators got their answers just by force of will. These types of interrogations were Lyons's favorite. There was no blood, there was no moral quandary, and the answers weren't the first lies screamed that made the pain stop. The Able Team commander was not a murderer or a sadist; he was a warrior and a seeker of justice.

"Well," Scalia began, "we took the shipment and

waited for them to bring their own trucks. We didn't look inside, especially since the bosses made sure we didn't fuck it up. They're scared."

"But you know who I come from, don't you?" Lyons asked.

Scalia looked down, breaking eye contact. His bald dome was beaded with nervous sweat that rolled down his forehead in rivulets. "I don't want to say his name."

"You do know my friend Mack," Lyons said.

Scalia visibly shuddered, his cheeks tingeing green as if he were fighting off a particularly violent bout of food poisoning. "Th...th...they said he was dead."

"You think you can kill the devil made flesh, come to collect the souls of you damned petty thugs?" Lyons asked, his voice dropping to a deep, rumbly baritone, tapping every movie about exorcism he'd ever seen as a boy. "The living spirit of murder and terror does not die, no matter how much you shoot him or burn him."

The acrid stench of urine suddenly filled the air as Scalia messed himself, tears joining the cascade of sweat droplets crawling down his face. "Oh, God..."

"If you had any pull with Him, I would never have found you," Lyons said, standing, leaning forward with his knuckles on the desktop. He was bent close to Scalia's face, his growl low and unholy. "Confession is your only salvation."

Scalia flinched, one eye squinted shut, the other a mere sliver. "Please, Father in Heaven..."

"Now you find religion, after moving illegal automatic weapons and drugs across the country?" Lyons asked. "Your hypocrisy makes you an even more tasty treat."

"Okay…okay…we sent out the crates to Idaho," Scalia said. "We figured they were machine guns for the militias."

Lyons nodded.

"To make their own state. You know how crazy they are," Scalia said.

"But they are honest in their hatred, if inaccurate as to the cause of their failures," Lyons returned. "Idaho. Do you know where?"

"Just that the drivers let it drop that they were headed in that direction," Scalia said. "They wanted to know the road conditions and such.…"

"How do you know that they weren't leaving a false lead?" Lyons asked, easing back down.

"Because I called the slip in, and an hour after that driver left, his corpse was found in a Dumpster three miles away," Scalia answered. "These fuckers didn't mess around."

"A Dumpster. You and your people take care of the body?" Lyons asked.

"Not my department," Scalia replied. "But his ass didn't go to the morgue."

"How long ago was this?" Lyons asked.

Scalia's eyes widened.

"How. Long. Ago?" Lyons repeated with a growl for each word.

"Three days," Scalia said. "So they should be in Idaho, even if they made rest stops, though I doubt it. There were multiple drivers for each rig."

Lyons grimaced. "We'll find them."

"And what about me?" Scalia asked.

"You can make it easier for me to keep an eye on this operation, or the next," Lyons said.

"Are you kidding me?" Scalia quizzed. "They know that I talked to you…"

Lyons picked up Scalia's 1911 and let out a shrill, frightened scream, firing the entire magazine through the door. Once the slide locked open, he turned to Scalia. "This is going to hurt, but you'll wake up."

Scalia was frozen in wide-eyed horror as the big burly blond pulled the biggest revolver he'd ever seen from under his leather jacket. With a flick of the wrist and a sharp, searing flame across his forehead, the mobster's fears vanished into the calming, accepting embrace of unconsciousness.

Lyons knew that he wasn't going to have a lot of time before the security teams would be rushing toward the door. Just to make things more convincing for Scalia, he punched the unconscious man to raise bruises and welts on his face. A couple of shots to the side and the stomach, and he was done with that. Scalia would look like he'd been put through a wringer, and the sound of the beating would be audible through the doors. Lyons just had to make certain that he left witnesses alive.

That wouldn't be too difficult for the Able Team leader.

The first two men through the door entered hard and hot, kicking through the weakened wood of Scalia's office entrance, pistol-grip shotguns held at the hip and each blasting out a thunder-load of buckshot into the air.

Obviously the two men must not have practiced much with 12-gauges without stocks as the recoil jerked the weapons in their grasps, but they'd been counting on the initial bellows of the weapons to cut down enemies in front of them, or the loud roars to act as a stun-shock grenade, overpressure hammering the ears of anyone who'd stayed out of the way.

Lyons had been standing to the side of the doorway, and he had been prepared enough to have a pair of electronic bud earplugs. They filtered potentially damaging sounds to manageable levels without compromising his ability to hear footsteps in the distance. The guard closest to Lyons looked over his shoulder to see the big blond ex-cop lunge at him. Lyons drove him face-first into Scalia's desk with a heel strike to the back of his head.

The other gunner turned in reaction to his partner's sudden crash, but Lyons was ready with a *shotokan* side kick that landed under the guard's sternum with sufficient force to lift the man off his feet before he crashed against the bookshelf behind him. It took a moment for Lyons to be certain that these two could give a corroborating story to their superiors about the assault on Scalia.

Never one to pass up a free weapon or ammunition, Lyons scooped up a stockless shotgun from the floor. It was a stubby tool, and he readily recognized it as an Ithaca Model 37 Stakeout Shotgun, a tool he'd used before. It only had a thirteen-inch barrel, but that gave it a magazine tube with room enough for four rounds of 12-gauge buck. Lyons also noted that there was a sidesaddle that held six spare shells on the side of the receiver. Lyons took one shell and inserted it into the magazine, then grabbed the other weapon after slinging the first over his shoulder. Making certain that the other shotgun had been topped off, Lyons was ready for serious business. Eighteen rounds of 12-gauge would make busting out of the building much easier.

He picked up the stomp of feet in the distance and barreled out into the hall, the stubby shotgun easy to maneuver through the doorway. With a hard kick, he entered the room across the way, a storage room loaded with filing cabinets. He'd ducked in just in time to avoid a spray of pellets that chewed off the doorjamb. Lyons knew that his Kevlar would hold against their onslaught, but the enemy gunners probably had their own body armor. He popped around the jamb, sighted down the barrel of the Ithaca and emptied a charge into the legs of the lead gunman. The load of buckshot tore his thigh and knee to shreds, turning him from the point of the spear to a snarl in the flow of guards moving toward Lyons.

As he ducked back in, the hallway resounding with the booms of shotguns discharging unintentionally and bodies and metal bouncing on tile, Lyons reviewed the brief glimpse he'd taken of the security team. They wore bulky vests, obviously heavy enough to absorb the impact of a 12-gauge load to the chest. It wasn't going to be a deadly blowout, leaving plenty to wonder what the hell had just hit them. Still, Lyons wanted these armed thugs to know that they were in the wrong line of business. One of their number was already maimed.

Lurching out into the open, he saw one of the mobster security gunners already up on one knee. Lyons triggered the Stakeout, its muzzle blast a mighty belch of flame and thunder. The guard whirled violently as his shoulder was smashed to a gory pulp of splintered bone and mutilated muscle. Lyons's target had barely hit the floor when a second man rose from both hands, utilizing the strength of his legs to turn into a human missile aimed at Lyons's midsection.

The ex-cop had played plenty of high school and college football in his days as a lineman. While he easily could have resisted the clumsy lunge, that would have tied him up too long to efficiently deal with the other two gunners who were recovering their wits and weaponry. Lyons sidestepped, bringing down his elbow between the tackle's shoulder blades. Only the guard's momentum had saved him from a severed spinal cord, but even so, he bounced off the tile floor face-first, teeth and blood flying everywhere from the messy impact. He wouldn't be getting up soon.

One of the last two gunners swung his shotgun up to eye level. The Able Team commando dropped to the floor, barely a heartbeat ahead of a blast that would have destroyed his face and vaporized his brains. Lyons returned the nearly fatal favor, triggering his Stakeout between the man's legs.

At a range of only a few feet, all nine pellets in a double O round of buckshot had little time to spread apart, so they struck almost as one, tearing and ripping through fabric and meat with equal ease. Unfortunately for the gunman, the pelvic girdle was made of tough, fracture resistant bone, which deflected the pellets through the man's bladder, lower abdominal muscles and the network of arteries that fed his legs. Brilliant crimson erupted from the doomed gunner's groin, horrific neural trauma making the dying man drop his weapon. He stumbled backward.

The last of the gunmen lurched to one side, avoiding his collapsing partner, but Lyons had racked the slide on his shotgun and blasted away again. The much more slender bones of this target's forearm shattered as the wave of buckshot ripped through them. Some of the pellets deflected off the barrel of his weapon, but most of them continued on into the guard's face, tearing furrows through cheeks and forehead. Slowed down by the man's arm, they hadn't proved fatal, but he was going to need significant reconstructive surgery for his shredded face.

Lyons got to his feet and headed for the stairwell that he had scouted before bursting into Scalia's office. He'd had several minutes to stake out the building, planning his escape route and the response of the security team. That kind of foreknowledge had been key in getting him and his team out of the narcoterrorist-filled jungles of Colombia or neo-Nazi ambushes in southwestern box canyons. He made a beeline for the stairwell, entering it.

He heard the stomp of boots even as he paused to feed the Ithaca the last five rounds in its sidesaddle, racking a shell into the breech before topping off the magazine. Normally, shotguns were carried with empty chambers, but this was the middle of a combat situation, so running around without a fully loaded weapon was beyond foolhardy.

Weapon full and ready to roar, Lyons dropped to the midpoint of the flight of stairs between the second and third floors. His two-hundred-plus pounds of muscle and extra equipment came down on the landing like the hammer of an angry storm god, surprising the group of security guards who were coming up from below. That sudden start gave Lyons all the opportunity he needed to cut through the men, working the slide of the Ithaca as fast as he could pull the trigger.

The leader of the group, the black man he'd spoken to, was bowled backward, his body armor absorbing the first charge of buckshot, turning him into an avalanche of muscle and sinew that crashed down on the gunners behind him. The rest of Lyons's 12-gauge thunder tracked higher under recoil, his brawny arms providing more than enough strength to resist the kick of the stubby weapon.

Faces and shoulders disappeared in clouds of bone-splinter-filled crimson mist, bodies tumbling out of Lyons's way as he continued down toward the second story. Lebron Devlin croaked as Lyons passed him, one hand clawing empty air.

"You bastard," Devlin gurgled.

Lyons dropped the empty Stakeout on Devlin's chest in a show of dismissal. He had no time to chat. The door guard had suffered broken ribs from taking a burst at the range of only a few inches, so there was little way he could put up any more of a fight.

The way to the first floor was clear, though booms

thundered from above as the gunners higher up opened fire in an attempt to catch up with the escaping Able Team commander. Lyons twisted and fired skyward to dissuade pursuit. There were screams as legs were peppered with .36-caliber pellets.

With a kick, he was in the lobby, stuffing new shells into the tube magazine of his remaining shotgun. He strode confidently toward the small security cage that Devlin had worked in. A single blast from the Ithaca opened the locked door, and Lyons was able to locate his Combat PDA lying in the middle of the desk. He checked to make certain that it hadn't been opened.

Schwarz was brilliant yet paranoid. He'd set up the small multipurpose communicators to melt down if someone tried to access the electronics within. Since there was no burned puddle of smoldering desk, things were all right.

Lyons had no qualms about entering a den of heavily armed smugglers, but even he didn't intend to anger Schwarz by leaving one of his prized creations behind in enemy hands.

He noticed that he'd gotten a message while he'd been dealing with Scalia.

Strike in Indiana. We're wheels up in thirty without you, the text read.

Lyons opened a link to his partners as he dumped his empty shotgun, exiting the smugglers' office. "Able One reporting in."

"There you are," Schwarz said. "I didn't see one bit of the Chicago skyline disappear, so I thought you were taking a nap."

Lyons knew that his friend's levity was concealing concern for his safety. "Tell Mott to hold up until I get there. I've got trouble brewing in Idaho now."

"At least four of the bombs landed in a little armpit of a town called Albion," Schwarz told him. "We're heading there to see what's up."

"Never heard of the place," Lyons answered, sliding behind the wheel of his rental car.

"Never will again," Schwarz returned. "Everyone in town was killed, including several sheriff's deputies."

Lyons glared at the offices. Now that he was back in his car, he had access to an M-4 with an underbarrel grenade launcher. If anyone dared to poke his face out the front door, he'd lay into the mobsters with high-explosive death.

Sadly, the smugglers were too smart to tempt fate. They'd hunkered down, knowing that to pursue Lyons would be suicide.

"Play now, pay later," Lyons snarled as a grim promise, driving off to the airport to meet with the rest of his team.

CHAPTER FOUR

In his younger days, David McCarter, the current leader of Phoenix Force, had earned the reputation of a hard-driving badass. He always seemed to be in a constant state of pent-up, impulsive action, easily growing bored, even with training exercises. He'd lived on the edge, primed and ready for battle. Back then, waiting for the start of conflict was something that ate at the young warrior's nerves.

These days, though, as commander of Phoenix Force, McCarter learned what had been missing. He'd lived his entire life seeking challenges that could match his phenomenal skills, taking to the cockpit of any new aircraft he could to master its maneuvers, testing out various martial arts to find their strengths in relation to others. He devoured books continually, starting out in military history but spreading out to political philosophy and analysis of current events. Far from a thug, he realized that the untamed fires within his gut were a strength that sought a task worthy of him.

Being the brains of Phoenix Force was that task, and the times when his impatience would get the better of him had disappeared as he applied his experience to plotting actions and reactions even before the first shot was fired.

So when the Syrians attacked, just as McCarter had anticipated, he was not only ready, but had also prepared Phoenix Force to deal with the sudden arrival. Experience had taught the Briton that there was little that could be done when a member of a country's covert-operations community came to harm or capture. He remembered avenging the deaths of colleagues, and he recalled when a Phoenix ally, Karl Hahn, was kidnapped by a terrorist group and the team went rogue to bring him home alive. The Syrians had lost men to Bezoar, and even if Damascus had sent orders for the hit team's comrades to pull back, anger and loss of friends were powerful spurs.

There was no way they were going to let this insult to their fellowship pass.

McCarter also knew that sometimes anger made men sloppy. From their approach to the front doors, ignoring even the obviously armed Hawkins strolling down the street, McCarter knew that they were focused on the job of bringing hell to Bezoar and his crew of fellow murderers. He keyed his hands-free radio to toss out the orders.

"Go time. T.J., even the odds should Bezoar's people or the Syrians seem to be winning. Keep out of the way, though. You're not packed for a proper dustup," McCarter ordered. "Gary…"

"Eyes in the sky, backing T.J. and monitoring you," Manning answered.

"Rafe, Cal, it's on," McCarter said. "T.J., remember, nothing gets past you to the public."

"On it," Hawkins answered.

Amid the chatter of automatic weapons, the men of Phoenix Force took flight.

THE SYRIANS HAD blown in, loaded for bear, especially if that bear wore tank armor and carried a grenade launcher, Hawkins mused as he found cover in a doorway, drawing the sleek Belgian P-90 machine pistol from under his jacket. Three SUVs screeched to a halt, windows open and assault rifles hammering at the windows of Bezoar's Parisian safehouse. The twisting, narrow street in front of the house was clogged by the big vehicles' presence. They opened fire on the windows of the storefront that Bezoar had set up as a diner so ramshackle that even the prostitutes didn't want a piece of it. The roar of big engines in the predawn had sent the women scrambling, their street instincts telling them that the trucks had either belonged to police or an organized hit crew.

Either way, they wanted nothing to do with that fight, disappearing between buildings or scurrying down the street past Hawkins. They studiously ignored him as the glass of the storefront diner disappeared in a solid wave of lead. Anyone who had been inside would have been shredded, and from what Hawkins had seen, there were a couple of men nursing cold coffee mugs as they cast anxious glares into the darkened street.

The Syrians weren't holding back. The unmistakable thump of a 40 mm grenade launcher echoed down toward Hawkins's doorway, its high-explosive message shaking the ground at his feet.

"Dave, the Syrians are going nuclear," Hawkins said into his throat mike.

"Heard that," McCarter replied. "Bide your time."

Hawkins grimaced, hating the wait, but the Briton had given his orders, and he had pulled the team through countless confrontations.

The Syrians piled out of their vehicles, a dozen strong, as their trucks idled, drivers and shotgun riders waiting behind them to secure their getaway transportation. A quick glance told Hawkins that he was smart to have brought along a 50-round magazine full of armor-piercing ammunition. The SUVs were solidly built, and the way the lights of the skinny road reflected off their windshields let him know that they were armored. He reminded himself that Phoenix had wrung the compact machine pistols out, and their 5.8 mm rounds could punch through a titanium plate backed by twenty layers of Kevlar out to two hundred meters and go through 9 mm of steel plate at fifty. He was barely fifteen meters from the lead SUV, meaning that no matter how resistant the glass, he'd be able to put rounds into the interior without much effort.

One of the men in the lead truck poked his head and weapon out of the window. This guy had a submachine gun, as well, and he'd noticed Hawkins's quick peek at the clogged road. Hawkins couldn't make out what the gunner was packing, but it sure as hell wasn't a folded newspaper and a cup of coffee. The roar of autofire filled the air as the doorjamb suddenly came alive with bullet impacts. Hawkins held his ground, enduring splinters of brick and old paint peppering his exposed face.

Whatever they were carrying, it was only a 9 mm, and for that he was grateful. Still, just because it couldn't penetrate into his cubbyhole didn't mean that Hawkins was free and clear to ignore the incoming fire. Once the barrage let up, Hawkins ducked low, rolled into the middle of the narrow road and opened up on a spot just above the SUV's headlights.

The sleek, hypervelocity rounds from Hawkins's PDW went to where he couldn't see them above the glare of the lamps, but the clatter of a machine pistol on cobblestones rewarded the American Phoenix pro. He pumped out two more bursts, sweeping the headlights and blowing them out so that his night vision could recover from their bright flare. The engine snarled to life, and he could hear the vehicle jolt into gear.

Hawkins knew that the enemy was going to try to ram a half ton of truck down his throat, so he leveled the muzzle at the driver and cut loose. The last half of the P-90's 50-round magazine elicited the crash and shatter of armored Plexiglas, but after a brief surge, the SUV no longer had pressure on the gas. The truck was idling forward, but its driver was dead.

Of course, that didn't mean anything to the trailing SUVs. The gunners for each had clambered out behind partially open armored doors, scanning for Hawkins in the darkened street. Without the blaze of the headlights, he was just a shadow, flat on the ground.

That wouldn't last for long, though.

He reloaded the machine pistol swiftly, all the while scrambling toward the idling, driverless SUV, keeping in the shadows from where the other vehicles' lamps blazed down the narrow road. Hawkins rested against the bumper.

"Gary, leave anything for me?" Hawkins asked, knowing that such a question was moot when it came to the Canadian sniper.

To MAINTAIN a low profile on this operation, the members of Phoenix Force opted for a set of tools that would help them look as if they were French special operations. This meant that their gear was typical police or military equipment. It allowed them use of familiar gear such as the PAMAS G1—a license-built Beretta 92-F—the FN P-90 and the suppressed rifle Gary Manning was currently riding, a PGM Ultima Ratio "Integral Silencieux" rifle in 7.62 x 51 mm NATO.

The Commando was a shortened version designed especially for urban operations teams. It was affixed with a 15.7-inch, integrally silenced barrel as opposed to the standard 24-inch tube, meaning that inside a crowded city, the Commando was handy and quick. Manning liked the name Ultima Ratio because it was Latin for "the last resort," a term that went with Phoenix Force hand-in-hand, and it was derived from the original term *ultima ratio regum,* which was "the final argument of kings." Since Phoenix Force had adapted their code names to variants of "king" and the phrase was a flowery synonym for "war", Manning felt it was tailor-made for his cover identity of Gary Roy.

As soon as T. J. Hawkins started to take fire from the three SUVs in the street, he swung the muzzle of the suppressed Commando toward the convoy. Only one gunner was actively shooting, and as soon as he stopped his fusillade, Hawkins was in action. Through the optics of the rifle, he could see the muzzle-flashes of the P-90 through the end of its blunt silencer.

The headlights went out and the SUV lurched into action, but more autofire erupted from Hawkins's position. Manning turned his attention to the other vehicles and saw that their gunners who had waited outside on security for the Syrian assault force were now looking for the source of the sudden, fierce combat that had erupted in front of them. The two gunmen were wary, but their attention was focused ahead of them, not behind and above.

Manning had complete surprise against them as he milked the precision trigger of the skeletonized combat sniper. The rubber recoil pad and suppressor made the lightweight weapon's kick feel like a tender caress against his brawny shoulder as he punched a hole through the neck of one of the Syrians. The rearmost man's death was instantaneous, spine severed and lower brain destroyed. He didn't even shudder, falling to the ground as if he were a marionette with its strings cut.

Only the chatter of metal on cobblestones alerted the second gunman, who whirled to see his friend lying facedown in a sprawl of loose limbs.

Manning worked the bolt on the Ultima Ratio swiftly, the finely polished steel gliding noiselessly as it stripped another .308 Winchester subsonic round off the top of the 10-round box magazine. The time between the first and second shots, which struck the remaining Syrian gunner in the bridge of his nose, was less than a second. The noise made by the subsequent rifle shot was softer than a polite cough, but on the receiving end, the armed commando's head burst like a melon.

"Gary, leave anything for me?" Hawkins asked.

"Get the middle SUV," Manning instructed as the rearmost vehicle ground into Reverse. He didn't have a good angle to see the driver of the truck, but Manning knew that a frightened driver would be a threat, not only communicating to the main assault team that they were under fire, but also tearing through the streets of Paris to escape pursuit. People could be run over.

Manning worked the rifle's action as fast as he could, firing round after round into the roof of the SUV, adjusting his aim so that his fire would lance down into the driver's seat. On his fourth shot, the escaping vehicle slammed its rear bumper into a storefront, glass shattering violently, metal crumpling as it met unyielding stone.

Hawkins ripped into the remaining Syrian escape car, his P-90 hammering at 800 rounds per minute, turning its windshield into a gaping hole and the driver into a mushy figure that resembled a deflating humanoid balloon.

"I hope to hell no one heard that crash," Hawkins said.

"With David and the rest inside, I doubt they'd hear the sky crashing around them," Manning answered.

RAFAEL ENCIZO WINCED, leaning back from the sudden slash of shotgun shells vomiting swarms of pellets like hungry, flesh-eating hornets. Bezoar's defenders had carefully chosen their place to make their stand, and with a stubby set of 12-gauge scatterguns, they were able to dominate the row of windows where Encizo saw an additional team of Syrians collapsed. Only one of the Damascus assault squad was still alive, but his cheek had been torn off his face, one eye leaking down into the gaping flesh.

The Syrian saw Encizo and reached for his sidearm, his main weapon lost in the initial conflagration that left him facially mutilated. The Cuban was not a man to take chances, but he couldn't bring himself to gun down a man, especially at such close quarters, and when he'd received terrible injuries already. With a kick, he disarmed the man and leaned his weight into the Syrian's chest.

"I'm not here to kill you," Encizo stated, pressing his forearm against the man's throat. "In fact, we're probably both here after the same man. Bezoar."

With lacerations down the right side of his face, the Syrian's grimace was hideous. "That…animal. He's out of…control."

Encizo could tell the genuine rage underneath the other man's words. "Where else are you hurt?"

The man tugged open his shirt, looking down at the glimmering copper discs embedded in dark blue nylon beneath. "Armor stopped the bullets."

Encizo let go of the man's arm and loosened his forearm from the Syrian's throat. "We're on the same side."

"Gunfire dropped off drastically," the agent said.

"I'm not sure that's a good thing," Encizo said. He handed over a small, prepacked wound dressing kit.

The maimed Syrian wasted no time, stuffing his pistol back into its holster and pressing a pad of gauze firmly against his torn socket. He'd never be able to save the eye. The best he could hope for was to keep out infection and prevent losing more blood. Micropore cloth tape held the dressing in place, especially one long strip wound three times around his head.

He'd live, but he didn't look strong enough to get back on his feet. He'd been rattled too hard by the blast that had laid open his face. However, there was one chance that Encizo could take by recruiting the man as a friendly intelligence asset. The Syrians and Phoenix Force had clashed on several occasions, but this wouldn't be the first time that the five-man team would work alongside traditional national enemies, especially in the face of a full-on crisis.

Whatever had caused Bezoar to become so instantly important to warrant not one but two attempts by the Syrian commando team, as well as garner the interest of Western intelligence, must have been big enough for Encizo not to regret the decision to rescue and aid a foe.

The Syrian commando took a fist full of Encizo's sleeve. "He's gone rogue."

"You told me," the Cuban replied.

"You don't know how bad it is," the injured man urged. "This is worse than anything your side could imagine. Even we didn't want it to exist."

"Exist?" Encizo asked.

"When Bezoar showed his test, it was too terrible," the one-eyed commando continued. "It's a deadly enzyme…some kind of infectious protein."

"We figured as much," Encizo returned. He didn't want to betray his knowledge of one of Bezoar's prior experiments, just in case the Syrians had a long enough memory to remember the destruction of a project that would otherwise have created a harvest hell throughout the Mediterranean.

"He improved on it," the Syrian told him. "But we missed."

"So you went after him again," Encizo answered. He kept his attention only peripherally on the wounded man; his main job was to provide security for the back door.

"No, we missed now!" the Syrian hissed. "He's gone."

Encizo looked down at the wounded man.

"This was a trap, and both of our teams walked right into it," the injured man croaked weakly.

Encizo felt his stomach twist at the news. "David, can you read me?"

No answer over the radio, nothing but a blanket of static that knocked out the radio network he was plugged into.

"David!" Encizo bellowed, hoping that his old friend could hear him.

Gunfire rose to a crescendo once more in a far part of the building.

DAVID MCCARTER GRIMACED as he realized that the tactical network that tied him to the rest of the team had gone silent. He waved to Calvin James, and the former SEAL nodded, acknowledging that his radio was out of commission, as well.

"We're in for a rough one," McCarter muttered as the gunfire suddenly died out. "Or maybe not…"

"One side's run out of targets," James commented. "We're never lucky enough for both sides to finish each other off."

"There's always a first time," McCarter mused.

"Yeah, right. I don't see you running out willy-nilly," James returned.

The Phoenix leader nodded, but he still took the lead as he moved toward the stairs. The old apartment building was pre-elevator technology, so its center was a spiral staircase decorated with black wrought iron that twisted from the ground to the upper floors. McCarter's ears were peeled for the sound of movement above, and he checked the steps. They were made of stone, so they wouldn't bend and creak like wooden slat stairs, meaning that they simply had to keep their footsteps soft and careful.

He moved up with catlike grace, James following several steps behind, preventing the pair from bunching up to be caught in the same burst or pattern of buckshot. McCarter, in the lead, knew he'd get most of the enemy attention, but despite his earlier assessment of how he'd matured in terms of no longer being impatient and addicted to action, he still was a man who led from the front, taking even more risks than those he assigned his own men. He had no illusions that he was bulletproof or immortal, but he knew his skills, equipment and reflexes. McCarter wasn't the kind of man to boast, yet he knew his odds of surviving a close combat situation were among the best of anyone on the planet.

Calvin James hung back for another reason: he'd supplemented his P-90 subgun with a sawed-off shotgun with a dull orange stock. The coloration wasn't a matter of fashion, but rather a means of telling this particular weapon from a live, fully-lethal 12-gauge. The orange-stocked weapon had a tube magazine, and its threaded sling was loaded with less-lethal munitions, specifically designed for the purpose of rendering opponents incapable of fighting while still leaving them available for subsequent questioning. Less lethal was not a guarantee, and if James had to kill in his defense, he'd be able to end a foe's existence with a direct hit to the face. Still, the majority of the loads were high-intensity neoprene slugs, flexible enough to yield when they struck flesh without penetration, but possessing all the horsepower of a regular slug. James had taken hits to the chest with one as part of his familiarization with the round's effects, and even through body armor, his chest was blackened with bruises.

Right now, however, the first three rounds were "ferrets," or compact capsicum suspension dispersal shells that could punch through a windshield or a door and vomit out several dozen cubic feet of tear gas. Capsicum was another effective tool in taking foes off guard, denying them their sight and smell, as well as limiting their ability to speak as their mucus membranes inflamed at the touch of the raw, powerful pepper extract. Bezoar needed to be taken down, and it would be beneficial to Stony Man to figure out who had spirited the mad scientist out of Syria and into Europe.

"Let 'em have it," McCarter said in a stage whisper

to James, and the Phoenix Force medic brought up the stubby shotgun, working the slide and trigger of the weapon as fast as he could, spearing the trio of ferret rounds toward the fourth and top floor of the building. Thick, cottony white smoke roiled from their points of impact, immediately followed by a fit of coughing and wheezing.

A figure stumbled into the open, his head wrapped in dark cloth, a machine pistol locked in both of his fists. McCarter reacted to the man's sudden appearance with well-honed, lightning-fast reflexes. A snarl of 5.8 mm rounds tore into the gunman just before the tear-gas-resistant foe could pull the trigger. While the FN P-90 didn't throw fat or heavy slugs, its lightweight projectiles moved at 850 meters per second and carried 540 joules per bullet. When McCarter opened up at 800 rounds per minute, ripping five shots into the gunman, ribs shattered and flesh parted as the high-velocity projectiles created havoc. With his lungs and aorta reduced to ribbons of slashed tissue, the only thing that the would-be killer was able to do was to tumble headfirst over the railing.

McCarter hoped that the hardman was instantly dead; otherwise the crushing impacts against the rails of the spiral staircase would have been additionally agonizing, limbs folded with ugly crunches as his mass and velocity vectors proved far too much for his skeleton to withstand. Forty feet down, Bezoar's hired gun stopped violently, his corpse accordioning against the floor, spine compressing, discs sliding off to the side from each other in their effort to accept gravity's loving embrace.

"It's not the fall—it's the sudden stop," McCarter mused to himself.

Other defenders had donned some manner of clothing to shield their nostrils and eyes from the brutal effects of the tear gas, but none had been so quick and efficient as to be able to charge out with their guns ready to blaze like their recently departed comrade.

As he took the steps three at a time, McCarter bounded to finish this encounter with the enemy shooters before the Parisian gendarmes arrived with a few heavily armed assault teams. While Phoenix Force proved that it was able to fight its way out of some of the most hostile environments in the world, getting into a direct conflict with lawmen only doing their job was something that the Stony Man warriors wanted to avoid at all costs. Shooting a soldier on the same side was a moral choice that each had taken. While that moral choice was made flexible in dealing with corrupt and crooked lawmen or troops, the French counterterrorism police were allies in the same cause.

With that in mind, McCarter let the P-90 drop to the end of its sling, withdrawing a collapsible ASP baton. He flicked his wrist, and the high-tensile steel tubes telescoped to their full length with an ominous snap. The sound caught the attention of one of the masked thugs, and he turned, drawing up his Steyr TMP machine pistol to deal with the sudden attack. McCarter batted aside the enemy gunman's barrel with one swipe of the locked baton, using the rebound off the gun's polymer frame to guide his next strike, a jaw-shattering stroke that whipped the cloth from his face.

McCarter could see that the enemy had East Asian features in the brief flutter of freed-up cloth, but he kicked the stunned or unconscious foe out of the way, whipping the point of the ASP down on the juncture between another gunman's neck and shoulder. Nerves overloaded under the assault, bringing a wail of pain from his target. A third gunner with a pistol was bowled over by a neoprene slug from James's shotgun, the three-quarter-inch cylinder of hard rubber breaking bones as the Phoenix medic hit the man right in the sternum.

James didn't wait to see if his target would stay down because the pistol hadn't fallen from nerveless fingers. The less-lethal shotgun proved quite deadly as James put another rubber baton round into the defender's face, blood squirting from his eye sockets.

McCarter had no time to comment on the gruesome demise as he was dealing with the fourth enemy soldier, lashing this one under his arm to make him drop his firearm. Instead of bringing the ASP around to administer a coup de grâce, the Briton jammed the heel of his palm under his opponent's chin, whipping his head back violently. The last of the defenders in this doorway were littering the walkway, their battered forms providing grim testimony to the efficiency of Phoenix Force.

McCarter let the baton drop to the floor, swinging his P-90 back into his grasp.

Lifeless bodies were strewed around the room, only one man still sitting upright. His white shirt was a bloody mess, and while at first blush he would have resembled Bezoar, a mouth full of mangled and busted false teeth yawned from the gaping gash of his lips. Bezoar's file read that he had perfect teeth and no dental work done to improve them.

This guy was a fake, and he was holding on to an unmistakable D-shaped object.

A dead man's switch equipped with a trigger that its wielder held down. Upon death and the relaxation of his fingers, whatever charge it was connected to would detonate.

The bloody, cap-filled smile broadened with the sight of McCarter and James. "And so…Paris dies."

A second later he was a corpse, head flopping forward, the dead man's switch tumbling to the cold tile floor.…

CHAPTER FIVE

David McCarter saw the dead man's switch begin to fall from the lifeless hand of a man who claimed Paris was about to die. His reaction was immediate and swift. He dropped his gun and leaped across the room, fingers clenching around the loosening fist of the corpse, keeping the pressure on the switch before it could activate.

"Cal! Get Gary now!" McCarter shouted. "I can't squeeze this geezer's digits all night!"

Calvin James took in the scene with a glance, then pivoted on his heel. McCarter could see that his partner was trying to raise someone on the hands-free radio even as he rushed to get the others, but communications had been knocked out.

It was a no-sweater for McCarter. The team was well coordinated, and had gotten along without the use of their hands-free communications nets before. The members of Phoenix Force hadn't been chosen because of their ability to get along aided by some of the best high-tech equipment and intelligence in the world. It was their ability to improvise when cut off from all other assets, relying on their vast wealth of skills and experience to minimize chances of failure and succeed where all else was lost.

Still, McCarter couldn't sit on the dead man's switch

indefinitely. The gunfire and explosions had to have attracted the attention of the Paris police, and no matter what, they would not take kindly to the Briton holding on to the trigger of a device that could unleash damnation upon their city, friendly or not. Barbara Price had been able to bail the Stony Man warriors out of trouble with local law enforcement before, but some incidents would be just too much and focus far too much attention on what was supposed to be one of the most covert operations in the world.

McCarter recognized Manning's tread as he raced up the stairs, and checked his mental clock.

"You must have broken position as soon as the radios went out," McCarter mused as the big Canadian came through the door.

"Cal met me halfway. He said you were hanging on to a dead man's switch," Manning replied, ignoring his friend and commander's comment.

McCarter shrugged. "What can I say? I've always wanted to hold hands with a corpse."

Manning looked at the device, then at the lifeless figure whom McCarter shared it with. "This could be one of two types of switches. One is that it transmits when it is released, in which case, our asses are safe, so long as they didn't booby-trap the power supply. The other is that it is transmitting, and we're on a countdown until the batteries fail, no matter how well we duct tape the trigger shut."

McCarter looked at it. "Considering that there's a jammer knocking out our radios, I'm not sure this is a live transmission that'll stop once the lever's depressed."

Manning's brow furrowed as he looked at it. "Perhaps it's on a shielded frequency, or the jammer isn't operating on that level."

"T.J. should be working our scanner to see which frequencies are open," McCarter said, referring to the radio communications bands. "Unless he's too busy…"

"He's on it," Manning returned. "He can keep an ear out for the cops while checking the scanner. In fact, he's determined that police bands are untouched by the jamming. We'd be on that wavelength, too, but…"

"Yeah, yeah," McCarter said. "The geezer I'm all chummy with said that when this goes off, Paris dies."

Manning leaned in closer to look at the crude electronic device. "David, you should know that I can perform multiple mental tasks simultaneously. Not to cast aspersions on…"

McCarter waited for Manning's lecture to finish, but the trailed-off sentence set his nerves on edge.

"What is it?" McCarter asked.

"T.J. managed to hit a clear channel for us. He says that Cal and Rafe located the 'bomb,'" Manning said.

"I don't like that you made it sound as if 'bomb' were in quotes," McCarter replied.

"Come on," Manning said. He pulled out his combat knife and severed the dead man's hand at the wrist, allowing them to take the trigger along with them to the roof.

"The roof?" McCarter asked. Manning reached over and reset the frequency on his hands-free radio.

"We've got three tanks up here," Encizo said as the two men arrived at the top of the building. Their Cuban ally had just torn open an air-conditioning unit and McCarter could see the canisters within the remnants of the housing. "We're lucky that no one put a bullet through one."

"Nerve gas?" McCarter asked as he stepped closer to the bomb. The canisters had been united by a bit of electronics with spray nozzles that pointed up into the night sky.

"There's not an agency or military in the world that doesn't have biohazard markings on their nerve gas delivery systems," James said. "Besides, these are traditional helium canisters, and as far as I can tell, they haven't been reloaded. They're fresh and unrecycled."

McCarter looked at the device that connected the three tanks. "What kind of dispersal could three helium tanks give to a spore or other pathogen?"

"I'm seeing we can get close to thirty square miles, effectively infecting all of Paris," Manning returned.

"Guys," Hawkins interjected over the radio. "I'm monitoring the police bands, and we're not gettin' any attention. They've got calls about fireworks going off, not gunfire."

McCarter and Manning looked at each other quizzically. "Staying away from this place under orders… like they know something bad is about to happen here," McCarter added.

Manning nodded. "T.J.…."

"I'm checking the scope for encrypted comms, and just linked up with the Farm," Hawkins answered. "They've got satellites looking down on the city, and there are no aircraft heading our way, marked or unmarked."

"Doesn't mean that they can't be arriving in a black van or two," Manning noted.

"My head's on a swivel down here," Hawkins replied. "Want to defuse whatever that thing is so we can beat feet?"

"Absolutely," Encizo agreed. "The longer we sit here thumbing our asses…"

Manning reached out to the box, his powerful yet sensitive fingertips caressing a smaller rectangular component on the side of it. With a powerful wrench of his wrist, the module popped off into his grasp and he closed his fist tight around it. Slender sheet metal buckled, the silicone board within popping as it was crushed in his powerful hand. "You can let go of the trigger now, David."

"How did you know it wasn't set to go off when its antenna was removed?" McCarter asked.

"It was just big enough to hold a transceiver, no booby traps. There's nothing inside of this part of the device that could trigger the dispersant without a regular command," Manning said.

McCarter nodded. "Get that shit off the helium tanks fast. We're taking it back with us."

Encizo spoke up. "You told us the guy holding that trigger said Paris would die."

James frowned as he leaned back, slipping a small tube into his vest. "Helium under high pressure was the dispersant. I've got the nozzles on both ends of the device sealed with epoxy."

"The superglue that you use to close minor cuts?" Manning asked.

James nodded. "Works on closing off tubing pretty well, too. It should retain its seal for a good stretch."

"Find a means of hermetically sealing it, too," McCarter said. "T.J., any more news?"

"I'm on my way up. A black van just pulled into view," Hawkins answered. "I made certain they didn't see me enter the building."

"We're roofing it," Encizo muttered.

McCarter tossed aside the severed hand, but kept the trigger unit, slipping it into a pouch for future study. If anyone could learn the origin of this particular bomb, it would be Gary Manning, if his keen observation of the strange dispersal unit hadn't already raised a few clues and flags.

For now, James had bound the device in a thermal blanket, duct taping the neck of the metallic cloth shut as it wrapped around the boxy unit. For something no larger than a shoebox, David McCarter didn't want to imagine what kind of monstrosity was within.

If one tiny bit was more than enough to kill a city, how much had Bezoar produced to deal with the whole world?

McCarter put such grim thoughts aside as he leaped from rooftop to rooftop, crossing the gaps between the tightly spaced buildings as he and the others trekked in a roundabout path to return to their own transportation.

HERMANN SCHWARZ KNELT at the edge of the bomb crater, looking around the scene with concern at the randomness of the single blast. The town of Albion, now a silent hole in the ground, had been nailed with several thousand-pound high-intensity bombs, turning the area into a lifeless wound in the Iowan countryside.

His credentials read FBI Bomb Squad, as did the identification for Lyons and Blancanales, but he was the only member of their team who had more than enough scientific background and qualification to study the forensics of a high-powered blast.

"Why here?" Schwarz asked.

"Maybe they missed?" Lyons offered. "As far as smart bombs go, sometimes one or two stray off course during a salvo."

"You don't think it was a miss, though," Blancanales added.

Schwarz shook his head, then stepped back. On his CPDA screen, he'd had a detailed report of Trooper Robespierre's observations. "This was a fruit stand that had turned into an apocalypse, according to our state cop."

"Trooper," Lyons corrected.

Schwarz looked at the Able Team leader, and was about to say something, when he remembered his own short response and correction of technical terms when Lyons made a mistake. "Trooper."

"There had been a gunfight here," Blancanales said. He'd read the report, as well. All of the federal agents on the scene were aware of what Robespierre had reported. Still, most of the investigation work was done around the shell-shocked town of Albion.

"Shell-shocked" wasn't the right term, Schwarz corrected himself. A bombarded town described as shell-shocked had pockets of destruction, survivors, damaged buildings. The wave of destruction that had come down on the tiny ville was complete. Not a single splinter of the town was still standing, bodies more than simply pulped, but incinerated and reduced to component atoms.

So far, no one had claimed responsibility for the bombing, the end of hundreds of American lives.

"Trooper Robespierre described something akin to a food riot, according to what was left over here," Lyons continued. "People rushed this fruit stand, and the owner opened fire. There was at least one casualty, and then the stand owner fell, literally torn apart, as if by an animal."

Lyons looked at his Combat PDA, pulling up dash camera images from the wrecked cruiser. The digital footage had been grainy, but Aaron Kurtzman had done his technical magic, providing Able Team with a clearer picture of the situation. "They didn't shoot the fruit stand owner with a shotgun. There's no burns or stippling such as from contact-range shots with a 12-gauge."

"So he was bitten and clawed apart?" Blancanales asked as he looked at the image Lyons referenced. "What, is this another group of crazies who think they're zombies?"

"I don't think anyone was pretending in this case," Schwarz said.

"Me, either. Look at this one. She's on the ground and her throat is distended, bulging with obstructions," Lyons said. "Kurtzman wasn't able to make out what is sticking from her mouth, but I'll bet you anything that she tried to swallow something whole."

"Throat and belly, that shirt's coming open across her stomach," Blancanales added.

Schwarz leaned in to look at the picture Lyons had on display. His lips pulled into a tight line, disappearing under his mustache. "Even at their hungriest, people don't try to eat each other," Schwarz said. "It doesn't make sense."

"They weren't trying to eat each other," Lyons said. "This was simply a gone-feral attack. He had a shotgun, and the rioters used the only weapons that they had— their teeth and nails."

Blancanales looked at the crater. "So the bomb was dropped here to prevent an autopsy."

"Even so, how would anyone be certain that things didn't spread, didn't get out of hand?" Schwarz asked.

"The same way the bombs were delivered," Lyons answered. "Aerial vehicles, manned or unmanned."

"That seems obvious enough, but you'd think that Albion's residents would have noticed extra aircraft hanging around," Schwarz mused. "I've had the Farm pull the FAA records about crop dusting in this part of the state, and none of the pilots even mentioned so much as a UFO."

Lyons looked at the blast crater again. "Maybe someone made use of local talent."

"Local pilots might work, but wouldn't they get suspicious?" Schwarz asked. "Could you drop a bunch of bombs on this town for us?"

"It wouldn't have to be as vulgar as that," Blancanales said.

"Observation during routine flights," Schwarz replied.

"It'd work for me," Lyons said. "That way you keep the bombers in reserve, but your experiment doesn't breach the security protocols."

"An experiment in what?" Blancanales asked.

"The closest I can figure, considering the reaction and the hunger so strong that they were willing to brave close-range shotgun fire," Schwarz began. "Man, even so, that's some fucked-up shit."

"What?" Lyons prompted. There was a hardness to his voice. Schwarz could tell that his friend was on edge. Everyone was on edge, considering that hundreds of people had been killed by a salvo of military-grade precision airstrikes. The trouble was, Carl Lyons on edge was dangerous and on the hunt for vengeance and retribution.

The blowout in Chicago had been proof enough of that.

When the Able Team leader became frustrated, results came quickly.

"A prion," Schwarz said.

Lyons frowned. "You're not talking about some kind of hybrid car. It's a protein, a dangerous one, right?"

"A dangerous, infectious particle composed mostly of

protein, much simpler than even a virus," Schwarz said. "There are a few that are known, but mostly prions are considered theoretical units of infection…a proposed vector to be eliminated when trying to identify an unfamiliar disease which may simply have mutated…"

"Right. And Striker recently encountered someone who had utilized weaponized versions of these proteins," Lyons returned.

Blancanales tilted his head. "It was an experimental process. What did this prion do, Gadgets?"

Schwarz pointed to the picture of the distended woman's corpse. "It shut down her ability to produce digestive enzymes."

Lyons's lower lip twitched. If it had been any other man, Schwarz would have dismissed the tiny tic, but on his friend's stoic face, it was the equivalent of shock. "She was starving to death, despite being surrounded by crops and fresh produce."

"That explains why there was a mob shooting it out with local county deputies in a grocer's parking lot," Blancanales said. "They wanted food, something to silence their hunger pangs."

"This had to have been quick, too," Schwarz added. "They had the strength and coordination to use weapons, to make attacks."

"So this isn't instant emaciation, just instant…hunger," Lyons translated.

"Maddening hunger as their minds couldn't cope with what was going on," Schwarz said. "But that's only a threadbare explanation. We don't have any evidence, nor an example of the prion that caused this situation."

"We would if there was something left of the town that hadn't been blasted to ribbons. The only clues we have of what happened are off the dashboard video," Blancanales mused. "Even that can't be conclusive, simply because of the necessary digital enhancement utilized isn't public technology."

"Blame the NSA for that," Schwarz returned. "Then again, No Such Agency doesn't even let the military that's defending it have up-to-date data, not without blurring what intel they do receive to keep the Army and others in the dark."

Lyons cut him off. "Now's not the time to bitch about jurisdictional fits. Besides, I doubt that the NSA would like knowing that we continually swipe their footage fresh off the airwaves."

Schwarz smirked. "If only I could pipe that kind of a feed into CENTCOM. Iraq and Afghanistan wouldn't have been considered clusterfucks and a whole lot fewer soldiers would have been injured."

"Would've, could've and should've aren't in our job description," Lyons countered. "What is in the description is fucking up the bastards who bombed women and children in a sleepy little town. We're not sure what happened here before the bombs hit, but we do know that someone utilized some heavy firepower—guided by tech that went through Chicago. So give me an idea where we go here."

Schwarz folded his arms, eyes cast toward the ground to focus himself.

"Don't forget, we don't have to worry about finding evidence, we just have to do our job," Blancanales said to Lyons.

Lyons nodded. "I'd still like to be sure of what we're doing. Beating up crop-duster pilots and barnstormers until we shake answers loose isn't my style."

Blancanales smirked. "But hitting a mob smuggling hub so hard it bounces…"

"That was different," Lyons said. "We knew those guys were crooked. They were armed and ready to kill anyone getting in their way. Besides, I showed restraint. I shot them in the body armor when I had the opportunity. Everything else was self-defense."

"Plus, it made your new contact look good," Blancanales added. "Just what we'll do with that kind of intel, especially if they find out about him…"

"We'll get at least one good use out of this," Lyons replied.

Schwarz looked up. "I've been doing the math. The crop dusters will only be operating inside of a normal size circle—they wouldn't be trying to stretch their fuel on their regular orbits because they'd want room to fly around to do their spraying."

"Need to look up ranges?" Lyons asked.

Schwarz shook his head. "General aircraft range is between five and six hundred miles. I looked up traditional, professional-grade agricultural aircraft and their ranges already in anticipation of what might have been local aircraft for delivery systems and such."

Blancanales nodded in agreement. "A crop duster could conceivably carry the weight of the kind of firepower that destroyed Albion."

Lyons frowned. "How much of a payload?"

"We're looking at 2.4 tons," Blancanales answered. "Given the fact that one gallon has the equivalent weight of eight pounds, and the AT-602 Air Tractor can take to the wing with a six hundred gallon payload. Another plane that's been in use for about fifty years, the SR2 Ayers Thrush has a maximum takeoff weight of 3.5 tons, 3200 pounds of that being aerial dispersant."

"Someone would notice the bulk of the bombs, wouldn't they?" Lyons asked.

"Maybe," Schwarz returned. "But who knows how the bombs were disguised. They could have been stored as external tanks on wing hardpoints."

"We're always thinking about high-tech aircraft like Predator drones and such, but something low-tech like a crop duster can be utilized to do a lot of harm," Lyons said.

"We're always involved in cases of high-tech weapons and aircraft, and we still are," Blancanales countered. "Remember, we were brought to this case because Albion was destroyed by laser-guided iron bombs."

Schwarz nodded in agreement. "We're still utilizing low-tech craft combined with high technology. Remote aerial vehicles aren't cutting edge—we've had radio planes for decades. Most drones utilize the simplest engines and body designs, combined with cheap, easy-to-replace camera transmission equipment."

"Will the FBI figure that out?" Blancanales asked Lyons. This was a valid question, because despite their credentials identifying them as Feds, Schwarz and Blancanales were both former military, not having much more than a passing familiarity with jurisdictional conflict and investigative protocols. Lyons came from a police background, having worked both for the LAPD and as an FBI operative.

"That ag planes were involved?" Lyons returned. "They might eventually, but we have a lot more leeway and can move without warrants."

"What about the Patriot Act bullshit?" Schwarz asked with unveiled disgust.

Lyons wrinkled his nose. Able Team and Stony Man worked outside of the justice system, doing their job without warrant, without sanction and without the necessity to take prisoners alive and unharmed. But they did that job to protect the system of freedoms and legal defenses the rest of the nation were guaranteed in the U.S. Constitution. The idea of the whole government having carte blanche to act on hunches and without need of judicial sanction was frightening. Giving law enforcement agencies far too much power was something they'd seen in action in places like Guatemala or the former Soviet Union.

Almost always, Lyons and his men had to put down the rabid, corrupt officials who were laws unto themselves. They fought tooth and nail to prevent the fall of the United States and its Constitution to the need for quick, easy persecution.

"Right now, things are just too fresh. We have some wiggle room. We just need to narrow down the duster who would have been servicing this area," Lyons said.

"If he's still alive," Blancanales brought up.

Lyons scowled. "If so, then God help the sorry bastards if they've hung around to clean up their tracks. Let's move."

CHAPTER SIX

David McCarter appeared on the wall screen in the Stony Man War Room. Stubble showed up clearly on his chin, whiskers that extended until he was two days past five-o'clock shadow. His eyelids were baggy and darkly shadowed, but his eyes themselves were bright, alert and full of energy.

Barbara Price could appreciate the kind of energy that kept the Briton going. He'd been in Paris on the hunt for Bezoar, and ended up stumbling into the middle of a war between covert operatives from Damascus and whatever group the Syrian had sided with in the wake of his defection.

"We've got some news here in the States," Price said.

McCarter's eyes focused tightly on the webcam's lens, growing even more alert with that message.

"Give it over, Barb," McCarter answered. "We're still waiting on whoever is going to analyze the crap in that device we defanged this morning."

"I'm trying to arrange someone to get to Paris without attracting the attention of the authorities," Price explained. "It's not an easy process, but we may have some clue as to what that secret weapon might be doing."

"It was released Stateside?" McCarter asked.

"Yes, in Iowa," Price told him. "We don't have any

bodies to autopsy, but we have some brief video imagery of victims of…something."

Price nodded, and Akira Tokaido forwarded an enhanced image to McCarter. It was a side-by-side comparison of the two fallen figures seen at the fruit stand that led Schwarz to his conclusion. The chilling visage of one woman who had literally distended her throat by jamming fruit and vegetables into her mouth, suffocating in an effort to abate her hunger, left McCarter with a grim jolt of recognition.

"Bloody hell, it's Bezoar's old trick with indigestible crops, except worse," McCarter said.

"It's only a theory, but these people were wildly starving if they were hungry enough to choke on their meals," Price added.

"If you hear hoofbeats, look for horses before saying they're unicorns," McCarter countered. "We and Damascus are on the hunt for a bioweapons designer who on at least one prior occasion set up a starvation plague."

"I was worried that Schwarz's conclusions might have been informed by his knowledge of your hunt. Bezoar's name wasn't known until recently, but he was one of the old-school lab monkeys who worked on projects for the hardline Soviets," Price stated. "We've had our own people working on this, too."

"So, we know it could be aerially dispersed, but is it breathable?" McCarter asked.

"That's part of my difficulty. We don't know how we're going to run a laboratory analysis on it, or if it's even safe to transport in a diplomatic pouch," Price explained. "Do we leave it there and get France uptight because we're bringing in American scientists to our embassy? Or risk it releasing on board a plane?"

"Touchy stuff," McCarter said. "I don't envy whatever decision you have to make. But whatever, we still need to figure out a few things."

"Like?" Price asked.

"Why the French police were told to deliberately ignore responding to shots-fired reports," McCarter said. "Has the cyberteam picked up any chatter? Top-level communications?"

"Still in the dark there," Price answered. "We're digging, though. Whatever caused it, they knew what was going down in their backyard. You don't have a group of Syrian special-ops guys suddenly appear in your city hot on the heels of the deaths of another bunch. Relevant agencies haven't been discussing the issue, and nothing's shown up in the newspapers. That means the government might be on a total lockdown of information."

"Complicity? Or blackmail?" McCarter asked.

"Only those two options?" Price quipped.

"If it was anything else, I'm sure their administration would be asking us for help. It's not as if we haven't gone scurrying to the rescue of European governments in the past. Sure, they wouldn't know Phoenix Force by name, but they'd know that they could ask Washington for those special Interpol investigators for assistance like they did when we took on ODESSA a long time back," McCarter explained.

"Do you think they'd ask us after the past decade's

worth of Chinese fire drills?" Price asked. "You've worked in France recently and only barely avoided getting fried while taking on another operation."

"We were poking around their nuclear reactors, Barb," McCarter answered. "They were on edge because of that, so we had to be working on the fringe. There's no way they could identify us with them."

"You've worked with these agencies before, David," Price said. "There's no way they could forget you."

McCarter looked around at the rest of his team, each of them unwinding and preparing for the next stage of their mission. He sighed. "We are a colorful bunch."

Price took a cleansing breath and looked at McCarter's face. He seemed to have picked up more of a glow, the bags under his eyes no longer seeming so deep, his stubble lying neatly on his jaw. "So what's your next course of action?"

"Gary and I are going to visit my French intelligence contact," McCarter said. "Meanwhile, Calvin's continuing to treat the Syrian survivor so we can get information out of him. T.J. and Rafael will be working security, keeping unwanted eyes off us, and making certain our visitor doesn't try to make a break for it."

"Damascus is not going to like that we took one of their number," Price told him.

McCarter shrugged. "We saved his life. What they're not going to like is the fact that T.J. and Gary blew their getaway drivers to ribbons. Once he's healthy enough to walk, we're sending him back home to Syria. We've kept things murky enough for any debriefing to be useless."

Price sighed. "Just be certain, okay?"

"We'll be careful," McCarter returned.

BACK IN IOWA, Able Team was in their Ford Explorer. Ordinarily, the vehicle had been designed to accommodate five people, with fold-down seats adding to cargo space at the expense of more room for passengers. However, most aspects of the SUV had undergone some form of subtle modification, either at the hands of John "Cowboy" Kissinger or the electronic and mechanical genius of Hermann "Gadgets" Schwarz. The Explorer had come with them from Virginia, as bringing a set of their own wheels was logical when it came to U.S.-based operations, or even across the borders into Canada or Mexico. Unfortunately, trips into Mexico either required full sanction and invitation from the Mexican government, or Able Team had to rely on their "border hopper"—another similar Explorer, except this one was designed to look completely ordinary, even in the presence of border police and contraband-sniffing dogs with items like a hermetically sealed weapons locker under the rearmost cushions.

Since they were on friendly ground, Lyons was glad to have the fully loaded Able Team SUV. The Explorer had a thin layer of electrically sensitive cells on its outer hull that could alter the hue of the vehicle at the touch of a button. There was the classic black look, but Able Team also had the options of fake textures from mud-splashed to rusted with holes in it or bullet scores on the skin and windshield, which had a similar photocel treatment. While the vehicle didn't have a built-in rocket launcher for utilization as artillery, it was packed with communications and surveillance technology designed by Schwarz, and layers of armor plating had been installed by Lyons and Kissinger. The Explorer was bulletproof now, but firearms damage to the skin would require panel replacement for the photocels to work in that particular area. Luckily, they were each on individual power circuits, so damage to one wouldn't affect the rest of their disguise, and the flat plates were modular for easy repair, even in the field.

The purpose of the SUV was to provide Able Team with the ability to disappear in plain sight, like now, when they were driving toward one of three airfields that Schwarz and the cyber crew back at the Farm had narrowed down as the possible source of the "borrowed" aircraft. At the moment the Explorer wasn't a shiny, imposing black Fed vehicle but a brownish red smeared with gray, indicating an SUV that had been rode hard and put away muddy.

Behind the wheel, Lyons accepted a pair of binoculars from Schwarz.

"This is the first one on your list," Lyons said. "You probably don't have any high hopes for the other two…"

"They're possibilities if we strike out here," Schwarz answered. "But given the field's position, its size and how low profile it is, it has the strongest possibility."

"Mathematically speaking," Blancanales added. "What's the cop gut say?"

"Other than no more doughnuts?" Schwarz interjected.

Lyons flipped Schwarz off without breaking his observation of the airfield. There was a hangar that was big enough for two airplanes, and they were both inside. Normally, that might not have seemed out of place, but there was one monoplane sitting on the grass beside the landing strip.

"You wouldn't leave your business aircraft sitting out in the open, would you?" Lyons asked. "Even if there was a fence around the field?"

Schwarz narrowed his eyes and studied the Air Tractor aircraft once more through his field glasses. "No. And the weird thing is that it doesn't look weather-beaten. As if it were only parked outside for the time being."

"And yet, I see the outlines of two aircraft sitting inside the hangar," Lyons noted.

"Cop gut says this place is crooked," Blancanales said.

"So, this field, normally registered with two aircraft, has three of them, one of those being a totally unassuming crop duster that doesn't look as if it's been left out in the open as it's stored now for evening," Schwarz concluded.

"So let's take a look to see what the other plane is," Blancanales said.

"How?" Lyons asked. "Kick down the gate, flashing badges?"

"That's one way to do it, but you already proved you can do sneaky," Blancanales replied. "Just follow my lead. Gadgets?"

Schwarz smirked. "Going in quiet."

With that, the Able Team genius slipped out of the

SUV, disappearing into the roadside foliage without more than a ripple. He'd grabbed his gear, and would make certain that he was hard to notice by the time he reached the fence. Both Schwarz and Blancanales had been part of a penetration team while in the military and as such, were as well-trained in scout work as open warfare.

Blancanales, meanwhile, slicked back his hair, tossed his hat onto the dusty road and gave it some stomps with his boots. Lyons didn't think that his partner had taken leave of his senses because he had suddenly begun pounding the living daylights out of his hat. Taking the cue, Lyons threw his "Fed" sport jacket into a storage area and slipped on his favorite, well-worn denim jacket. He flipped his tie in after it and checked himself in the mirror.

"Couple good old boys," Lyons murmured.

"Never meanin' no harm," Blancanales added, a twinkle in his eye.

"If I remember, you were the only one of us that's been in trouble with the law, Politician," Lyons countered.

"You never had problems with your chief?" Blancanales asked innocently.

Lyons sighed. "So, what's the role?"

"Couple good old boys," Blancanales said.

"Drunk 'n' stupid?" Lyons asked.

"Wouldn't be good if we weren't," Blancanales answered, slurring his speech a little.

Lyons shrugged. "Newp."

The two friends went on to provide a brief distraction for their friend, making certain to put their weapons away.

This was an intelligence-gathering operation, and if there was trouble, neither Lyons nor Blancanales would be wanting for the ability to respond to violence swiftly and acquire a firearm. It was a risk, but then so was every mission that Able Team had ever been on. The presence of a pistol on the hip was not an automatic guarantee of combat ability any more than holding a paintbrush made someone van Gogh. Lyons and Blancanales, however, were truly dangerous men, both not only having received thousands of hours of martial arts training, but actually having used their abilities in combat across the globe. If their ruse failed, then they would be in good shape.

Even so, each wore a low-profile undercover Kevlar vest. They weren't reinforced, and wouldn't do a single ounce of good in the face of a rifle or a shotgun, but the vests would buy them precious seconds if fired upon by a handgun.

If it came to that, however, all of their subterfuge and Schwarz's stealth would have been wasted, not only because of the efforts taken, but they'd also potentially set off any traps left behind by the mysterious enemies who'd destroyed the town only a few miles away. Able Team had encountered enough opponents who had left all manner of ambush, and the explosives and potential biological weapons on hand could spell doom for thousands of investigators and support teams in nearby Albion, even if a spread of the contagion didn't carry death on the wind to larger nearby towns or crop fields.

This was a case for silence and intelligence, not guns blazing.

With that knowledge, the two men approached the gate, seeming just lit enough to pass as a couple of farm hands who had whiled away the afternoon with a case of beer. Having given their partner enough of a head start, the two Able Team men went to raise a small ruckus.

THE SECURITY at the small airfield was nothing less than laughable, its fences rusted and in ill repair, but that was to be expected. The pilots out here didn't have much left out on the field when it came to valuable equipment. Everything that could be damaged by the elements or stolen was secreted away in the hangar, office or locked sheds. As such, Schwarz didn't even need to use his cutters to get through the chain link, which already hung in tatters between gritty brown poles. He was able to keep himself low to the ground, slithering along at a pace that minimized his profile but gave him enough mobility so that he could scurry across the ground fast enough to be in position at the hangar the minute that Lyons and Blancanales began to draw their heat.

Schwarz was pleased to see that his partners had changed the appearance of the photocel shell of their SUV to a green, muddy and rust-riddled vehicle, the windshield grayed by the same translucent, color-changing material. From a distance, it didn't look like anything special, just a previous generation Explorer that had been used hard. There was even an outline of clearer glass duplicating the windshield wiper patterns that swept away mud, grit and dust. Up close, it would certainly never pass a touch test, or even perusal at short range. For this work, especially with the setting sun, that was not going to be a problem.

Once he got within the perimeter, Schwarz lay prone. There appeared to be no sentries patrolling the airfield, but they could have been hidden or using some manner of remote camera. He turned on his Combat PDA, sweeping for signals, hoping that if his targets were rich enough to use black market laser guidance systems, they would be tech savvy enough to utilize wireless cameras rather than hardline. Nothing in operations was ever certain, but even if the cameras were Wi-Fi, then there would be a signal as they broadcast back to the central hub.

He set the CPDA where he could observe its screen, then turned on the thermal optics of his weapon, a compact SIG 556 SWAT carbine. The weapon combined the best features of the AK-47, such as its efficient, works-dirty piston and folding-stock capability, with the best of the AR-15 platform, like its high-powered 5.56 mm round and rail capabilities. In this instance Schwarz had his rifle set up for snoop-and-poop, a covert observation rather than all-out fighting. The SIG had a suppressor, a long-range thermal scope and a directional microphone that fed directly into a digital recorder for future intel gathering. This wasn't to say that Schwarz wasn't armed for a fight. The rifle would rip an opponent in two at the blistering rate of over 800 rounds per minute, its 5.56 mm projectiles tearing through flesh and fluid mass like miniature buzz saws, or exploding against bone to produce shrapnel in the form of bone splinters and shattered lead and copper. Schwarz had heard that there was doubt as to the efficacy of the 5.56 mm round, but he'd been able to stop an opponent.

Then again, Schwarz was a trained rifleman; he kept his rounds on target and could put them in an enemy where they'd do the most damage. However, if it came to a fight, Schwarz realized that he'd have his friends and partners left hanging out in the cold, and there could be a contagion breach.

No enemies showed up on thermal, and the CPDA showed that there wasn't a sign of wireless communication between cameras and a central computer. Schwarz's brow furrowed at this development. There was a plane on the scene that didn't belong, but no one was working the perimeter to keep the mystery craft from being investigated. Every instinct went on full alert, and Schwarz did a follow-up sweep of the terrain with the thermal scope, searching for any signs of camouflage from its infrared lens. It was hard for Schwarz to actually see a negative, so he improvised, keying in his hands-free communication set to listen to the parabolic microphone.

Immediately, he could pick up the rustle of the evening breeze rushing in, jostling the grass gently. The audio filters prevented the sudden chirp of a cricket from deafening him, but it had given him a slight start when it cut through the microbud speakers placed in his ears. He continued his sweep until he heard hushed but recognizable breathing.

Schwarz looked through the thermal scope at the spot where the breaths came from, and he caught the odd, shadowy outline of a figure, nothing more than a ghost against the background warmth of the cooling terrain. There was a slight turn of the ghostly figure's head, and Schwarz could see the sliver of uncovered face showing from underneath an insulated hood.

"Gadgets to the gang," he whispered. "I've got one sniper hidden and insulated against infrared optics."

In the distance he spotted the Able Team SUV screech to a halt at the gate to the airfield. If there was one hidden opponent, then there would definitely be more. His partners were still within their armored vehicle, but Schwarz himself was relatively exposed. He hadn't thought to cloak himself against infrared cameras, and if the enemy was using measures against such devices, there was the strong possibility that they possessed such technology themselves. Schwarz hated like hell to be stuck in the middle of a field with no more cover than uneven berms of soil surrounding him.

Schwarz turned the camera toward the hangar and noticed movement within. The parabolic mike picked up quick, hushed words, too soft and rushed to be decipherable even with the microphone, but definitely orders about an impending attack. A silhouette blocked the form of the plane that had drawn them in, and he could see the man was clad in a parka.

Worse, he had a rifle and was raising it to aim at Schwarz, who was stuck without any cover nearby.

CHAPTER SEVEN

Hal Brognola surrendered his sidearms to the Secret Service agents at the entrance to the Oval Office. Even a highly ranked member of the Justice Department—a man who had been entrusted with nothing less than the covert operations of Stony Man Farm—wasn't allowed within spitting distance of the President of the United States while carrying firearms. These days, he'd traded his old Smith & Wesson .44 Special revolver and backup snubnose .38 Special for a Glock 22 and a Glock 27, both chambered in .40 S&W, but it was still the same deal. Brognola had been through his share of administrative changes, and while there were those who decried disarming any officer of the law, the Secret Service had seen too many attacks on presidents during the twentieth century to ever leave anything to chance.

Cleared, Brognola entered the Oval Office to see the Man standing at the window. He had gone from rich, dark hair to gray in a short time, but then, the head Fed hadn't known a single President who hadn't been tasked and tried by the chair he sat in. Being leader of the free world meant that he was exposed to things that most people were not meant to know. As such, gray hair was only one small thing to worry about.

"Sir," Brognola said in greeting.

"Hal," the Man replied. "Have you ever had to make a decision to let your own people die?"

Brognola remained quiet for a moment, wondering how to answer that. "We've lost more than a few good people at the Farm, sir."

"I don't mean to send them on missions where they can't at least fight to survive," the President said.

"You're talking about blackmail on a global scale," Brognola answered.

The President turned and looked at Brognola. Under his eyes, sagging, heavy bags made the President seem ancient. "You've got a hint as to what's going on?"

"We have rumors of Syrians hunting a renegade mad scientist through Paris and a town disappearing in a fireball in the Midwest," Brognola said. "Someone is sending a message, and this likely isn't an isolated incident."

"I forget how in touch your people are," the President said, looking away.

"So, what are the demands?" Brognola asked.

"The United States has been asked to enter an auction," the President told him. "I've been asked to make a decision by a group of people who have a terrible weapon."

"How did they get the terms to you? You never even mentioned this during the morning threat matrix meetings," Brognola replied.

The President looked down, chagrin coloring his features. "I know we're not supposed to be using our own personal communications devices, but my digital assistant is very hard to give up."

"I know how much of a tech enthusiast you are," Brognola agreed. "They got to your personal account?"

"I was told that if this video were shown to any of the heads of the major agencies, the consequences would be genocidal," the President responded.

"Like what happened to Albion," Brognola said.

The man in front of Brognola looked as if someone had let all the air out of him. Shoulders sagged, head lowered, he was gaunt and harrowed. "I had to act as if I were surprised by what had happened. Here."

He handed over the small device.

"Keep it," he whispered as Brognola held it. The screen had been paused at the beginning of a video. Brognola slipped on the hands-free wireless mic and earbud so he would be the only one listening, then hit Play.

There was no reason to further distress the President.

Brognola sat for a horror show.

IT WAS EASY to recognize the man on the screen, the resolution of the video being high quality, and Brognola had been familiar with his face from the briefing he'd only just received a while ago when Phoenix Force had been dispatched to Paris for the purposes of pursuing him. The face was olive in complexion, with a dusting of a thin beard running from the sideburns down to the chin. His hair still had streaks of black in it, but it was losing the war with time and age, having been taken over by silvered locks. The eyes were dark but keen. The man was known as Bezoar and, until recently, had been assumed to be one of Syria's top defense-initiative biochemists, which really meant he was a mad scientist in charge of weapons of mass destruction.

Bezoar was addressing the camera, and took careful note that this particular video had been personalized for the administrative official who owned this phone.

"Greetings. Your intelligence analysts may identify me as Bezoar, that is, if you do not follow the stipulations by which we will punish you for betraying this video and these demands within," the Syrian said. "They would also inform you that I worked for the Russians and the Syrians, but now, I am my own man. For too long I have seen this world run by incompetents such as you and your predecessors, fools who have allowed civilization to slip from the edge of greatness.

"You see, my allies and I have realized that, for humanity to survive, the so-called first-world nations, the countries that burn fossil fuels and play with nuclear reactors as if they were toys, would have to disappear. Do not feel singled out by this message. Not even my own homeland, Syria, is immune to this criticism, and they, too, will be receiving this message. The only way for us to stop the incessant damage wrought upon this world is to deal with the sickness infesting it. That disease is known as modern man."

Bezoar turned from the screen. There was a video cut, and Bezoar and his simple dark backdrop had been replaced by a dark-skinned man in a glass cell. The individual had been sleeping, though not comfortably. He must have been hit with some form of sedative, because when he started to come around, his pallor changed quickly. Nausea overtook him, and he leaned over the arm of the chair, emptying what little he had in his stomach on the floor of the cell.

There had been no sound of retching, so Brognola assumed that this part of the video had been dubbed over. "I'll let you rack your brains over this information, but I will now show you the means by which everyone in your nation *could* die, unless you win your auction."

Brognola looked up from the smartphone at the mention of an auction. He was tempted to ask the President the stakes of such a purchase, but instead held his tongue. The video would explain everything that Bezoar wanted.

"As this man dies, I will explain the purpose of the group I've assembled—Greenwar," the Syrian scientist continued.

The captive lurched from his seat, feeling his upper abdomen. Brognola understood the universal gesture for hunger, but was surprised that the man was so ready and willing to eat only moments after vomiting. He saw a table full of food, a bountiful spread that would make most caterers envious. Fresh fruit, sliced cheeses, but no beef products as far as Brognola could tell, nothing that would go against the dietary prohibitions of a Hindu.

He picked up a piece of fruit and bit into it with the abandon of a starving man, gnashing it to the point where pulp and juices flowed over his lips and down his chin. Even as he tore into the fruit, his other hand scrabbled for another piece. Brognola had never seen a man suddenly succumb to so voracious an appetite, let alone so soon after vomiting, but even as the prisoner shoveled food toward his mouth, crumbs and drool gushing from the corners, there was a look of horrified realization as he continued.

A wave of violent frustration, even as he still chewed, washed over him and he kicked over the table. He tried to say something, shouting it actually, but there was no audio recording of this scene. It happened in silence, a pantomime even as the poor guy raged against the impossible position he'd been put into. He turned and kicked the glass, which resisted his efforts even as he stomped with all of his weight behind his foot. The frantic effort to escape was so frenzied that the glass bent under the force of his kicks.

Having gotten nothing more than a limp for his work, he looked back at the food that had been strewed on the floor. The prisoner whirled and lunged at it again, grabbing handfuls, fingers crushing the items he grabbed, reducing it to unrecognizable mush. He opened wide, trying to take in more than enough to fill him, and this continued for minutes when his stomach started to distend. He had first been seen wearing a loose white button-down shirt, and now the buttons were starting to stretch over his belly.

The man dropped the food, gasping for breath, the bulk that he'd swallowed having visibly stretched his abdomen. Brognola didn't have to wonder why he was having such a hard time sucking air into his lungs, especially with such a mass pressing against his diaphragm. Fear compounded with each ragged, helpless breath, and he began to scream out for assistance.

Bezoar spoke up, breaking Brognola from the riveting sequence. "There is no cure for this. He's pleading for an end to his maddening starvation, but there will be no respite for this. We have shut off the enzymes and neurological processes by which the human body can metabolize food. He's digesting it, but the nutrients he received from the food aren't being absorbed into the bloodstream. Without the protein code to unlock the cells and transmit those vital nutrients, nothing comes through to sate his appetite."

"Jesus," Brognola swore, watching as the prisoner clawed at his own face, fingernails breaking as he dragged skin off his forehead, drawing blood. He returned to the window, fists hammering against the heavy polymer. The crimson on his fingertips spread, ugly, chunky splotches appearing where his hands struck the glass. He was screaming, pounding at his prison, and Brognola could catch the detail of one of the man's pinky fingers flopping alongside his fist, dangling like a mashed rat's tail, bones crushed and shattered by the fury of his blows.

Finally, the victim of this "experiment" took to beating his head against the unbreakable transparent barrier. Skin split, and he slowly disappeared behind an ever-growing splotch of messy blood smear. By the time the gore dripped, thinning enough to be seen through, Brognola saw that the man had been laid out. His face was a crimson mask, features mashed and distorted, as much by the self-inflicted impacts as by the fear and hunger that had claimed him.

"This was one man alone. He had food, he had comfort, there was no need to harm himself, but the hunger was simply the first symptom of what would kill him,"

Bezoar continued. "We've also tested this on fully re-strained subjects, and the lack of digestive enzymes ac-celerated the rate of starvation from nearly a month to a matter of days."

Bezoar appeared on camera again, face grim and se-rious.

"Mr. President, you have heard about the disappear-ance of the town in Iowa called Albion. Powerful bombs have leveled every structure and smashed everybody down to their component atoms. Try as you might, your investigators will never find anything as large and co-herent as a tooth, so chemical analysis will prove futile," Bezoar continued.

Brognola hadn't doubted that each of these video messages had been individualized for the world lead-ers they had been sent to, and this statement was fur-ther evidence of the extent of the planning. The town in Iowa, every man, woman and child within it, had been doomed from the start.

"Allow me to show you what happened when a small town, cut off from cellular and landline telephone com-munication with the outside world, experiences this kind of hunger," Bezoar offered.

It was then that Hal Brognola witnessed the truth be-hind what had happened in Albion in the hours before it had been destroyed by thousands of pounds of TNT. It had been a riot. People, maddened by fear, took to the streets, their faces smeared with caked, drying food, eyes wild. Some battled each other, fingers hooked like claws ripping at skin. Others seized rifles and shotguns. When a food delivery truck pulled up to a local warehouse to pick up crops, a swarm of people attacked it, opening fire. Dozens crawled into the trailer, seeking sustenance within, while others engaged in battle with sheriff's deputies who arrived to rescue the truck driver after he called for help on his CB radio.

All of this was taken from a high angle, a familiar camera mount as on an airplane or an unmanned drone. Another scene of mayhem appeared when a roadside fruit stand, not far from the town, was attacked by more of the starving people of Albion. The owner's shotgun spoke, people fell, but they continued their attack. The need to quell the hunger burning in their bellies was more important than the fear of a 12-gauge and its deadly buckshot message.

Brognola watched as townspeople turned against each other, charged at the blazing guns of deputies and store owners, died and killed with abandon.

The footage ended.

"Imagine that happening to every city," Bezoar offered. "Could you imagine the sheer suffering as New Yorkers or Washingtonians grew so desperate in hunger that they would kill their own children or go to war with neighbors for the slightest morsel that could sate their commanding appetite?"

There was a pause, and even though he tried to resist it, Brognola could imagine the rioting, the carnage. The city would be in flames, and there would be little need for a bomb to be dropped to ensure destruction. Already, from the footage of Albion, Brognola could see that buildings had been set ablaze, burned to the ground in a spasm of insanity.

"I only require two things of you in this auction," Bezoar said. "First, keep this quiet or no part of your nation will be spared the wrath of Greenwar. Second, you must bid higher than your opponent. The opening bid is one fifth of your nation's population. Those willing to sacrifice the most of your people will survive total extinction. Those unwilling will be completely exterminated."

Bezoar smiled, though there was no mirth or warmth in it. "Have a nice day, sir."

The video ended.

Brognola felt as if he had to scrub himself down. He'd only been watching for ten minutes, but the horror carried the weight of hours. He set down the small smartphone, plucked out a handkerchief and mopped his brow.

"They either have someone inside Homeland Security or they have good spies. Given the aerial footage…" the President began. He rested a hand on Brognola's shoulder. "Stony Man is our only option. Bezoar is insane, asking for me to kill one in five people."

The smartphone beeped. The two men looked at it.

It was a text message.

France has bid to kill one of every two of its citizens. Make up your mind quickly.

The Oval Office grew silent as the specter of doom hung over the big Fed and the leader of the free world.

"WE'VE GOT NOTHING for you, David," Morlun said as McCarter and Manning sat with him in the open-air café. To the civilians walking past, even to the diners who were seated right next to the three men, it looked like a reunion of friends simply having a friendly, casual conversation.

Gary Manning, however, was on full alert, keeping his sharp eyes on rooftops looking for snipers, either from the Syrians, Bezoar's people or, most importantly, the French authorities who had told the police to steer clear of the prior night's raging gun battle between the two organizations.

"Nothing," McCarter repeated.

Manning could sense the frustration in his friend's voice, and before the British Phoenix Force pro had been mellowed by the responsibilities of leadership, the Canadian would have expected to have to restrain McCarter. Even so, he could see the anger that had crept into the team leader's face, and despite being in public view of bystanders and witnesses, there was some doubt as to whether McCarter could hold his infamous temper.

McCarter managed a smile. "All right. Thanks for the assistance."

With that, the fox-faced Briton stood, placed a few euros on the table as a tip and nodded to Manning. The Canadian joined his friend as they walked away.

"I was expecting you to beat the hell out of him," Manning said as they moved out of earshot of McCarter's French intelligence contact.

McCarter shrugged. "It seemed like it would be fun, but we received the same stonewall from your mate. Now, either two men we both trust, from different branches, have both turned into complete berks, or we're looking at them being given the same amount of trouble that we have been."

Manning nodded. "Morlun looked as if he wanted to jam us."

"Of course he did. He has some egotistical issues, the foremost being that he wants to be the number-one man who knows everything about France's intelligence scene. Your guy, Gaspard, is as honest with you as the day is long, and he was completely in the dark," McCarter said. "Put those things together, and we've got the French agencies scratching their nuts over why they've been told to piss off by their higher-ups, and the higher-ups are probably just as in the dark as they are. Probably more so because Morlun keeps his finger tight on the pulse of his division and his higher-ups. You picked a contact you could trust, and I picked one I could read like an open book. Morlun wished that he knew what was going on, and now that there's something he doesn't know, he's pissed, and so he's passing that on to us."

"A fair observation. What next?" Manning asked.

"Hopefully, we're making enough of a spectacle of ourselves to draw some outside attention," McCarter stated. "There's always the possibility that who we're searching for might want us eliminated."

"So, basically these meetings were just to make us look like tasty, attractive bait," Manning returned.

"You're a little nervous about taking fire?" McCarter asked.

Manning shook his head. "No. But there's a fine line between playing a lame duck and having a death wish. When the bad guys come, one day, bringing more firepower than we can deal with, we'll be wishing we hadn't pulled this."

"When the day comes that they bring enough firepower to bring down the two of us, they're bloody well welcome to take over the world," McCarter growled, a bit of the old Cockney warrior pride flaring through. "Until that time, Phoenix Force is the line in the sand between hell and Earth, and no one's crossing it on my watch."

Manning clapped his friend on the shoulder. "Just when I thought you were growing soft with authority..."

McCarter shrugged. "It's a matter of principle."

With that, the Phoenix pair took a long, leisurely stroll back to their safehouse, waiting for someone to make their move.

They didn't have to wait long before a van screeched around a corner.

CHAPTER EIGHT

Hermann Schwarz rolled as soon as he saw the rifleman lock on, and he winced as the ground where he'd been lying only a moment ago exploded with the impact of a high-velocity, high-mass round. As he twisted through the grass, he tucked the SIG rifle against his chest so that he was able to land prone with it wedged against his shoulder. The instant he stopped, he held down the trigger, sweeping a full-auto scythe of 5.56 mm projectiles at his target. Through his thermal scope, Schwarz could see the rifleman duck out of sight, his rounds sparking as they struck the doorjamb where he'd appeared from.

"Guys," Schwarz called.

At that moment he spotted Blancanales and Lyons exit the SUV. They had thrown on their combat harnesses, retrieving their weaponry in response to the sudden announcement of snipers in the grass. Schwarz hoped that they had better luck at spotting the hidden gunmen when he remembered that there was a ground-effect radar setup installed in the vehicle. While the enemy might have been insulated against thermal-optic discovery, they and the weapons they wielded would have been very visible on radar. There were few means by which the close-range-radar setup would have missed the metal frames of the firearms by pure dint of the fact that most stealth systems relied on distance and diffusion of signal to lower the radar signature of the craft. When dealing with less than a few hundred yards, the simple emitter was close, and hearing the signals.

It wouldn't be enough to pinpoint the enemy snipers, but Schwarz saw that his partners had armed themselves in anticipation for an area effect battle. Blancanales, Able Team's grenadier, had chosen to mount an M-203 grenade launcher on the rail beneath his SIG's barrel, while Lyons forewent the assault rifle altogether and had readied his AA-12 assault shotgun loaded with a 20-round drum magazine, making the weapon appear like an overstuffed Tommy gun.

Blancanales started the show with a looping 40 mm shell that he fired at a clot of thick grasses, the spinning grenade arcing only barely. The impact fuse jarred, and seven ounces of high-density, high-velocity explosive core went from inert material to a full flush of energy. Expanding on a wave of concussive force and heat, the notched-wire casing of the grenade ultimately splintered, turning into quarter-inch-long slivers of metal that rocketed along at hundreds of miles per hour, moving swiftly enough to pass through flesh as if it were butter. Kevlar body armor fared little better against the high-speed razors that didn't so much seek out skin and muscle, but simply wanted to accelerate in a straight line, hurled by the explosion that released them. Two riflemen now visible as the grasses were bowed over on the shock wave writhed in agony as their bodies were riddled with deadly splinters of metal.

There was nothing like a 40 mm grenade to get a fight

started on your own terms, and figures suddenly moved, scrambling as their rifles chattered to lay down suppressive fire against the wily veteran warriors of Able Team. Blancanales hadn't stood still, but disappeared into the uneven waves of grass. The enemy's suppressive fire wasn't meant for effect, Schwarz was glad to see, so their aim was high and wide.

In contrast, Carl Lyons's fire was aimed and deadly efficient on target. His AA-12 thundered off a 3-round burst, and one of the scattering riflemen was slammed hard in the chest by a 12-gauge storm of heavy buckshot. The gunman's run turned into a scrambling somersault, his body pitching head over heels as Lyons's auto shotgun hammered the life from his body. The fireball put off by the automatic shotgun was huge, and it was as if someone had turned on a giant spotlight, singling out the Able Team commander as a living target. Lyons, however, had taken a path leading him behind the Explorer and, by extension, behind the heavily armored hull of the modified combat vehicle. Even as he took cover behind a fender, one of the ambusher's assault rifles barked, bullets smashing against the heavy steel plate and raising sparks. The gunman who'd taken a pot shot at Lyons had lit himself up. Schwarz was about to take the shot when Blancanales's SIG snarled, 5.56 mm rounds slicing that gunman down.

"Don't worry about the two of us, check that plane," Lyons growled. "We'll take care of these assholes."

Schwarz noticed that he no longer was the center of attention. With a pivot, he sped toward the hangar. Maybe the gunman who'd lined up on him was still present, waiting for the Able Team member to move, or perhaps he was quickly working toward the aircraft that Schwarz needed to investigate and neutralize if it was capable of carrying the contagion. All of this raced through his mind as his feet pounded the ground, shoving him along through the long grasses. If there was going to be a release of a deadly bioweapon, it would instantly infect Able Team. Schwarz knew that he'd die in the field, but he didn't want to be the cause of the deaths of his friends because he was just a moment too slow.

Schwarz exploded across the field as fast as he'd ever run in his life, letting his high-tech, tricked-out SIG rifle fall behind his back on its three-point sling. If he was going to burst through a doorway and engage in close combat, he wanted a handgun out for maximum mobility and better weapon retention. A part of his mind measured the time it took from his start to the end of his charge to the hangar entrance, did the math and registered that he'd crossed fifty yards in five and a quarter seconds, which was less than optimal for Olympic world records, but it was just fine for someone humping with full battle gear.

He entered the hangar swiftly since the door had been left ajar by the gunman who'd tried to take a shot at him. His return fire had punched holes in the metal surrounding the doorjamb, and there was a splatter of blood across the floor, indicating a slight injury that left its recipient still able to walk and retreat. Schwarz had his pistol drawn, gripped in both hands, leveled at the floor. The .45-caliber Smith & Wesson had an M6X combat light attached, and his off-hand thumb was rest-ing against the activation switch, finger hovering near the trigger. With a flinch, he would have the gun up and firing, its Xenon lens pumping out 125 lumens that would slice through the darkness and burn the eyes of anyone hiding in the dark. He didn't want to use either the light or its submounted laser sight to make himself a greater target, especially after being backlit by the doorway he'd just entered. It appeared he'd injured his opponent, which was why this was now a case of hide-and-seek, but Schwarz knew better than to simply stand like a beacon.

The pistol came up, and he tapped the rocker switch to illuminate the airplane. It was an ag plane, painted bright yellow, the better to match with the rest of the crop dusters in the area, and it even had tail markings that indicated that it was part of the agricultural aviation firm that ran this field. This gave Schwarz a moment of doubt, even as he sidestepped after dousing the combat light. There was movement in the shadows, attempting to take advantage of the momentary night blindness that Schwarz would have experienced utilizing the lamp mounted beneath the Smith & Wesson's dust cover, but the Able Team veteran had kept one eye closed, shielded from the night-vision-destroying glare that his light would have thrown off.

Schwarz was tempted to fire a few shots after the shadow, but he knew better than to make himself a target for what might have been a feint. Outside, more grenades and shotgun blasts signaled that Lyons and Blancanales were tearing apart the ambush team. The Able Team electronics genius didn't know why the enemy had left such a blatant trap, but whatever was in the planning, he wasn't going to make a wrong move, not when there was the potential for a few hundred gallons of chemical weaponry nearby that would have been the spark for a wave of new deaths. He continued to crabwalk through the hangar, keeping his head low as he ducked beneath the wing of the second craft. At close range, even in the dim light of the building, he could see that this plane was the same color as the one that he'd assumed was not part of the local company's setup.

"Carl, Pol, stay away from the plane on the strip," Schwarz said. "Don't fire close to it!"

"Got you!" Rosario Blancanales answered. "The gunmen we have on hand are retreating past it as some form of sucker play."

"Baiting us, so they might not know what they're running past," Lyons said. "These could just be idiots culled from some local militia or gang."

"Explains why we weren't cut to ribbons before," Blancanales added.

"Gadgets, what's your position?" Lyons asked.

Schwarz didn't answer as he caught movement out of the corner of his eye. With a pivot, he brought his elbow up hard and quick, bringing it toward the center of a shadow he reckoned was his opponent's head. The impact was cushioned on his own joint by the polycarbonate plastic shell he wore to protect it, and the same tortoise-shape guard amplified the impact, sending the man stumbling across the floor with a single stroke. Schwarz turned on the M6X, blasting the man in the face with 125 lumens. His target writhed and twisted under the sudden harsh spotlight, but Schwarz already could tell that this wasn't the man he'd tagged with his assault rifle in response to the sniper shot.

Schwarz exploded into evasive action, pivoting out of the sweeping path of the hard buttstock of the rifle that had been fired at him. The tube-steel collapsible stock would have had the same effect as a sledgehammer, the unyielding metal capable of crushing bone. A spatter of mist sprinkled on Schwarz's cheek, even as the killer stroke missed his head close enough to cause the hair on his head to waft aside. A few inches closer and Schwarz would have been sporting severe cranial trauma, accompanied by subdural hemorrhaging, unconsciousness and eventual death, if the guy simply didn't use the steel stock to continue to crush his brain.

Schwarz turned the muzzle of his Smith & Wesson .45 toward the belly of the shooter and squeezed off a single round at contact distance. Though he was a fan of the .45's legendary stopping power, he knew that it wasn't a death ray, and that he might need follow-up shots if he wanted to kill the man. But he wanted answers, not corpses right now. A full load of 230 grains of copper-jacketed lead struck his foe in body armor, something that the cloaked men outside had been missing during their ambush of his Able Team allies.

The armored assailant staggered backward, clutching his lower stomach. The .45 slug hadn't cut through the Kevlar, but at mere inches from the muzzle, it carried the power of a prize-fighter's jab, which left the man gasping for breath. Schwarz followed up with his shielded elbow connecting with the attacker's chin. There was a loud crack, bone giving way under the strike. Schwarz pushed forward, swinging the Smith & Wesson around, and hammered the butt of the gun against the man's temple. The counterattack ended as he collapsed into a jumble of limbs across the floor.

Schwarz turned back to the other man, who was currently trying to fight off the fireball of the 125-lumen spotlight that had just struck him in the eyes. The attacker had pulled his pistol from its holster, but the Able Team commando kicked his gun hand. Carpal bones shattered under the force of Schwarz's steel-toed boot, forcing the gun to drop from limp, useless fingers.

"Hangar is secure," Schwarz said. "Check the damn plane on the strip!"

"Why is it the one out here that's rigged?" Lyons asked.

"Because a hangar would contain a cloud, but an explosion on the tarmac…"

Lyons cut him off. "Say no more. Pol…"

"On it," Blancanales answered.

Schwarz turned on the light and swept the man he'd taken out with the elbow and pistol-whipping. The unconscious attacker had a bloody smear sticking his uniform shirt to a lacerated biceps, and there was broken electronics dribbling out of a pocket just over the injury.

"You always secure detonators in protected pouches on your vest," Schwarz said, kneeling and tearing out the batteries from the tiny transmitter, just to make certain that no errant spark would suddenly send a deadly message to the plane his partners were dealing with. "What's in the plane?"

"I'm no biochemist," the man slurred with difficulty, thanks to his broken jaw.

"What kind of explosive?" Schwarz asked. "Or do I have to get mean?"

Blurry eyes glared at him in the hard spotlight. "You're not going to torture me, weakling."

"No, I'm not," Schwarz returned. "But I have someone outside who will not be so squeamish."

The man blinked, but Schwarz was not quite certain that there was enough fight left in him that would warrant calling on Lyons as his bluff.

"Gadgets, you might want to get out here," Blancanales interrupted. "This is some elegant bombwork here."

"I'll be with you," Schwarz answered. "Talking to a reluctant prisoner."

"Want me to send in Carl?" Blancanales asked.

"You wriggle something out of him first. I'll deal with the plane," Schwarz responded. "Tag team it."

"How many are in there?" Blancanales said in followup.

"Two," Schwarz answered. "One with a busted hand, the other with a broken jaw. Brokejaw is the one I want to talk to."

Blancanales was at the door in a moment. He looked at the scene, then put up his hand for Schwarz. With a clap, the two men handed off responsibilities. Now, it was Blancanales's turn to deal with the situation.

"Be gentle with him," Schwarz called.

Blancanales shrugged, then put on his best Colombian-hitman swagger. "I can't promise you anything."

"Then don't get blood all the fuck over everyplace," Schwarz returned.

Blancanales tossed his friend a grim smile, striding toward the fallen man.

"Look like a redneck," Brokejaw said.

Blancanales looked him over. "I've dressed to blend in around here. But enough about me."

"What are you going to do?" Brokejaw asked. "Cut me up? Give me a Colombian necktie?"

Blancanales shrugged again, nonchalant. "You want one? I'm always good for a little haberdashery, but really, why should there be pain and suffering on your part? This is just work for me."

Brokejaw winced. Blancanales had leveled his light at the floor, using the wash of its reflection to illuminate the scene. This was a much less harsh means of allowing the two men to see each other, and Blancanales could tell that the fallen man was having an easier time seeing, even though he rubbed one eyeball.

"It's just a job for you, too, isn't it?" Blancanales asked. "Nothing worth losing your life over, right? Not like the chumps you set up to ambush us."

The captive winced, grimacing at the implication.

"Come on. You hid them out in the open without a single lick of cover. They weren't even given the opportunity to dig foxholes, which would have given them protection against incoming fire," Blancanales added. "They were sacrificial. You weren't—otherwise you and your buddy here wouldn't be sitting inside a building with closed ventilation units."

"You're pretty smart for some cocaine cowboy hired

to kill people," Brokejaw murmured, slurring his words. "Especially if this is your way out of a death sentence."

Blancanales smirked without mirth. "Oh, you think that I work for the U.S. government? That's just precious."

"Then who are you?" the man asked.

"Someone who thinks that destroying millions of people would eat into his fucking profits, idiot," Blancanales said.

Brokejaw stiffened. "This is just blackmail, man."

"Really?" Blancanales quipped. "You've got a biological weapon sitting on the tarmac, positioned just so that it could be hit by stray bullets during a firefight, and it would release…how far?"

"I wasn't told how far it would disperse. But it's just a threat," Brokejaw grumbled.

"Like the bombs against the town?" Blancanales inquired.

Brokejaw grimaced. "What deal can I make?"

"Tell me who hired you," Blancanales snarled. "And make it quick."

"And you'll make it quick? Because these guys are scary. Really scary," Brokejaw mumbled. Blancanales could tell by the wan color of his face that he was in agony speaking this much, but there was very little that could be done to soothe his pain. The other man was still blind, his retinas knocked out of commission by the powerful strobe of Schwarz's gun light. As a precaution, when handing off custody of the pair, Schwarz and Blancanales made certain the prisoners had been secured with nylon cable ties.

"You might not even have to die," Blancanales answered, menace dripping from his words. "But if you do have to die, it's not going to prove merciful."

"I understand," Brokejaw slurred.

Warmth seeped into Blancanales's cold, killer's smile as the injured prisoner began to speak.

SCHWARZ MOPPED his brow after he removed the detonation charge on the tank. He could tell by the detonator that it was meant to breach the shell of the tank and a secondary dispersal charge without an ignitor. Whatever was within wasn't meant to duplicate the power of a fuel-air explosive, which was a bit of a relief, as five hundred gallons of aviation fuel going up as a thermobaric detonation would have produced an explosive just short of a one-kiloton atomic bomb, only without the radiation.

On the other hand, the lack of ignition charge, just a pressure-based dispersal charge, meant that whatever was within the tank was a lot more dangerous than the equivalent of a one-kiloton nuclear explosion.

"Is it clear?" Lyons asked him.

"This tank isn't going to pop," Schwarz answered.

Lyons ran his fingers over the skin of the tank. "Is this a thermobaric?"

"No," Schwarz said brusquely.

"So it's loaded with bioagent, the kind of thing that made the people in Albion go completely apeshit," Lyons mused. He took his hand off the metal skin of the tank, but only for a moment, a minor reflexive act against the possibility of infection. Even Lyons was stymied by the fear of something so small, so insidious, as a dangerous strand of DNA, a simple viral organism or even tinier, the molecule of a bad, self-replicating protein. Against something he could touch, he could see, Lyons was fearless, and he would never admit to being panicked by biological or chemical weapons. But he still had the instinctive, primitive terror of disease.

Fearless was the wrong term, Schwarz knew. All people felt fear, but Lyons, Schwarz and Blancanales were able to use their fear, not give in to blind terror and loss of reason. They could retain their focus, use the adrenaline caused by the ancient human fight-or-flight reflex to move faster, react more quickly, deal with the danger that frightened them.

But again, that had to do with focus. The invisible nightmare stored within the tank wasn't a man or a rifle or mechanized equipment, something that could be dodged or counterattacked. It was ephemeral, an idea, something real but untouchable and, by dint of its very existence, unstoppable by the means by which they could usually fight.

"We've taken on these kinds of things before," Schwarz said, as much to reassure himself as Lyons. "We've stopped them cold."

"I know," Lyons said. "But every time we do, we've got to worry about the whole world going extinct."

They looked at the formerly booby-trapped chemical tank.

"That's a heavy burden," Lyons added. "No matter how strong you are."

CHAPTER NINE

Rafael Encizo looked over the unconscious Syrian, Fadi, from the assault on Bezoar's town house. He'd been asked questions under hypnosis, thanks to Calvin James's training, that confirmed that the team from Damascus had been sent to clean up a terrible mess, not instigate new troubles inside of France. These commandos were monster hunters, though they hadn't been too concerned about public safety considering the mass of firepower they'd brought with them.

Sedated and with his features bandaged and taped back to a semblance of normalcy, Fadi seemed almost peaceful as he lay in the bed. Encizo knew that Phoenix Force had been in Paris without sanction, so keeping a prisoner, no matter how friendly to their cause, was an inconvenience, but he didn't regret rescuing the young soldier. None of the members of the team was a cold-blooded murderer, so taking him out of combat without lethal force was something any of them would have done.

Fadi not only had been reduced to half a face, but he was left half-blind by the destruction of his right eye. Even if the Syrian had been able to pull the trigger, Encizo would have been able to avoid harm. Kicking the pistol from his fingers was an act of mercy. James came into the bedroom where the wounded man slumbered, checking on Encizo.

"He's still sedated?" James asked.

Encizo nodded. "This kid is going to be fine…at least until he's home."

"His bosses will wonder why he was the only survivor, or why he was let go by a nominal enemy," James said. "We could turn him over to the law…"

"Who might have to hand him off to local intelligence services, who will not be any more gentle than vengeful Syrian secret police," Encizo responded. "He'll be sent home, where at least his special operations community will give him some shielding."

"That's one small favor for him," James said.

Encizo looked up at James. "Is T.J. all right?"

"He'll be fine," James answered. He didn't want to directly refer to Hawkins and his battle with the gunmen who were driving the Syrian commando team to the site of the battle. Even asleep, the human mind was able to process conversations, so the less they said, the better the chance that the Syrians themselves wouldn't consider Phoenix Force's "interference" to be an act of war. Though even that bit of hostility would have to be kept under wraps, for operating a military team in the European Union would attract intense controversy and political sanction.

"Everyone makes mistakes," Encizo said. He got up and walked to the doorway. "You going to keep an eye on Fadi?"

James nodded. "Get some rest."

Encizo managed a weak grin of agreement, scratched

the back of his head and lumbered toward his cot. He'd been guarding Fadi since the team picked him up, and he had kept a constant vigil, assisting James in his treatment and interrogation. It was a case of Encizo taking up the burden of his prisoner in an effort to make things easier for his teammates. However, working himself to exhaustion was not going to do any favors for Phoenix Force. He was glad that James had given him leave to get some sleep.

Mental and physical exhaustion were something even the most trained and physically fit warrior had to worry about.

With a skill that each of the Stony Man warriors had learned over their careers, Encizo was asleep the moment his cheek touched the pillow, his worries and doubts shoved aside to keep him from being kept up and deprived of further slumber. The ability to fall into a quick catnap was necessary, and it was simply a matter of a combination of focus and meditation, dispelling the sensory input around oneself to slip into a restorative snooze. The ability to ignore outside stimulus was key, a shutdown of the senses through concentration that also produced the kind of zenlike single-mindedness that made sleep easy. Once unconsciousness took over, the concentration filter disappeared, allowing Encizo to wake at the sudden spur of any new, loud sounds.

Encizo wasn't certain how long he'd been asleep when Hawkins shook him awake, but since he'd dropped into a deep rest, he opened his eyes and was mentally clear immediately. "'Sup?"

"It's David and Gary. They just warned us that they're

under attack," Hawkins said. "They said to watch our own asses."

"Who was it?" Encizo asked.

Hawkins looked to the window. "No idea. But we just had a couple of SUVs show up on our perimeter."

Encizo tugged his pistol out from under the pillow. "We're under attack? Why?"

Hawkins's face grew grim. "Seems like our President got a video saying the highest bidder wouldn't end up being hit by the wasting plague. Bezoar himself was talking, and he said that any interference from official intelligence or law-enforcement agencies would only spur reprisal from Greenwar, Bezoar's group."

"So the SUVs could be this group, Greenwar?" Encizo asked. He did a press check on his HK P-30, then pressed the decocking lever, lowering the hammer safely on the live round in the chamber. One pull of the smooth, slick, double-action-only trigger and the 9 mm pistol would fire, but the pressure needed was enough that it wouldn't be tripped by an inadvertent flinch. "Or whoever the French president or the EU have as their version of us?"

"Allies or enemies, they look like trouble," Hawkins answered. "Ready to rock?"

Encizo clipped his spare magazine pouches to his belt and slid on his paddle holster for the P-30. "Woke up ready. Cal know?"

"He and Fadi are up and ready," Hawkins replied.

"Fadi?" Encizo said with some surprise. "Cal woke him up?"

Hawkins handed the Cuban one of the team's Nomex

protective hoods. "He's got his hood on, and when I informed Cal, I stayed out of Fadi's visual field. His lack of binocular vision is going to be a detriment in anything but close-quarters combat, so we outfitted him accordingly."

Encizo spent a moment tugging his cowl on, then opened the rifle case he kept beneath his cot. Inside was his personally issued MP-7 PDW. The stubby little chatterbox had a curved 40-round magazine sticking from the base of the pistol grip. Spares were stuffed into the load-bearing vest he'd kept beside it. "What's the plan?"

"Break and disengage," Hawkins said. "No telling if these are our European allies, or if it's going to be Greenwar."

The team had set up a rendezvous in case of trouble while they were separated or if their safehouse was raided.

Encizo secured his load-bearing vest and grabbed the bug-out bag he'd set up. "Then let's get the hell out of here and meet with David and Gary."

DAVID MCCARTER'S REFLEXES were honed to a razor's edge, as were Gary Manning's. The two of them knew that the moment the van pulled to a screeching halt there was going to be trouble, and neither of them was willing to start a gunfight in the middle of an open street with bystanders around.

The British Phoenix Force leader was the first into action, but only by a hairsbreadth. As soon as the side door started to crack open, McCarter charged in close, grabbed the lip of the sliding panel, then added his strength to the force of its opening. The maneuver took the guy within off balance and he toppled forward onto the curb, striking the sidewalk with his face. The jolt had been magnified by McCarter clutching his shoulder and shoving him down, making the face-first landing into a tooth-breaking, nose-mashing splash on the ground.

The assailant had been dressed in dark BDUs, with a shoulder-holster harness, but there was no weapon in his hand. Even so, there would be someone else working security, or perhaps even ready to make his attack as soon as the door had been yanked fully open.

Manning, only a fraction of a second behind, suddenly loomed through the opening, a hamsize fist rocketing into the chest of someone who was holding on to some manner of weapon. The Canadian's heel-palm strike to the sternum was nothing short of a sledgehammer blow to the gun-wielding man, and had been more than sufficient to jar the object from his hands. The big Phoenix Force sharpshooter had only been striking to disarm and incapacitate; otherwise he would have struck the man in the jaw, snapping his neck. The gunner tumbled back in his seat, bowled backward under the force of the punch.

McCarter saw that there was a third man in the back, and two in the front, one driving and one literally riding shotgun. The Briton saw that the third of the crew was clawing for a pistol, which made the man an instant target. With a cobra-swift lunge, McCarter was on top of the man, shoving the muzzle of his weapon against the wielder's own body to tame him. The guy was a professional, because he instantly released the handle of the gun as soon as he no longer knew where his bullet would go.

McCarter had a raised level of respect for his assailant, but that didn't mean he was going to let the man run rampant over Manning and him. He launched a powerful elbow block up under the assailant's jaw, whipping his head around in a stunning blow. The gunman shuddered, but McCarter could feel the stunned opponent's other hand reaching back toward a backup weapon. The Briton pistoned a second punch, this one over the kidney in a paralyzing strike. The man would wish he was dead, but he would recover.

Manning, on the other hand, pivoted hard, bringing his elbow against the headrest of the passenger's seat. The head cushion broke loose and caromed off the side of the passenger's head, knocking him wild. There was a moment of stunned shock on the operative's part as the sudden, improvised missile rebounded off the side of his head and down against his shoulder. Manning grabbed a fist full of the enemy's hair and pushed his head violently against the dashboard, taking the last of the fight out of him.

The driver stomped on the gas, and the van jolted, but McCarter and Manning had already made their way aboard.

"Ditch or stay?" Manning asked.

"Stay," McCarter replied, grabbing one of the stunned men in the back and shoving him through the open side panel. Manning lunged his bulk between the driver's and passenger's seats, bringing a numbing karate chop against the wheelman's left arm, dislocating his shoulder.

Pain caused the driver to swerve, the front fender grinding against a parked car. In response to the sudden pain and the crash, the driver hit the brakes, but Manning had been so well braced against the passenger side seat, he was able to grab control of the wheel.

McCarter rose, stabbing his thumb under the driver's ear. The sudden jab was a prisoner-control method that was not only extremely painful, causing swift compliance, but it was also capable of rendering someone unconscious within a matter of moments by pinching off the blood supply to the brain. The driver's eyes swam crazily for a few moments, Manning holding him still until he collapsed into stillness.

"We're taking the van," Manning surmised. It wasn't a question. He knew McCarter's knack for turning an ambush into an opportunity.

"Heave that bloke onto the street," McCarter said. "We'll have enough with the driver and this geezer."

"Questioning," Manning added.

"Got it," McCarter answered. "I'm calling the others to make sure they're to our fallback, provided they don't get caught."

"They won't," Manning assured him. "They're as good at avoiding trouble as we are."

McCarter appreciated that the Canadian would remain quiet during his quick message to the others back at the safehouse. It was a hurried, hushed conversation that was bare bones and quick.

"Avoiding trouble, or getting away from it?" McCarter

asked. "Because we tend to drop right into the middle of this shit often."

"Sometimes you literally hang us out like bait," Manning reminded him.

McCarter shrugged, taking a seat behind the wheel. "I'll own up to that."

Manning secured their two prisoners with the very nylon cable ties that the snatch team were going to use. He picked up the initial weapon that the gunmen had leveled through the open side panel. "Looks like an update of our bio-innocular guns, but with multiple barrels for more than one target."

"So they wanted to take us nonviolently," McCarter said, looking at the pair who were trussed up. "Too bad we left them all bonked up."

Manning shrugged. "If we'd done the same, they might have been just as harsh, or used lethal force. I mean, we have guns, and would have been well within our rights…"

"I really don't need to deal with this kind of headache," McCarter replied. "We find out who these asses are, and we dump them off somewhere neutral."

"French government or EU?" Manning mused.

"Either way, it means that we have someone who's scared people enough to attack an American operations unit on their terrain," McCarter said. "I'll give Barb a shout to see what she knows on the situation."

Manning nodded. "Want me to spell you on the wheel?"

McCarter frowned. "You call. I'll drive, just in case."

"Great, so if we're under attack, you'll bounce me

off the walls of this van," Manning mused. "But we'll be free, so no big."

"Just get on the horn to the Farm," McCarter grumbled.

Manning chose not to egg on his friend any more. Things had gone too strange in comparison to their other missions. It wasn't often that Phoenix Force had to operate as outlaws, legitimately on the run from local authorities, unless they had actually parachuted into the country on a hard military probe. There wouldn't be a problem with the team avoiding trouble and evading capture, but they were still in a state of criminal trespass.

Something that could turn the U.S. against their own allies was a nightmare that neither Manning nor McCarter—both international citizens—particularly favored.

McCarter looked back after about two minutes of conversation between the Canadian and Stony Man Farm, his curiosity piqued by the lack of updates.

"What's all on, then?" McCarter asked.

"The opposition, the ones who have control of Bezoar, has asked the President to engage in a bidding war against other governments. The winner gets to keep his country alive," Manning answered. "The losers get the plague released."

"And if the governments say sod off?" McCarter asked.

"The plague is released anyway," Manning explained. "And it's something even more advanced than the last starvation plague we ran into in Greece."

McCarter grumbled. "More advanced?"

"It cuts off the body's ability to metabolize. They're stricken with intense hunger almost immediately on exposure," Manning replied. "We just don't know how it's transmitted."

"Just what effect it has," McCarter surmised. "Any video?"

"The President and Hal both saw it, and sent it to Barb. She hasn't had a chance to review it," Manning answered. "We'll look at it in a bit."

"The President didn't call us in on this, and he sat on the video evidence?" McCarter asked. "That doesn't sound good. Usually, if things are desperate enough to call us, he has no problem giving Hal a shout."

"This time, Hal says the Man was shaken to the core," Manning said. "That really can't be good."

McCarter frowned. "Damn."

BARBARA PRICE COULDN'T have been more perfect for the job of Stony Man Farm's mission controller if she had been bred and schooled in every detail of the job, the necessary components added to her genetic structure from birth. She had become accustomed to the kind of nightmares that washed across her eyes on an almost daily basis, from murderous ethnic cleansing in eastern Europe to monstrous massacres in the region of the Congo, where innocent children and their families were butchered by machetes. She knew full well that the world was a dark and dangerous place, just as she realized that the majority of humankind was bright and true, living only to make themselves better.

Still, Price knew horror, knew truth when she saw it.

And the death in the video sent to the President was one of the most demonic assaults on humanity that Price had ever experienced.

"Aaron, can we figure anything out from the footage without letting this out to any federal agencies?" Price asked.

Kurtzman, the wheelchair-bound yet still burly computer genius and head of Stony Man Farm's remarkable cyberteam, had sat watching the video forwarded from the President's personal smartphone. His eyes were locked on the screen, and Price could already see the gears spinning in his mind as he applied his phenomenal intellect to the dilemma posed by the short video. He broke himself from his reverie, turning to Price, even though he'd picked up a pencil and started scribbling on a small scratch pad of paper.

"I'll see what I can do about checking the video footage itself. The programming for the video data should have some origin information embedded within the code, but that might take hours, even days, to dissect."

Price nodded as Kurtzman's hand seemed to have taken on a life of its own, jotting down figures and equations even though his attention was on her. Price had been around enough genius-level intellects to know that their minds could work on myriad levels. Hermann Schwarz had once explained that he did his best work while listening to music, and when his teachers complained that the audio stimulus was a form of distraction, Schwarz had agreed. It was a distraction for the artistic part of his mind, leaving the rest of his intellect free to work as an unfocused segment found its anchor.

"What about from the footage itself?" Price asked. "We can tell that the victim was from the Indian subcontinent, but without the original audio, we're completely out in the cold with potential locations where this had been filmed."

"I've got Akira and Carmen scouring Europe for Bezoar," Kurtzman told her. "They're trying to see if he passed between countries after Syria sent their first recovery team after him. It might turn out fruitful, but Bezoar isn't the kind of man who's easy to follow, especially if he was able to ditch Damascus spec ops and espionage for this long."

Price nodded. "What's Huntington working on now?"

"He's running the plane that Able Team captured in Iowa," Kurtzman said. "Tracing the craft won't be easy, as a lot of these planes have been rebuilt, and in the process could have had their registries falsified to facilitate sales between pilots. The tail number was simple gibberish, a random code put out by an alphanumeric generator that made it seem legitimate. Hunt's also working on people who might have put together such a program, but since a lot of these keygens tend to be freeware, that could end up being a blind alley."

"And what are you working on there with the paper?" Price inquired.

Kurtzman looked down, almost as if he was surprised at the automatic writing. He chuckled and looked over the notes. "It's a list of the symptoms evidenced in the video, as well as what I know about digestive enzymes and the human body's metabolic processes. Do we have anyone on the Farm who has a degree in biochemistry?"

Price pursed her lips. "It'll take me a few minutes to go through my own notes, but I'll get back to you on that. You're going to try to trace the chemical processes involved in this?"

"If possible. Once we can figure the kind of vector by which the victims are made into starving, panicked maniacs, then we can do something that will either provide a cure or block it," Kurtzman said. "There's also a good chance of narrowing down who helped Bezoar with the creation of this compound, and where this originated."

Price nodded. "It's a good idea. What else have you got in mind?"

"Right now? I'm also running programs regarding money transfers," Kurtzman answered. "Bezoar and Greenwar are going to need some way to receive their payments, and there's also the possibility that these other governments might have their own black operations trying to hijack and utilize the money that someone else is using for their own auction bid."

"So, we could be looking at places like France or Russia engaging in an electronic war for their survival," Price asked.

Kurtzman nodded grimly.

Price looked at the incoming data on possible similar incidents to what had happened to Albion. So far, there were at least six other small communities, spread across the globe, that had disappeared inexplicably. Investigators from these countries were trying to figure out exactly what happened, but the governments had been silent. She saw there were two in the subcontinent itself—Pakistan and India had each lost a village. She chewed her lower lip. "There was nothing on our particular video that indicated who else was in the bidding for a buy."

"No, but the President just received a new MPEG," Kurtzman said. "Hunt's working on tracing it, but it's most likely sent from a roboserver."

Price took a deep breath. "I don't think that Greenwar wants money. Look at Pakistan and India."

Kurtzman glanced at the map, then let his pencil drop. "We didn't receive any information about a town going dead in North Korea, but below the 38th Parallel, there was another town taken out. They didn't blast the village to oblivion because South Korea isn't known for its forensic technology."

"Can you spare either Akira or Carmen for looking into North Korea and into mainland China?" Price asked.

Kurtzman frowned. "China is already struggling with population control. Do you think that they might get into a shooting war to outbid another country?"

"Or it could just be a case of Beijing finally wanting to be done with the Taiwan situation once and for all," Price said. "Like a jilted, crazy ex-lover—if China can't have Taiwan, then no one can."

Kurtzman grimaced. "So this is just an excuse to depopulate the whole world. The blackmailers might not even have the means of wiping out entire nations…"

"Or they could, but they don't have enough to enforce the kind of extermination pogroms that they want," Price concluded.

"A global nuclear war would actually cause more

harm to the planet," Kurtzman said. "Both Pakistan and India are packing atomic heat, and I don't have to remind you that China's stockpile of nukes…"

"The Earth has survived worse extinction events," Price said. "The thing is, Greenwar and Bezoar don't happen to believe that mankind going the way of the dinosaurs is the worst fate for the planet."

Kurtzman looked at the map and the spacing of incidents of Bezoar's attacks.

"Nuclear weapons might not be what Greenwar wants to launch," Kurtzman said. "Able Team has been scrambling after laser-guided weaponry."

"And we naturally assumed that this was something that could turn dumb iron bombs into precision terror weapons," Price added. "But what if there is a bomber that could deliver high-altitude airbursts?"

"Special Ops laser tech is capable of doing that as easily as dropping a thousand-pound iron bomb into a terrorist's backyard grill," Kurtzman answered.

"The thing is, how many bombers do they have?" Price asked.

Kurtzman wheeled his chair away from the conference table with a shove of his powerful arms. "Even one plane might be enough to disperse more than enough to kill millions."

"I've got a few phone calls to make," Price said as her face locked into a stern countenance. "No one is going to make their bids. We're stopping this now."

CHAPTER TEN

Carl Lyons's biceps bulged as he pulled the heavy plastic tarp—designed to shield aircraft from the harshest elements, such as tornadoes—over the ditch in which he and the rest of Able Team had stored the tank that Schwarz had defused only hours before. While his great strength was used to do the heavy lifting, Blancanales and Schwarz worked together to neutralize the deadly threat contained within that tank. Schwarz was an expert in rigging spectacular demolitions devices, and with the materials available at an airfield, he could make some truly terrifying explosions given only a few minutes. Now Blancanales and Schwarz were busy pouring aviation fuel into a hole in the ground that they had lined with another such tarp. The flammable liquid filled the bottom tarp as if it was a gigantic bowl, gas sloshing against the sides of the tank.

"You're sure that this will sterilize whatever's inside that tank?" Lyons queried Schwarz one more time as he tugged the plastic tarp into place, sandwiching the tank so that it would be sealed off from open air.

"The overtarp will contain any dispersal from the initial shell-cracking charge," Schwarz answered. "When the av-gas burns, it'll produce 550 degrees Fahrenheit in open air, and without a means of circulation, the heat will grow even worse. Liquid chemicals and enzyme compounds just can't take that kind of sustained heat. The plastic will ignite, as well, and when it melts, it'll add to the temperature, killing just about anything inside this pit."

Lyons nodded as the three men swiftly set about securing the edges of the top sheet around the pit. It would be hard to get a perfectly airtight seal, but they didn't need a perfect closure. The breeching charge was low velocity, much too weak to move the heavy plastic sheet, and when the av-gas was lit, the fireball would vaporize everything. "If I suddenly begin to starve, I'm literally going to eat your face off, Gadgets."

Schwarz looked to Blancanales for support.

"Don't look at me. I'll chew your ass out," Blancanales added.

"Thanks for the vote of confidence, guys," Schwarz responded as he took out his remote detonator. "Great, the two of you already have decided how to cannibalize me and where to start off."

"Just blow that shit to hell so we won't have to worry about being cannibals," Lyons responded.

Schwarz triggered the two-stage explosion. The initial charge sounded like a soft crack that simply made the center of the sheet bubble upward with a light punch. Even as the tarp sagged back down, billowing from the concussion that broke open the tank and exposed the chemicals within, the second ignition blast went off. The trigger generated a brief burst of 410 degrees Fahrenheit, causing the cauldron of fuel to autoignite. As the wave of heat ripped through the liquid fuel, vaporizing it, then releasing the stored energy within the molecular mixture, tendrils of hot fire burst through the plastic, searing the heavy tarp and shredding it.

The blast wave was impressive. The fuel utilized contained 42.8 megajoules per kilogram, and a kilogram of fuel equaled one liter. Schwarz and Blancanales had emptied the entire fuel tank of a single aircraft into the pit, in this instance more than 740 liters. The earth shook with the force equivalent of seven and a half tons of TNT, the heat energy substantial enough to turn the night sky into a blazing lance of fire that made Lyons and his allies turn their heads from the column. They'd gotten more than enough distance from the blast to be safe from shrapnel, and even if there had been, the ditch had been dug so that any projectiles produced by the empty tank or burning plastic would go straight up, not flat in a radius.

Lyons wiped one eye, which had been forced to tear up thanks to the wash of hot air across his face. "Gadgets, that had to be one of your best explosions to date that didn't involve a nuke."

"Better than Colombia?" Schwarz asked with a smirk.

"I said one of your best," Lyons countered. "Now we just have to wait and see if any of that crap survived the heat."

Blancanales grimaced. "You know, if the shit can survive that kind of heat, it's welcome to take us out."

Lyons regarded his partner. "I'd rather have a bullet."

Schwarz sat still, concentrating on the air. Lyons could tell that the man had emptied his mind of all preoccupations, casting his senses out like a net, looking for the tiniest of anomalies. There were times when the Able Team leader thought that his partner might just have been almost superhuman in his perceptions.

"No hunger pangs after a minute," Schwarz said. "Going by the footage Barb forwarded to me, we might be okay."

"But we're going to sit here, waiting for symptoms for how long?" Lyons asked.

"Ten more minutes," Schwarz answered. "We can't expect to wait here all night, but if we're all right after ten minutes of breathing this air, we should be fine."

"And if symptoms show up only after hours, or days?" Blancanales asked.

Schwarz shrugged. "And what if we don't dodge a bullet, or if the bad guys detonate their nuke while we're in their headquarters, or what if an asteroid hits the planet?"

"I'm just saying, we could have unleashed something bad," Blancanales responded. "Or we could end up as contagious carriers."

"Enough of this bullshit," Lyons growled. "Even if we are infected, that means we've found a way to transport a specimen back to the Farm. This stuff might be spread by airborne means, but the cops who responded to this situation didn't report symptoms themselves, and Robespierre hasn't been suddenly shuffled off and put into quarantine."

Schwarz frowned. "I'll have to get on Barb about a follow-up for that. But if that's the case, we can further narrow down the symptoms... I'm sure the rest of the Stony Man crew is working on it."

As quickly as the fireball had flared up, it disappeared, the aviation fuel having expended itself in releasing thousands of BTUs and an equal bolt of kinetic pressure. Scanning the field around the ditch, the three men could see that the ground had rippled under the concussive force that fought to shatter the very earth itself.

"Get on the line with Barb and make sure our assessment of the communicability of this disease is right," Lyons said. "We don't need to be driving into a populated area and spreading disease around like fucking Typhoid Mary and her ugly sisters."

Schwarz nodded. Blancanales continued looking around, half-distracted as he tested himself with each step. It was that fear reaction once again, but not one of panic and self-preservation. It was the combination of uncertainty as to their physical state and to whether he had simply become a menace to all the world because of his existence. It was that niggling core doubt that came with them whenever they encountered bioweapons in the field.

Was the microbe dead? It wasn't like a Taliban trooper whom you could identify as out of commission thanks to the gaping head wound where you'd put two rounds into the bad guy's central nervous system. Dead microbes, inert proteins, they were invisible, and the way that Schwarz had explained it, some of these organisms or molecular structures were never really alive in the first place, not by the definition of multicellular complex creatures such as humans.

They were either active or inert. A blast of intense

heat would usually do the job, and the kind of explosion that matched seven and a half tons of TNT affected matter on the molecular level. That level of pressure could restructure a prion. It wasn't reliable, but for now, it appeared to have done the job.

The two prisoners, trussed up, had been secured in the back of the Able Team SUV. The doors were left open, so anything that the team members breathed in, so would they. Lyons was not a cold-blooded murderer, someone who'd shoot a helpless opponent, but considering that these two had been intending to release the very weapon that had left them with all of these doubts, if anyone deserved to be exposed to the starvation plague symptoms, it was them.

It was poetic justice for those who'd facilitate mass murder with the cruelest of symptoms.

The two had given up information to Blancanales, but it was vague; they had been hired through blind drops, which had segregated them from any solid contact. Following the trail enough to be viable within a court of law would have required leaps of faith and violation of evidentiary rules making any case worthless. It would only be slightly easier to make a trail that Able Team could track themselves, even with the remarkable skills and technology available to the Stony Man cyberteam.

Lyons would keep them alive for further questioning and imprisonment, but what they had would provide a running start for Kurtzman and his computer geniuses.

"We're going to have to get some attention on us," Lyons declared. "That means we have to make the bad guys think we know exactly what they're up to."

"But we have to do it without letting it out that we're privy to information only the President has access to," Blancanales replied. "Luckily, you've got me to figure something out."

Lyons smirked. "That's why I said it to you. You're great at diplomacy, but you're just as good at manipulation, like you did with the two turds we have in custody."

"We can use them," Blancanales responded. He dialed the Farm. "Barb?" he began when the mission controller answered.

"What is it, Pol?" Price asked.

"I need a couple of favors pulled in," Blancanales said. "We're going to try to draw attention to the fact that we've got two prisoners who have at least peripheral knowledge about Greenwar. We'll need hospital facilities, but nothing too close to any real patients."

"Got a city in mind?" Price asked. "We can finagle something in either Cedar Rapids or Dubuque."

"Dubuque seems too small," Blancanales said. "But it does have more major medical facilities…"

"You go to sleep reading guides to the states you're visiting?" Price asked.

Blancanales cleared his throat. "I'm Able's medic, Barb. I have to know where we're going to need to get medical attention in case we're injured. Thing is, Cedar Rapids is large enough to warrant federal agents preferring it, just because it's got twice the population of Dubuque."

"Dubuque is closer to your current position. It'd make

more sense," Price said. "What kinds of injuries are you thinking about listing for these two?"

"List them as both having gone into shock without external injury," Blancanales replied. "Unknown symptoms should give just enough of an alert that their plague might have backfired. I'll personally need credentials as a CDC investigator brought in. Chances are Greenwar is monitoring the U.S. government agencies, and my presence will also be a good flag."

"What about Carl and Gadgets?" Price asked.

"We'll keep them low profile. They'll see me as a gray old doctor who hobbles along with a cane," Blancanales responded.

"I'm looking through Dubuque hospitals right now, and I'm seeing that Finley Hospital's campus has some expansion. There are a couple of unused buildings that have the facilities for contact isolation, as well as lab facilities," Price said. "The campus hasn't done anything with the empty building yet, as its board of directors is trying to ascertain whether to turn it into an outpatient clinic expansion or more office space."

"That indecision will give us the room we'll need to bring in the bad guys for a trap," Blancanales answered.

Price paused for a moment before asking the question about the elephant in the room. "How are things going with the contagion?"

"We've neutralized it," Blancanales said. "Whether it's bacteria, a virus or just a prion, while it might be immune to drugs, three hundred gallons of aviation fuel set off in a fuel-air explosion renders it harmless."

"So that's what that tremor was picked up by seismologists," Price responded. "Still no symptoms after… looks like twelve minutes."

"Nope," Blancanales answered. "And we waited until there was no prevailing wind to spread a contagion breach."

"Hal's going to be glad he doesn't have to sweat that out," Price said. "Just so you know, things have gotten hairy for your counterparts."

"What happened?" Blancanales asked.

Price sighed. "Apparently with the auction for countries not to die, we've found that the Commonwealth of Independent States sent a black-ops team to Paris. They caught wind of Phoenix and tried to snatch them, but you know how that happens. French authorities were also called in and nearly caught the rest of the team at their safehouse."

"So Phoenix is on the run," Blancanales concluded. "I bet David's going to love that."

"I wouldn't put money on that," Price returned. "Sure, it's going to give the team headaches, but as long as Phoenix is catching the heat, it means he's doing something right."

"Which means we might expect more of the same here in the States," Blancanales replied.

Price made an affirmative noise. "That's why I told you."

"Wouldn't be the first time someone sent the law after me and Gadgets," Blancanales said.

"Just be careful," Price warned. "Bad enough Phoenix is on the verge of causing an international incident…"

"Remember. If either of us blows it, there's not going to be an international community to raise hell over this," Blancanales countered.

Price chuckled. "By the time it gets to the Farm, we're pretty much at the end of the line. The court of last resort."

"We'll start for Dubuque. Tell us exactly where to go when you finish the arrangements," Blancanales responded.

"Got it," Price replied.

With that, the men of Able Team loaded into their SUV and drove toward a confrontation in Dubuque.

MIKAIL GROZNA WAS SURPRISED to see a Syrian among the small group of men who held him captive. Battered and bruised, the Russian wondered just how he'd ended up a prisoner when he and his Spetznaz team had actually ambushed the two as they left their meeting with their French intelligence contacts. The nylon cable ties around his wrist were tight, but left with just enough slack not to cut off the circulation to his hands. He knew full well that trying to twist his way out of them would only end up leaving his hands numb and strangled, useless for defending himself the moment he got free.

The American-employed team seemed to have its act together, although the Syrian wore fresh bandages and new stitches over one eye and down the cheek, ending at the livid, red jaw. The Syrian held a Makarov PM, finger off the trigger, but safety off and hammer cocked. Grozna, being Russian, knew full well how light and easy the trigger of a cocked Makarov was, and he'd seen the power of the 9 x 18 mm Makarov round at a range of a foot. While it didn't have the same power as the 9 mm parabellum to cut through body armor, the stubby little bullet could still cause massive trauma at this range and break through the thin bones of a human face to reach the vulnerable brain within.

Perhaps the Syrian was actually an American-born Arab, but the way he spoke had too much of an accent for someone raised in the States. Still, considering the British and Cuban accents that Grozna had heard, it wasn't unlikely that the man holding him under the gun was actually part of some manner of American covert-operations foreign legion. Grozna had worked with Russian intelligence teams with a similar setup, groups made up of expatriates hired simply because of their loyalty and their ability to disappear into foreign countries.

The burly man, one of the pair that Grozna's team tried to capture, entered the room. A white T-shirt stretched across a barrel-thick chest, arms hanging down at his sides rippling with relaxed muscle that still was wrapped like heavy rope around iron bars. He didn't have an accent at all, at least from what Grozna had heard, and except for the phenomenal strength shown in his bare limbs and tight shirt, he was otherwise nondescript.

"I will tell you nothing," Grozna answered.

"Shame, because we're actually hoping to work with you," Gary Manning answered. "You didn't try to kill us, which is precisely why you're still alive."

To emphasize his point, Manning clenched his fists,

tendons popping in those big hammers made of meat and bone. Grozna felt the throbbing ache reminding him of what had happened when that wrecking ball had struck him in the center of the chest. "You're being a lot more courteous than my team would have been."

It wasn't a lie. Had someone made an effort to snatch him or his partners, the Russians would have drawn their guns and begun blasting away. This one, and his fox-faced, British-accented friend, had moved so swiftly that they broke the ambush and turned the situation into their own acquisition of prisoners.

"You're lucky that you came on us now," Manning said. "Your side and our team had some run-ins in the past, and my partner would have gladly skinned you back then. He's settled down."

Grozna swallowed. "I kind of know who you are talking about. We never knew the name of your group—"

"You won't." Fadi spoke up, cutting him off. "But we don't have to know their real names. We're all in the same boat, which means that any posturing can be tossed away now. We're allies."

"Why would Damascus work with Washington?" Grozna asked.

Fadi's mouth tightened into an angry, thin line for a moment. "Politics doesn't matter when all of humanity can end up dead. You know the stakes just like we do. Fuck squabbles with Israel and Egypt or the U.S. This shit counts for real."

Grozna nodded, then saw a blade snap open under his nose. The Russian turned and saw the fox-faced Briton who the burly man had told him would gladly skin him in a previous life. The folding blade flicked forward, biting into Grozna's nylon wrist bindings rather than seeking flesh. In moments his hands were free, and the Briton gave him a clap on the shoulder.

"You right, mate?" McCarter asked.

Grozna rubbed his chest where Manning had punched him. "As long as I didn't break any ribs when I stopped that fist…"

"We had our medic check you out," McCarter returned. "He has a portable ultrasound that we used to check for fractures and internal injuries."

"I pulled that punch," Manning added.

Grozna smirked, releasing a nervous chuckle. "I'd hate to see if you weren't holding back. So you're enlisting me?"

"More like we're making this a group effort," McCarter answered. "One-eye over there is right. Political divisions don't mean shit when it's mankind's extinction that's the end result."

"So you think the same thing we do," Grozna said. "That Greenwar and Bezoar intend to release their weapon, no matter what kind of bid they get."

Manning set out a laptop and pressed Play on a stopped video file. "They don't want money. They want who can prune their own population the most, and they also want a commitment of resources to release biological weapons on allies and enemies."

Grozna watched the video in rapt silence. The others had obviously watched it before, and Fadi had turned his one remaining good eye away from the screen. It was like a car wreck, watching Bezoar asking the American President to unleash a salvo of deadly, weaponized diseases against Canada and Mexico.

Nothing was said about what different countries were asked to do, but he saw that Bezoar said that the minimum "bid" of eliminating America's population was now four in ten people.

"Four in ten Americans," Grozna repeated. "Which means that he's gotten a confirmation from Moscow that we must sacrifice thirty percent of our countrymen. And it might not even be the whole of the Commonwealth of Independent States. We could see the complete annihilation of Georgia, Mongolia, Azerbaijan…"

"That's what we're assuming," Manning said. "Note, Greenwar wants a biological weapon used."

"To minimize environmental impact," Grozna agreed. "Kill the people, leave the remains. Trouble is, what happens to the cities? Natural gas, petroleum, all manner of toxic chemicals…"

"Greenwar are maniacs," Manning answered. "They don't care about the real effects of sudden, traumatic depopulation and the kind of environmental damage it would cause. All they know about is that mankind is a parasite and we all have to die to fit some twisted set of rules they made up."

McCarter handed Grozna his sidearm. "Saddle up and give your team a call. We're going to need all the help we can get."

Grozna slid the weapon back into its holster, then

accepted the cell phone that they had confiscated from him.

The Russian dialed his partners. "Comrades, we need to talk."

CHAPTER ELEVEN

Rosario Blancanales had changed from the field. He was now wearing a powder-blue dress shirt, a loosely knotted tie and black slacks underneath a white lab coat. There were several blacksuits—military and law-enforcement members who had been recruited by Stony Man Farm for the purpose of serving as security, as well as learning advanced officer and combat survival tactics. Here in Dubuque, some of those men and women had been set up as nursing staff while others were purely security for the otherwise unoccupied building. That the group had come out of federal vehicles and moved in quickly was a bonus. It looked exactly as if the Feds had obtained prisoners experiencing an unknown set of symptoms, and were keeping them isolated but still somewhere that the men could be cared for.

Blancanales, to further fit the role of noncombatant medic, leaned on his cane, affecting a limp that made him seem older and weaker, belying the .357 Magnum snub-nosed revolver tucked into the pocket of his slacks, or the fact that his cane was actually an ironwood *jo*-stick, the central weapon of *jo-jutsu*, Japanese stick fighting. Blancanales was a master of the art, and he was able to turn the slender yet sturdy and flexible stick into a deadly tool, capable of ripping flesh from bones or shattering limbs with a flick of his wrist.

The .357 Magnum was a Smith & Wesson Night Guard—the 386 model. No larger than the classic Model 19 snubnose, it held seven shots, and kept the weight down with a proprietary alloy frame with stainless-steel reinforcement. Everything had been cast in nonreflective black, given a low-profile rubber grip that cushioned recoil and was topped with tritium night sights, giving Blancanales a fearsome seven rounds for initial combat. The 125-grain semijacketed hollowpoint rounds had been extensively battle proved since the 1970s, and shown to be highly effective in firsthand experience at the side of Carl Lyons, so he didn't worry about not stopping an opponent with a single shot.

Blancanales rapped on the hospital room door. There were negative air pressure and contact isolation warnings all over the place, and to keep up appearances, the Able Team pro had put on a disposable gown, latex gloves and a mask. He opened the door and entered, seeing Lyons and Schwarz lying in their beds.

Schwarz was occupying himself with a computer game built into his Combat PDA while Lyons kept his eyes shut, listening to music through earbuds.

"How're my patients?" Blancanales asked.

"Tired of being waited on by frumpily dressed nurses," Schwarz said. "We want boobies, and we want them now."

Lyons opened one eye. "That would blow our cover, Gadgets. Behave."

"You know how hard it is for me to do," Schwarz answered. His face lightened. "Ooh!"

"New information?" Blancanales asked.

Schwarz shook his head. "No, I found a stack of diamonds. Now I can make a pick to mine obsidian!"

Lyons snorted. "That damn digging game is the sole reason why he hasn't invented the teleportation portal."

"Funny you should say that, because with the obsidian blocks I can…" Schwarz began. He looked back at the screen, his good cheer disappearing. "Silent alarm activated at the loading dock. The blacksuits got their signal."

"I know. My music cut off as soon as it got the alert," Lyons answered. He still had his hand under the blankets, and Blancanales figured that the fist was now filled with the grip of a Remington MCS shotgun. Being in bed, under sheets, Schwarz and Lyons were able to conceal larger weaponry. Schwarz himself had a mini-Uzi submachine gun nestled against his thigh.

"Looks like they're making their move," Blancanales replied. "Good. I got tired of playing Dr. Casa."

"Just a few more minutes, Pol," Lyons returned. "We want answers."

Blancanales leaned on his cane. "I don't want to get too fancy—we don't need to get our blacksuits killed."

Lyons checked his CPDA. "We've got it so that the staff has moved away from the silent alarm. I've got it set so that there's a path of least resistance that these bastards will love to take. The crew has body armor and Kevlar headwear to minimize injuries."

"This all depends on what their tactics are when they

hit," Schwarz said. "The entrance they've taken, they're avoiding confrontation with guards. I'm porting their movements to you from the motion detectors set up."

"Got it," Lyons said. "We'll still lay back?"

"Looks like it. They'll come straight to us," Schwarz said. "We've got four contacts…hang on. Rooftop sensors went hot."

"They're coming down and through the windows," Lyons said. "They're literally on top of us."

Schwarz tossed the covers aside, as did the Able Team commander. Blancanales reached into the room's closet and pulled out an M-4 carbine. Lyons and Schwarz worked together to flip the near window bed onto its side, its steel frame and mattress able to provide more than sufficient bullet resistance to an initial wave of enemy autofire.

"Stony One to all blacksuits, fall back and form perimeter. Code Black!" Lyons ordered into his hands-free communicator the moment the bed frame slammed into the floor. He turned in time to see Blancanales toss him a bandolier of magazines for his converted pump shotgun.

The Remington Model 870 Modular Combat Shotgun was a great little weapon, designed to be field customized for operator usage, as either a backup door-breaching gun firing lock-and-hinge-busting slugs, or cut down to stockless, short-barrel use for out-of-the-way storage at the ready, nimble in the hand and less likely to snag while rapidly exiting an automobile or charging through a doorway. This one, however, had been optimized to make it truly full-battle worthy. It was outfitted with a converted Knoxx Breacher's grip, a design with a built-in pistol that halved its recoil, making it faster and less punishing for its light weight in combat. To stabilize the weapon, Lyons had a three-point sling drawn tight, providing active resistance to his pushing against the weapon. Under the slide action was a Choate pistol grip, which added to the amount of grip Lyons could apply to the weapon, increasing aiming control and weapon retention. Finally, there was a box-magazine conversion for the stubby MCS, allowing it to be reloaded instantly without interfering with the original tube magazine under the barrel. Now, in addition to the normal five plus one rounds in the MCS, Lyons had access to 7-round boxes of 12-gauge, as well as a 20-shot snail drum for serious firepower.

"Contacts no longer measured on rooftop motion detectors," Schwarz announced before he set the GPS aside and gripped his mini-Uzi with both hands, having put a forward pistol grip on to replace the stubby handguard.

The three men of Able Team knew that they had only seconds before the enemy arrived through the windows, and they sought the cover of their improvised barrier. Lyons pointed to his eyes, then made a chopping motion, a lightning-fast, silent message to Schwarz to put his Uzi's gun light into strobe mode. A flick of the switch on the handle, and the Able Team electronics genius now had a blinding beacon under the machine pistol. Anyone charging into it would be dazzled by the Surefire M900A flashlight and unable to see to fight back.

Lyons had pulled a specially marked box mag out of his bandolier and slapped it into place, making certain that it was secure. The building's lights went out immediately, but it was nothing that he and the others hadn't anticipated. The attackers were going for the element of surprise, and there was the sudden rattle of automatic weapons, the windows to the isolation room blown inward by the high-velocity slugs, which tore into the mattress and rang against the steel base of the bed.

Schwarz was up first, triggering his strobe light, releasing 220 lumens of light energy at the men swinging in. The dazzling burst was enough to cause them to jerk in reflex against the sudden flash. In the brief flicker, Lyons could see that the men wore tinted goggles, something to protect them from both the effects of their own weapons' muzzle-flashes and external light source surprises.

Even so, Schwarz had caught their attention with providing a minimal target, pulling them off balance just enough for Lyons to blindside the two gunmen with a sudden wave of less-lethal neoprene baton rounds. One of the shooters who'd burst through the window was jerked back out by reflex, flailing wildly on his rappelling rope, while the other one absorbed two sledgehammer blows. The first dislocated his shoulder, and the second caromed off his helmet, literally tearing it off his head.

Blancanales lunged into view, hooking the stock of his M-4 behind the helmetless attacker's neck to drag him off his feet and face-first into the Able veteran's rising knee. There was a sickening crunch as facial bones fractured, but Blancanales dropped to his knees, pinning the stunned commando. There was another crackle and a yelp of pain as Blancanales's knee forced the shoulder back into its socket, and suddenly the man dropped unconscious, his senses overwhelmed by the jarring pain he'd received in the space of only a few moments. The second man, out on the rope, was still dealing with the sudden agony of multiple impacts against his face and torso. His goggles were askew, and he'd dropped his weapon and was now dazedly bouncing off the ledge.

Schwarz pointed to the wall that adjoined the hospital room on their right. Blancanales swiveled his M-4 and cut loose with a salvo of 5.56 mm NATO rounds that bit into plaster and drywall. One of the Able Team warrior's rounds must have struck a detonator, because a fist-size explosion vomited broken material and dust back into the room.

"Six contacts. Two initial strike, and four in backup on the other side," Schwarz said.

Lyons nodded, dumping his empty, less-lethal magazine and affixing a new box of rounds, this one standard 12-gauge double O buckshot. It was more than enough to cut through the drywall of these particular hospital rooms, and he blasted another fresh, fist-size hole in the wall. There was movement on the other side, and their automatic weapons returned fire in a haphazard manner. These men hadn't expected to have receive so much resistance to their plan, their breaching and flanking maneuver meant to overwhelm what defenders there were.

But with Lyons's shotgun and Blancanales's carbine cutting through the wall, seeking them out, their momentum had been broken. Their panic fire was high, fortunately for Able Team, but it was more than enough to leave sections of plaster hanging like shredded cheese-cloth. Schwarz and his partners were prone, and they returned fire in unison, aiming for the focal points where enemy guns had erupted.

Schwarz's mini-Uzi was loaded with high-intensity submachine gun ammo, each round twenty-five percent faster than normal parabellum rounds, but far too high in pressure to use in handguns. The full-metal-jacketed rounds were flat-tipped, shaped like barrels, making up for the notoriously bad round-nosed profile that had given the 9 mm a bad reputation for stopping power. The blunt slugs tore through plaster and support studs easily, their profile making them immune to being plugged with material that would have impeded their velocity. The trio of weapons tore through to the attacking commandos, smashing bone and ripping flesh with the same aggressive power that turned a wall into raggedy gossamer dangling between chewed supports.

"On them," Lyons ordered to Blancanales, even as he rose and rushed to the window and the hapless, hanging attacker.

Schwarz turned his attention to securing the prisoner whom Blancanales had knocked out. His nose was folded over from its violent introduction to Blancanales's kick, but other than that, he was still breathing through his mouth and he had a strong pulse. Nylon cable-tie restraints came out of Schwarz's vest and bound the man's wrists and ankles in mere moments.

Lyons, at the window, smashed the grip of his shotgun against the dazed, dangling enemy's jaw with sufficient force to put him out like a candle. The Able Team leader let his weapon drop on its sling, pulling his knife to cut the rappelling rope and haul him into the room. With a speed that would have impressed a cowboy, Lyons trussed the man up quickly with his own cable ties.

In the meantime, Blancanales went through the hallway, as the gunfire might have perforated the wall, but it didn't make any openings large enough for a man to squeeze through. He let his rifle dangle on its sling and pulled the Night Guard out, gripping a Smith & Wesson Galaxy LED light with the other. The 9 LEDs in the lens lit up with the brightness of a sunny day, and he swept the room, wrists crossed, the muzzle of his battle revolver following his aim even as he looked over the quartet that they had engaged.

All of them were prone and bloody from where they had been shot. Only one was still moving, but he was jerking, rasping as he tried to breathe. Blancanales knelt closer to the man, and he saw that bloody, frothy bubbles were burbling over his lips, eyes twitching in agony and terror. There was little chance that the enemy commando would live. His rib cage was a crater where he'd taken multiple hits that defeated his body armor. Trying to control that bleeding would be impossible.

Blancanales rolled back the hammer on his .357 Magnum and put a mercy round right at the bridge of the dying, suffering man's nose. His spastic jerking stopped instantly, his life released from the broken shell that used to be his earthly form. He looked around, ensuring that the others were down for the count, not wanting to waste time, given that there was a second opposing force already in the building.

"Heard a gunshot," Lyons said as he appeared at the door.

Blancanales nodded as he plucked his spent shell from the 7-round cylinder and thumbed in a new one. "Ended some suffering."

Lyons looked around, contempt flaring his nostrils. "We're still tracking the others. They haven't retreated."

Blancanales put the Night Guard into its holster, transitioning back to his carbine. "Gadgets turned this building into a cone of silence already."

Lyons nodded in agreement. "They don't know what happened to their allies, and no one is going to get anything short of flashlight semaphore or good old twentieth-century landline telephone out of this place. Throw in a rusty camp lantern, and it'll be just like the old days for you when you lived in the little house on the prairie."

Blancanales snorted. "I'm old, but at least we had TV and electric lights back then. Granted, we only had three channels on the tube—"

"C'mon," Lyons cut him off. "We've still got work to do."

CARL LYONS TOOK POINT as Able Team advanced down the stairwell. It wasn't going to be easy, as the building had been constructed with only one central stairwell, along with a single elevator shaft. This made the building a fatal funnel, as both sides could only approach each other from one direction. Lyons was in the lead, his shotgun quick, handy and capable of producing a volume of death and violence to greet any ambush they faced. With double O buckshot in both the tubular and box magazine under the barrel, Lyons had thirteen shells, each packed with nine .36-caliber projectiles. Emptying the stubby blaster would put 117 projectiles in the air, turning any corridor, stairwell or doorway into a slashing rain of copper-jacketed lead, the equivalent of emptying four Uzi submachine guns at once.

According to Schwarz's security network, the opposition had entered through a basement window, and hadn't exited the way they had entered. It made sense, as there was a maintenance room in the basement that had the panels necessary to control the telephone lines and electrical wiring for the building. The sudden blackout showed that the men in the basement had done their job, but now it was simply a matter of the two teams hooking up together. There was little chance that the teams had a snatch in mind, but Lyons was curious to see if they were in communication with outside support. If that was the case, it would simply give them more intel to gather and to examine where they had come from and who had hired them.

There was the scuff of a boot on a concrete step's lip. Lyons and his partners froze. The enemy was within earshot, which meant that silence was necessary right now. The stairs would provide cover as their stone-and-steel reinforcement rebar would stop most bullets cold, but then this would turn into a standoff. He glanced back and saw that Blancanales had taken out a small canister from his battle harness.

Lyons knew full well that it was a flash-bang grenade, capable of producing enormous noise and light, capable of blinding and deafening foes. In the close quarters of a stairwell, it would also produce sufficient pressure to cause long-term injury.

Lyons gave his partner the nod, and Blancanales eased out the cotter pin, held the arming spoon under pressure and released it slowly. Blancanales was cooking the fuse down to make it almost impossible to catch and throw back. Once he reached his countdown number, he hurled the canister over the railing, releasing a loud bellow to equalize the pressure inside and outside of his ears. Lyons and Schwarz echoed their friend's yell, knowing full well the pain produced by explosions and gunfights in close quarters echo chambers like these had the potential to permanently deafen them. The trio lost nothing in terms of the element of surprise as the flash-bang detonated only a few moments after it had left Blancanales's hand.

The minute the bang went off, Lyons charged down the stairs, knowing that even in the tight confines of the stairwell, he could count the seconds of total incapacitation inflicted on the enemy commandos slipping away. Once those seconds were gone, he and the others would be facing armed and shooting opponents, not dazed and easily corralled targets.

Within a few heartbeats Lyons found the first of the enemy gunmen, holding his ears, nose pouring blood. Lyons spared him some suffering by whipping the muzzle of his shotgun across the man's jaw, breaking it and knocking him out cold. In the same instant, Schwarz leaped over the railing and landed feetfirst into the chest of another marauder who had managed to pull himself up by holding on to the railing with both hands. The would-be ambusher took Schwarz's full weight in the ribs, and there was an ugly snapping and breaking of ribs as he and Schwarz struck the wall simultaneously. With a kick, Schwarz dropped away from the man as he slid down the wall, folded over and in agony.

Blancanales spotted the last two of the gunmen, both of whom had taken the brunt of the flash-bang explosion, and knew instantly that they were not going to recover their senses before he could cross the distance to them. Drawing his *jo*-stick as if it were a sword, he lunged forward, catching one of them in the solar plexus as if he was running the gunner through with a rapier. The blow struck the man's xyphoid process and froze him up, gasping for breath.

The other man felt his partner stagger against him and cut loose with a blast from his carbine. Only Blancanales's swiftness with the fighting cane had been enough to prevent the gunfire from claiming any lives, whipping the muzzle upward to where the enemy's bullets would pulverize themselves against concrete and not sink into his comrades or their unconscious targets.

The rifleman had felt Blancanales's presence, lashing out with a back fist that swept in an arc that would have caught the Able Team diplomat, dead and blind or not. Unfortunately for the enemy commando, he was facing a man whose athleticism belied his gray hair and lined features. Blancanales brought his forearm up and blocked the blow, feeling his body jarred by the force of the enemy's swing. Had the blow connected, Blancanales would have been nursing a broken jaw of his own. Countering the attack, he whipped the cane hard into the back of his foe's knee, buckling him over and off his feet. A swift knee-strike to the chin ended the brief, brutal conflict as quickly as it had started.

"That was quick," Schwarz said.

Lyons grimaced. "Not quick enough. These assholes have information, and we need to get it out of them before the bastards who sent them decide that the President's shitting on his parade."

"I'll do what I can," Blancanales replied. "I've got something that will loosen some tongues fast. In the meantime, Gadgets, get your digital camera to work."

Schwarz nodded as Lyons helped Blancanales remove the men's goggles and protective hoods. Photographs and fingerprints were gathered from the current crop of unconscious opponents within one minute, the data hurtling across the ether back to Stony Man Farm.

CHAPTER TWELVE

Phoenix Force had reconvened, and from the looks of things, the Stony Man international operations team had doubled in size. In addition to Fadi, the wounded Syrian, there were a couple more Middle Eastern operatives, something that McCarter and Manning had expected. James, Hawkins and Encizo were aware of their guests, Grozna the Russian and his driver.

"Do either of you have names?" McCarter asked.

"Only if you tell us yours," responded a squat, stocky Arab with a slight British accent and a thick beard. "Just call me Yoneh." He jerked his thumb toward his tall, slender partner. "He's Haji."

"David and Gary," McCarter responded. "You know the stooges over here."

"And that Slavic geezer with you," Yoneh answered.

"Syrians and Jordanians working together," Grozna said, looking at Fadi, Yoneh and Haji. "I would have thought…"

"We all know the beefs that each of our little families bring to the table," Hawkins interjected. "If you want to pour salt into wounds, wait until the fuckers ransoming the world to kill chunks of its population are dead and harmless."

"We're gathered here to keep humanity in existence,"

McCarter added. "So if you're wagging your chins, say something useful or bloody well shut your gob."

Yoneh nodded in agreement. "I'm assuming our bosses received their threats at the same time."

"And the video footage of the Indian man dying of starvation," Manning answered.

Yoneh grimaced, and Haji's eyes flared with anger.

"He was my asset." Haji spoke up. "We were working together once Damascus dropped the hint that one of their own had gone rogue."

"Bezoar," Grozna said. "Moscow takes his involvement seriously."

"So do we," McCarter said.

Grozna looked askance at McCarter, a hint of recognition showing on the Russian's features. "This is not surprising."

"Again, what T.J. said," Haji reminded. "We know about our past conflicts. This must not get in the way of the prevention of mutual destruction."

"No one has an idea how these madmen intend for our governments to make these 'sacrifices'?" Fadi asked. "I would think that the jig would be up the moment we started murdering our own citizens."

Yoneh took a deep breath. "This might simply be a red herring, but Khan, the man who was in the video, had gotten information that there were generals in Pakistan who had been asked to provide airspace security for some aircraft, no questions asked."

"It makes sense that this would be dispersed as an aerial vector, but it just doesn't seem quite right," Manning surmised. "Cal?"

"I've been racking my brain about metabolic disorders and their transmission," James answered. "Still trying to figure out how it would be done."

"You calling bullshit on the video evidence? Don't forget their demonstration back home," Hawkins said.

"No. I know it's possible, I've seen that. It just doesn't seem right," James explained.

"You're not the only one thinking about it, Cal," Manning said. "My field is more chemistry than biology."

Grozna's thick brow wrinkled, and McCarter seized on that.

"What crossed your mind?" he asked the Russian.

Grozna shook his head. "The video showed the man driven to insatiable hunger. It showed him unable to sate that hunger, and then it showed him driven to such great suffering he caused himself violent harm."

James jerked alert at that statement. "David, I'm going to call home. The rest of you, if you have quick and secure links…"

Fadi spoke for the Middle Eastern group. "On it."

Manning looked after James, then lowered his gaze to the floor. McCarter had seen the brawny Canadian do this before. It was his means of stepping out of himself, shutting down outside stimulus to concentrate on a particular problem that had been eluding him. After a few seconds he looked at McCarter.

By then, the summit in the safehouse had spread apart so that each of the representative teams could have privacy, both in planning and communicating with each other.

"What did Cal and Grozna find?" McCarter asked.

Manning smirked. "We're looking for diseases or rogue proteins that can actively shut down the human body's need for digestion. As such, we're dealing with an infection that would have left corpses available, leaving behind a record of such research."

"Incineration," McCarter said.

"Possible, but releasing a prion isn't like releasing a nerve toxin. There are few antidotes for it," Manning replied. "As such, why would Bezoar's people have remained in the safehouse?"

"And why would the enemy be so quick to eliminate evidence of the plague?" McCarter asked. "All we have is aerial footage of the reaction. There was a lot of destruction, rioting in Albion, and at the end it was a group of starving people fighting county sheriff's deputies for the contents of a food delivery truck."

"Would the enemy have wanted to keep us from thinking about why the deputies weren't experiencing the same hunger reaction? Or even the delivery driver?" Manning asked. "And when Carl and the boys hit the airfield where the weapon had been launched, they managed to capture people who felt as if they were safe inside the hangar, while outside there was a device ready to go off."

McCarter grimaced. "It looked like a bioweapon, it acted like a bioweapon, and we've seen what has happened from the efforts to weaponize prions like the ones responsible for spongiform encephalopathy."

Manning raised his eyebrows. "I don't doubt that Bezoar has the means of releasing a weaponized protein capable of making people starve to death despite taking in food," he said. "We've seen another of his efforts with such an attack. But this, we're hearing hoofbeats and looking for horses…"

McCarter grimaced. "But someone is smuggling zebras past, not horses."

Manning nodded. "Of course, we still have to know exactly what's being used."

"What does that mean?" McCarter asked.

"It means that the enemy could or couldn't have the means of releasing an actual starvation plague, destroying people's metabolism, or they are using something to make people simply think they're starving to death. And now that this information has opened up some new hope for us, we have to know if it's a hallucinogen or an enzyme that merely overrides the body's need to recognize that it's processing nutrition."

McCarter sighed. "I was hoping that this was all a smoke-and-mirrors ploy with something along the lines of LSD."

"Either way, people won't actually be left to starve, but that doesn't matter. As long as they are consciously aware of their hunger, a bottomless, endless need to feed, they're still going to be in a state of panic," Manning answered. "We saw what happened to a small rural community. Imagine the kind of carnage that would occur in a place filled with armed, stressed-out civilians like Los Angeles or Chicago."

"It's not necessarily guns," McCarter replied. "You saw some of the squad car footage. People literally took bites out of others in their rampage."

James returned from his brief conversation with

Stony Man Farm. "No good news about Robespierre. He wasn't exposed to whatever agent caused the chaos in Albion, or if he was, he was left incapacitated long enough that it had worked out of his system. Still, the Farm and the CDC are working quietly and running a full toxicology screen on him, as well as a metabolic function test."

"But he hasn't shown signs of actual metabolic shutdown," Manning returned.

"Nope. He's been given intravenous glucose and he's been processing it," James answered. "He hasn't shown any signs. Robespierre is in a coma, so we don't know any psychological effects, but physically, he looks completely normal."

"So whatever the effect is, it won't linger in the air after a short while if it does make first contact, or it doesn't operate on a metabolic level," Manning mused.

"You figured out the hallucinogen possibility after me and Grozna?" James asked.

"Did you consider an enzyme 'message' that blocks off the body's feedback that it doesn't require extra nutritional intake?" Manning shot back.

James tilted his head, a look of consternation flashing quickly across his face. "Ninja, please!"

Manning grinned. "I'd have been disappointed in you."

"Grozna might not be aware of that," James said. "All indications showed that he's a layman in terms of biology and medical matters. That's what helped him see past our consternation over proteins and poisons."

"Can you blame us?" Manning asked. "They handed

us a biochemist with a track record for working on this kind of thing and had him talk it all up."

McCarter looked toward the Russian and his driver, frowning.

"Now what's wrong?" Manning pressed.

"Grozna had hints that we tussled with Bezoar before," McCarter responded. "And then he comes up with this option..."

"Misinformation that he didn't really give us," James said. "Aw, shit."

"He could have been peripherally attached to Bezoar back in the Greek operation," Manning said. "As such, he would have known that we, or at least our agency, went after the Proteus Enzyme and had that knowledge in our pockets."

"Bezoar knows how close the old, hardline KGB came to turning Greece into hell with Proteus," McCarter added. "And he knows we shit on that parade. He'd be a fool to think that round two would go unnoticed."

"Did I fuck up and send the folks back home on a snipe hunt?" James asked.

"No," McCarter said. "We're looking at all the possibilities now. This could be the same old Proteus Enzyme, this could be something new or it could just be something that only makes people insane with hunger. Either way, it's enough of a threat to make a town implode and fearlessly engage in a gun battle with law enforcement for a truck full of hamburger patties and frozen onions. We're not omniscient, and neither are our buddies back home. All we can do is anticipate what's going on and look for solutions. If we were looking for the wrong solution, we'd end up dooming everyone. Tunnel vision doesn't do anyone good."

"I'll get back to the Farm, see if Grozna's legit or someone we have to grill." James spoke up. "He might have an old grudge with us, or he might be working with Bezoar."

"I've already got that started," McCarter said. "Just reinforce to the cybercrew that the hallucination part is only a possibility, something extra to look for."

James nodded. "I'll amend that right now."

McCarter looked over at Grozna. If he were a plant, it would stand to reason that he would be working to cast doubt on those trying to oppose Bezoar's plan.

PAK ZUO RAN HIS WRIST across his forehead, looking around Qingshuihe. The town was cramped, crowded and dilapidated thanks to a billion-dollar project to develop a new high-tech city twenty kilometers to the north. Zuo was not the kind of man to shirk his duty, but he and thousands of other workers had been sitting on their thumbs, unable to work since Hohhot, the capital of Inner Mongolia, had run out of money for this project.

It would have made sense for Hohhot to have asked Beijing for recompensatory funds to continue the project, but only when the paychecks stopped coming and thousands had sold their farms and small businesses was it learned that no authorization had come for the sake of this building. The government of the republic allowed Inner Mongolia to run itself as an autonomous region, though it still passed down orders through their puppet government in Hohhot. Right now, there were only a few government buildings and a single hotel that had been constructed in the "new" Qingshuihe—all of which sat empty, surrounded by empty lots excavated to start new buildings, and the half-formed shells of other structures.

Now the county of Qingshuihe was completely broke, having squandered $880 million. Zuo thought of it in American money because six billion yuan was far too depressing a number to contemplate. The old town was overcrowded—a city that had been planned to house more than 120,000 people had drawn fresh blood into the community, and the old Qingshuihe had room for only 80,000. Now, swollen by more than half again as many people, in a city which had no money for new, local construction, the city was in a state of chaos.

Gunfire cracked in the distance—jobless young men turning to the violence they so often fell into when economic times were tough and they were surrounded by slums. Zuo had grown up in old Qingshuihe and grimaced at the thought that his hometown had gone from quiet, gentle little city to distressed, jobless ghetto.

The only thing keeping the peace were three companies of Chinese Mongolian forces—actually composed mostly of Han Chinese just like the whole of Inner Mongolia—with PRC advisers overseeing that nothing would happen to inconvenience the People's Republic in terms of civil rights violations by the troops.

The whiff of a cracked sewer pipe assaulted Zuo's nostrils. A truck had finally hit a pothole hard enough to break through the street, creating a new source of stink to add to the pressure cooker that was the crowded neighborhood. The gunfire in the distance couldn't continue fast enough to lessen the overcrowded conditions of the city.

Zuo lowered his head in shame and self-reproach. Such a thought was beyond the pale of common decency. He knew that things were out of hand when he actively wished for the deaths of the thousands around him.

The rate of gunfire increased, and Zuo looked out the window. This was unusual, even for the cramped Qingshuihe. Worse, it was automatic rifles, like the ones used by the army. Now Zuo was really on edge. Had order finally broken in his town? Did the unemployed, impoverished youth finally snap and steal weapons from the military?

An airplane was soaring above the crowded city, a crop plane by the look of it. Zuo's brow furrowed. Most of the agricultural aircraft had been sold off in anticipation of the movement toward the new, larger city, and to make money for the farms to make adjustments to their new delivery locations. The sound wouldn't have been unusual years ago, before the project started, and even up until last year, when the money completely ran out and the county was struggling to make up its cash shortage.

Zuo tilted his head. He could remember the buzz of its engine before the recent spat of violence crackled to life. Maybe the aircraft was working as a spotter for the army, targeting gang activity for the military to swoop in.

That thought disappeared in the thick, cottony cloud dumped from the dispensers on the crop duster, a wash of chemical smoke that struck Zuo full in the face and nostrils.

"Madman!" Zuo shouted, raising his fist to the sky in impotent anger. "Women and children live down here, you idiot!"

Releasing pesticide over a city? Zuo wished that he'd had a rifle. That would have given him the opportunity to swat that maniac out of the skies.

Zuo looked down at his hands. "I've never been this... angry. What's going on?"

The rising ire had been something that had snuck up on Zuo. He was Han Chinese, a descendant of the glut of people who expanded into Inner Mongolia, making the Mongolians themselves a minority in the southern part of their very homeland. Inner Mongolia had become popular with people as it was not directly under the Communist state, and was therefore more lax in the occasional spats of religious persecution that had been directed toward Buddhism. Zuo had been glad to grow up in a Buddhist society, and he was an adherent of its message of peace and enlightenment.

Now fury boiled in his blood, fury mixed with an insatiable hunger. He turned from the window, feeling as if he was starving. He threw open his meager cupboard and grabbed what would have been his breakfast—bread. He shoveled it into his mouth, trying to assuage the hunger that churned within the pit of his gut, but no matter how quickly he swallowed, there was no relief.

The bread he'd devoured was substantial, a full loaf that would have lasted him a week of breakfast meals, but there was no end to the deep, seething hunger. It was as if his body stopped digesting, but still wanted more.

The anger that had been rising was more than frustration with an overcrowded, bankrupt county. It was a cruel, snarling fury that burned deep inside of him, making him want to lash out. He turned and scooped a butcher's knife off the counter.

He was starving, and his body trembled with rage. Someone was going to pay for this.

"What...would they...pay for?" Zuo asked himself out loud, attempting to retain some semblance of his humanity.

A tremor rolled through his entire being. Had Zuo seen the being that replaced him, he would have run in terror. Blood-rimmed eyes were framed in a twisted, strained mask of animalistic rampage. The knife in his hand gleamed, his shakes having disappeared, muscles no longer struggling against themselves.

"They'll pay for everything."

Zuo kicked open the door. The hallway of his apartment building was suddenly crowded with similarly enraged people. Zuo lashed out with his butcher's knife, its point slicing through flesh. He felt minor stings through his body as other weapons, even simple fists, struck at him. Down the hall, flames suddenly roared to life, the top of the corridor filling with smoke.

This should have turned the riot into a rush to escape, but the violence in the hallway had risen to a fever pitch. The flames were simply a backdrop for the insane melee occurring between what used to be neighbors.

Across Qingshuihe, other buildings, other blocks

erupted similarly, hunger and rage seizing the population of the cramped city, turning homes into infernos and spilling corpses into the streets.

AARON KURTZMAN'S COMPUTER monitor lit up with a fresh alert. He turned and clicked on the new subwindow and watched as Chinese characters were pushed through one of his translation programs, turning the kanji into something that could be understood by the Westerner.

What Kurtzman saw turned his complexion ashen. He snapped his fingers.

"Akira! I need translation confirmation over here!" Kurtzman called out.

Akira Tokaido, in addition to being a genius in the realm of computer programming, had also worked hard to understand Chinese dialects, at least in the form of reading comprehension.

"On you, boss," Tokaido said, rushing to Kurtzman's workstation. Rather than view something forwarded from another monitor, the cybercrew remained mobile—especially Kurtzman with his wheelchair—so as not to risk any alterations or degradation of signal by continual forwarding.

"'The 34th Company requests permission to drop artillery bombardment into Qingshuihe to contain sudden attack,'" Tokaido read out loud. He turned to Kurtzman, then at the translation on Kurtzman's secondary monitor. "The commander is reporting that he has received casualties from a violent uprising. The entire city has been turned into a war zone without any warning."

Kurtzman frowned. "What kind of casualties?"

"Three squads completely lost contact. Others have reported rioters taking to the streets and attacking anything that moved. One fire team reports that it has completely exhausted all ammunition and has been forced to lock bayonets," Tokaido responded. "This shit sounds bad."

"Thanks for the confirm," Kurtzman replied. "I'm pulling up what satellite imagery I can from this area. It's going to take some wriggling, but…wait. I've got the feed."

"Jesus!" Tokaido cursed. "It looks like a cooling volcano on thermal imaging."

"I'm zooming in for a closer look," Kurtzman told him. "At this distance, multiple thermal contacts tend to blur together. Raised resolution…"

"Multiple individual fires. It looks as if there isn't a block in the city that hasn't got a blaze going on it," Tokaido noted.

"Aaron, Akira, I've got a newsfeed from South Africa." Huntington Wethers spoke up. The tall, distinguished professor had set aside his pipe, his lightly dusted jaw set firmly as the blue glow of his monitor painted shimmering highlights on his chocolate-colored features. "Diepsloot, the community on the northern edge of Johannesburg, has exploded in riots. Local police have been overwhelmed by armed and unarmed assailants, and dozens of officers have turned on their cohorts who are responding to assist them."

"Getting the same from Gary, Indiana," Carmen Delahunt interjected. "It's getting real serious there."

Kurtzman grimaced. "Greenwar must have gotten

the clue that we're after them, and they're demonstrating what they can do in some fairly good-size communities."

Tokaido was back at his station. "Running the numbers. The dispersements seem to be in towns with average populations of about 125,000, and stuck in close quarters. The size of living quarters in Diepsloot is only two by three meters, and the huts are right on top of each other."

"That explains why we're seeing rational responses from people who are nominally on the outskirts of these areas," Delahunt noted. "Indiana State Police and the Illinois State Police are rapidly putting up roadblocks into the city. They don't want the rioting to extend toward Chicago."

"Diepsloot is a lost cause. The place was built as a slum for people too poor to afford to get into Johannesburg," Wethers stated. "They have a small, incorporated government, but it's nothing in comparison to what 'first-world' countries like China and the U.S. have. Even Gary, for all of its economic ruin and violent crime, isn't a write-off that can be cordoned off like Diepsloot."

"It doesn't matter," Kurtzman said. "Right now we have people dying in droves. I'm getting on the horn to Hal."

Kurtzman remembered a line that popped up after the horrific events of Hurricane Katrina. Humanity was just three meals away from the collapse of civilization. New Orleans had been taken over by savages, predatory thugs who found the new chaos to be their greatest ally the moment people were left homeless and hungry.

The starvation plague, whether an actual metabolism-killing disease or a brain-altering hallucinogen, was very real, very deadly and was beginning to light up parts of the world now.

This was simply a message sent to the world's leaders.

Give us what we want or your nations will burn.

Unfortunately, what the psychopaths of Greenwar wanted was nothing less than the extermination of the humans who were choking off and poisoning the planet.

CHAPTER THIRTEEN

McCarter and his Phoenix Force colleagues had retired from the summit with the other operational teams hunting the Greenwar blackmail group in Europe. Each of the organizations wanted to run through their data and possibilities without influence or interference from their counterparts. The Middle Eastern contingent was functioning as a unified force, but McCarter knew that it was more a factor of their being thrown together in a country that hadn't been amenable to groups of armed Muslims. A few members of that crew could actually pass for European in France, which meant that they had to cleave together.

McCarter had been tempted to stay with the Arabs, but Fadi said that there was not going to be a lot of love in the group for Phoenix Force, simply because of the explosive first contact that had been made with the rest of his Syrian contingent.

Right now, Phoenix Force had other responsibilities as Germany was suddenly caught off guard by an eruption of violence. A heavily populated suburb of Berlin was undergoing what appeared to be a race riot that had been so ferocious, elite German counterterrorism troops had been called in to control the perimeter.

Added to the mayhem occurring in Gary, Diepsloot,

Qingshuihe and now apparently Mexico City and the neighborhood of Ajami in Jaffa-Tel Aviv, McCarter knew that something had blown up in their faces. He was in a van, racing toward the section of East Berlin that was full of immigrants, and the rising tide of cultural-purity thugs who were in opposition to their presence in Germany. Ostbanhof was already the beginnings of a powderkeg, but hell had broken loose. It was so hot on the heels of the other riots that it couldn't be a coincidence.

Calvin James and Rafael Encizo were the only other members of Phoenix Force in the van, and the two men were preparing their grenade launchers with less-lethal munitions to minimize casualties. Gary Manning and T. J. Hawkins were back in Paris, trailing Grozna in the hopes of determining his true loyalties. Behind the wheel of the van, McCarter had the vehicle practically flying down the autobahn in a mad dash. With phony credentials, they had been able to sweep through the border between France and Germany without raising alarms. It was going to be close, but James, Phoenix Force's medical expert, wanted a rioter specifically for the purpose of blood tests and metabolic monitoring to determine the kind of weapon that had been released across the world.

That, of course, meant that James, Encizo and McCarter were going to have to enter the old train yards and the surrounding community, diving into the midst of a riot and possibly having to deal with quarantine containment forces.

"Hell of a trip, eh?" McCarter asked.

"I don't know about you, David, but if there's the chance to save any of the victims of this madness, then I'd assail the gates of hell armed with a toothpick if that'd give them a chance," James responded as he slipped the last of his less-lethal shells into place on his vest.

"Still notice that you've got live and very dangerous 5.56 mm ready for your rifle," Encizo returned.

"I'll defend myself," James told him. "But we've never been the kind to pump hot lead into people, no matter how over the edge they've gone."

"We do what we can," McCarter said. "Chances are, we might not even break through. The rioting might be over by the time we get there."

"And if it's not, then we can rule out actual enzyme interruption," James returned.

"Because if they were actually starving to death, they wouldn't retain the kind of energy necessary for sustained violence," Encizo mused.

"On the nose," James said. "They need nutritional processing to keep up their strength. They only believe that they are starving to death."

"That narrows it down, but this doesn't give us anything in terms of whether it is an enzyme, a hormone or a hallucinogen," James said.

"Hormone?" McCarter asked.

"Hormone, pheromone, some sort of chemical message that sets them off and inspires them to act on strong emotion," James explained. "Some of the behavior we're seeing can possibly be acting out of fear or from anger."

"So that's why we're hanging our arses out into the riot zone," McCarter said.

"You'd do it just for fun," James countered. "This at least gives you a purpose to head butt someone in the face for good cause."

McCarter smirked. "You had me at head butt."

The van continued on, hurtling toward the next conflagration that would soon engulf Phoenix Force.

T. J. HAWKINS WAS the youngest member of Phoenix Force, and as such, had the least experience. Though he hadn't engaged in outside scientific studies unrelated to his military experience, he was a military historian, an expert in electronic telecommunication and had been a quick study at languages to better understand the original philosophies and writings of the famous generals he followed. While he wasn't an innovator in creating new technologies like Hermann Schwarz and the other members of the Stony Man cybercrew, his facility with the technology, plus his linguistic acumen, came in handy.

Hawkins still knew Russian well enough to follow Grozna's conversations through the shotgun microphone. The man who'd been the leader of the snatch team against Manning and McCarter was careful, but Hawkins himself was a hunter from his early days. While he had a decade less experience than his comrade and costalker Gary Manning, he had been born, almost literally, with a rifle in his hands. The skills he'd picked up deer hunting made urban surveillance as close to a breeze as any other mission he'd been on for the Stony Man group.

The SUV he was packed into had only slightly tinted windows and was filled with cleaning supplies. Across the side of the light gray vehicle was a banner that was comprised of mixed letters assembled in the approximation of a slavic name. While Paris wasn't as well-known an immigrant stop as New York City, the former Eastern bloc nations sent teeming thousands out, anywhere, looking for employment. If anything, Paris was a much more likely spot for immigrants from all corners of the world, both Asia and North Africa, as well as the Middle East.

Disappearing in a large city was nothing more than putting on the right scent. In Texas and Georgia, it had been deer urine that would mask his presence. In a city, it was an appearance that people wouldn't afford a second glance to.

Two blocks away, bracketing Grozna on the other side, was Manning in a similar clandestine setup. The mission right now was quiet observation and the tracking of a potential enemy without letting him know that he was in their sights. As such, both Hawkins and Manning weren't just looking at Grozna, but were also keeping an eye out for his security teams or any of the Greenwar operatives that Grozna could be in contact with.

Hawkins watched his CPDA, waiting for more contact with Stony Man Farm regarding Grozna's background, but any such search would prove difficult. The members of Phoenix Force were in a similar position to the Russian, if he was indeed part of a clandestine operations agency. Their histories had been erased, any profile that they had raised in their lives before becoming members of Stony Man disappearing from files. There were still personal contacts, but even when they tapped those assets, such things were kept in the dark. No mention of the Farm, the Sensitive Operations Group or the identities of their new comrades could or would ever be brought up.

It was a hard line to keep, but for the safety of the Farm, and by extension, the safety of America and the free world, it was adhered to. His old friends could make assumptions about his current position, but Hawkins had to remain a hint, a rumor, rather than a fully formed fact.

It was a good thing that the men of Phoenix Force were more than just a team. They were friends, quite nearly family. Their camaraderie kept loneliness at bay, made them feel alive and vital, connected to something more than just a life of gunning down the enemies of civilization and order. Grozna would be in a similar situation, and depending on the truth of his purpose in Paris, would be as much a phantom as Hawkins and the rest of Phoenix Force.

"This isn't getting us anywhere," came Manning's voice over the CPDA.

Hawkins looked at it as if the Canadian had released a long burst of flatulence over the airwaves. "You're getting impatient?"

"I'm seeing vital time disappear," Manning returned. "We already have riots occurring around the world, and each passing moment we don't knock something loose, we get closer to the weapon spreading. Without the capture of samples, we're just looking at mindless mayhem with no cure in sight. We're supposed to protect people, not watch them get shoveled into mass graves after they've been cut down."

"So you're going to push the envelope," Hawkins said. "We've got circumstantial evidence at best. Thing is, we don't have to take this to any court of law."

"The best way to figure out who's on the wrong side is just to offer yourself as a target and let them come at you," Manning said.

"We're doing that in the middle of a city, though," Hawkins replied.

Manning made a grunt of assent. "I won't be sloppy in my shooting, and I'll make certain I'm the focus of their attention, not bystanders."

"So you're coming at them through the alley," Hawkins concluded.

"Got it. How long do you need to get into position to cover?" Manning asked.

"I'll take a minute," Hawkins said. "Going hands-free communication."

"Copy and copy," Manning returned.

Hawkins reached into his kit bag. He already had his sidearm with him, a Beretta M-9 A1, an update of the classic 92-FS utilized by Phoenix Force for some time, this one outfitted with a picatinny rail and coming standard with tritium insert night sights and a reinforced slide. It was loaded with its standard, new 17-round capacity magazine, giving him 18 shots. As a Ranger, Hawkins was well versed in the pistol's use, and it came naturally to him. For a backup, he had an alloy-framed Smith & Wesson .45 ACP Revolver, giving him six fast and heavy-duty shots in an exceedingly accurate package. It also had a rail beneath its stubby four-inch barrel, but being in concealed, backup duty, in case the M-9 A1 was lost or ran dry, it was naked of accessories. It was meant for lightning-quick point-and-shoot action. Being raised in Texas, the idea of having a .45 revolver as one of his sidearms was something that appealed to Hawkins on a genetic level, despite his birth in Georgia. The Scandium alloy double-action revolver, fed by lightning-quick full-moon clips, was as far from the old Cowboy Peacemakers of the Old West as his M-4 carbine with Aimpoint optics and laser/illumination module was light years more advanced than the old lever-action Winchesters. But the basic concept was the same. Hawkins didn't have any delusions about being a twenty-first-century cowboy, and it was far from his personality, at least in terms of being a "shoot-from-the-hip, wild-living" stereotype. Despite the prejudices of some self-anointed intellectuals, Hawkins hadn't joined the military or Phoenix Force out of an urge to kill foreigners.

He'd joined because he loved his fellow Americans, because he had the fire in his belly that drove him to give up a life of comfort so that he could safeguard those who couldn't fight for themselves. He was precise, determined and selfless when it came to the performance of his duty.

Grozna, if he was guilty, would be brought down. Anyone who came between Phoenix Force and the Russian would be swept aside, gently at first, but with finality if he or she turned out to be a true menace.

Hawkins checked his M-4 rifle once more. Since it was in the city, he had the Aimpoint zeroed to fifty yards, insuring that he would be able to thread a single 5.56 mm round through the nostril of his target of choice if the situation warranted it. The carbine was locked to semiautomatic. Full-auto firepower was more of a hindrance than an asset when fighting inside of a community. While full-auto was highly controllable with the weapon, at the close quarters he'd be operating within, the 5.56 mm round would be highly effective, and he wouldn't have to worry about a bullet going through both a body and a wall beyond it to hit bystanders.

"Hawk." Manning's voice cut in. "Twenty?"

"Time of arrival, fifteen seconds," Hawkins answered. The carbine had been hidden inside a gym bag, allowing him to carry it through the city streets unseen, avoiding a panic and preventing Grozna's watchers from being alerted. He sidled into a doorway and let the bag hang on its strap, his hand surreptitiously inside its zipper on the grip of the rifle. "In position."

"Moving in. Cover me," Manning said.

Hawkins had his eyes peeled, and he watched as his teammate walked openly down the alley. Manning's coat concealed whatever firepower he carried, a benefit of being a man with a barrel chest and massive, powerful shoulders. The fabric of his coat hung loosely, and Hawkins knew that among his friend's battle gear was a sawed-off shotgun with a ten-inch barrel, giving it only a three-plus-one-round capacity, and a long-barreled revolver. Riding backup was an update of Manning's favorite 9 mm pistol, the Walther PPS. Its predecessor, the P-5, had been a traditional alloy-framed 9 mm auto descended from the old P-38, one of the two legendary German sidearms of World War II. While the striker mechanism and the polymer frame were themselves developed from the much newer P-99, the PPS had much more in common with the flat, concealable service P-5 than the higher-capacity P-99.

Lack of large magazines was never going to be a detriment to Manning. With him, accuracy was king, and accuracy backed up with powerful impacts were the Canadian's specialty.

Hawkins was aware that the man who was acting security on the alley doorway that Grozna had entered took notice of Manning, who walked forward in an unassuming, friendly manner. The guard focused hard on Manning, one hand drifting toward a concealed sidearm.

"Tango is hot and ready to party," Hawkins whispered over his hands-free microphone.

Manning didn't visibly act as if he'd heard the Southerner, but that was simply because of Manning's discipline and coolness under fire. Through his earpiece, Hawkins could hear his Canadian friend speaking French, a slurred, tipsy voice that was another testament to the burly man's vast array of abilities. The drunk act had been good enough to pause the guard, and with a sudden burst of explosive speed, Manning lunged at him.

Sledgehammer fists struck the guard in the chest and stomach, folding him up and leaving him unable to do more than croak painfully. With practiced speed, Manning disarmed the man and tossed his weapons into a garbage bin. The machine pistol that the guard had been packing was a nasty surprise, and Manning had taken a moment to look at the magazine of the weapon.

"This guy's using armor-piercing ammo," Manning said. "No regard for urban combat settings. The Russians are hardasses, but they wouldn't be loading tungsten cores in a foreign city for site protection."

"But that's what a terrorist group would have handy for putting away local SWAT and counterterror ops," Hawkins said, jogging up to stack with Manning at the entrance to Grozna's safehouse.

Manning looked at the M-4 that Hawkins had pulled from its gym-bag covering. Hawkins didn't have any such concerns about the danger of his weapon. Anyone who would be on the receiving end of its deadly message would be hit, but the spoon-tipped hollowpoint rounds were designed specifically not to cut through hard cover like a brick wall. Marines in the recent Gulf Wars had vetted the 5.56 mm 69-grain hollowpoint as a perfect close-quarters cartridge for use in neighborhoods where there were likely to be friendlies on the other side of a wall from the bad guys being engaged. Stray rounds simply would not cut through a building and hit noncombatants on the other side.

The terminal effect and increased accuracy of the long bullet's barrel-contacting surfaces complemented the lack of danger to innocents on the battlefield.

The big Canadian drew his cut-down Remington 870 MCS. Six shells rode on its sidesaddle, and he fished a cartridge from his belt to slide it directly into the breech.

The shotgun was now ready, ten rounds of 12-gauge ready to tear into enemy forces. The buckshot that Manning had loaded wouldn't be lethal upon penetrating a wall any more than Hawkins's rounds.

"Keep Grozna alive. At least leave him able to talk," Manning said. "Anyone else is fair game."

"Got it," Hawkins replied. Seeing the doorway's narrowness, he knew that he would be snagged by his rifle's length. Reluctantly, he cinched the M-4 across his back and drew the Smith & Wesson 325 revolver. With that in hand, Hawkins would be able to cut through close quarters with greater speed and agility.

Manning nodded at the wisdom of Hawkins's last minute change-up. The M-4 had been ideal for countersniper overwatch in an alley. Door-busting, however, required something smaller and much more handy. "At will, Hawk."

The Southerner reared up and kicked just under the doorknob, shattering the door's latch and swinging it open hard. Hawkins went low, .45 revolver tracking to the left, while Manning remained standing, his shotgun sweeping the right side of the entrance. The sudden racket of their safehouse being invaded caught the two guards inside flat-footed, their eyes wide with surprise.

The time for pulling punches was long gone, especially since these two men were not Russian—they were Chinese, judging by their features and their sudden curse words. One lunged toward his assault rifle, propped against the lip of the table they shared while the other one clawed at the pistol he had jammed into his belt.

Manning's Remington boomed, nine closely packed pellets slamming into the side of the Greenwar soldier who went for his rifle. Upon encountering fluid mass, the copper-jacketed lead balls bounced off each other and off rib bones, shooting wildly through the man's vital organs. Holes were torn through heart muscle, lung tissue and blood vessels, ending the Chinese gunman's fight before his fingers did more than brush the handle of his rifle.

The Greenwar fanatic with the handgun was Hawkins's target, and he cycled the slick trigger of his revolver, two fat 230-grain hollowpoint rounds roaring down the S & W's barrel in quick succession. Either one of those two shots would have been enough to anchor the Chinese handgunner in place, one .45 slug tearing into his heart, the other shattering his breastbone before coming to a violent stop at his spinal column.

Hawkins used two shots anyway. He was only using a handgun, and even the vaunted .45 ACP round wasn't an instant death ray.

The two Greenwar sentries were gone in the space of three shots, only a few seconds passing as they went down. Of course, those three shots had raised the alert for the conspirators. Their edge of surprise disappeared swiftly.

Manning and Hawkins were going to have to work to fight their way to Grozna.

CHAPTER FOURTEEN

The helicopter flared out, coming down to a smooth landing at the police line circling Gary, Indiana, allowing Able Team to dismount with their cases of equipment. The three Able Team operatives, bristling with gear, held the attention of the men assembled at the roadblock overlooking the city in the middle of its self-destruction.

Carl Lyons recognized Captain Robert Macingham from the quick info dump sent by Aaron Kurtzman. Able Team, like Phoenix Force, had been dispatched to retrieve one of the "infected" in the hope of locating the actual Greenwar weapon and its transmission vector. As such, Lyons had replaced his 12-gauge shotgun with something a little more appropriate for preventing mass slaughter rather than being a close-quarters death machine. The FN 303 looked skeletonized from the rear, black polycarbon forming the bones of a shoulder stock, while the front end was a 15-round disk underneath a fat-barreled launcher with a high-pressure air canister to propel the fin-stabilized shells within.

Since the air bottle was charged sufficiently to fire 110 rounds, Lyons had a pouch of six more disks of .68-caliber less-lethal shells. In most instances, this would have been enough to repel even the most ferocious riots, but an entire city was currently in uproar. Even with a 303P sidearm, itself packed with 6-round box magazines, he wouldn't be able to dent the mayhem going on.

"I heard that you guys are Feds," Macingham said as he looked over Lyons and his similarly equipped partners. "What's with the sci-fi gear?"

Lyons nodded to the captain. "We're here to find solutions, not leave bodies."

Macingham smiled and extended a hand. "Good to know. A lot of my men have families in that hellhole. We're almost out of tear gas, and the fire hoses are only barely enough to bowl over whatever crowds are rushing the perimeters. Who are you guys exactly?"

"We're a CDC hot-zone intervention squad," Schwarz told him, pulling one of their quad bikes out of the back of the National Guard MH-58 chopper that had brought them. "The cool motorcycle wear we have is equipped for hostile environments."

"Which is why we've been told to stay put. Thing is, we've lost communication with only one of the roadblocks that's downwind from the city," Macingham said.

Blancanales pursed his lips. "Only one? Can I see it on a map?"

Macingham nodded and directed him toward a command tent full of Indiana State Police and National Guard comm officers. So terrible was the Greenwar weapon's potential that not even helicopters were allowed entry into Gary's airspace.

"It was a National Guard unit, and they rushed a state trooper roadblock," Macingham said.

Lyons frowned at the report. "Five dead, a dozen wounded. The guard went crazy, but they remembered how to load and use their rifles."

"It's pure insanity," Macingham muttered. "I never thought I'd see a mess like this outside of a zombie movie. There are big sections of the city that look like they're on fire right now, and we are getting reports of gunfire."

"Local lawmen and criminals?" Blancanales asked.

"And law-abiding citizens," Lyons added. "This isn't Illinois, Pol."

"So we could run into something worse than clubs and pointed sticks," Blancanales murmured, looking at the map. "Has anyone tried to rush to the roadblocks?"

"We've got men with antimatériel rifles knocking out engine blocks," Macingham said. "We don't know what sparked this, but we were told not to let anything escape."

"Which includes people who might not be infected," Lyons mused. "You haven't done anything to knock out windshields, have you?"

"Just engine blocks or tires," Macingham said. "These people aren't terrorists."

Lyons nodded. "Can you tell if any of the vehicles were driving erratically?"

"Most of them," Macinghame returned. "Some that we hit in the engine, though, the people inside remained still."

"Too frightened to evacuate their vehicle," Blancanales noted. "And the erratic drivers?"

"They unassed pronto," Macingham said. "That's

why we're keeping a watch on the stalled, occupied vehicles."

Schwarz rejoined the team after setting up the ATVs. "Well, that means you might have a chance to help the occupants. We're going in with no more actual protection than regular riot squads interacting with riot control gas."

"If you guys are fine, we can send in retrieval crews for the people," Macingham said. "I'll dispatch some paramedics with the retrieval crews. They'll have oxygen masks, which could help the captives."

"Good idea," Lyons told him. "We've dealt with this particular contagion only a few hours ago. It dies out fast in heat, and some of the men responsible were certain that they could ride out a breach of the stuff inside an airtight hangar."

"So it's a chemical? Or an organism?" Macingham asked.

"We're going in just to find out," Blancanales said. "We need to capture a prisoner or two to figure out what's set this all off."

"Word from above says we're not to enter the city and make physical contact with the people within," Macingham countered. "They told us you're the only ones with clearance to enter. Three men…"

"Less personnel to lose if we're overwhelmed," Schwarz told him. "But we're coordinated enough to have a chance of survival."

"You have real weapons in case?" Macingham asked.

Lyons patted his six-inch .357 Magnum, then directed Macingham's attention to Blancanales's 1911 and Schwarz's Beretta 93-R. "I hope we don't have to. These are citizens."

"God bless and Godspeed, Fed," Macingham returned.

Lyons nodded and his partners mounted up on their Honda ATVs. In a city that was in turmoil with crashed vehicles and burning wreckage, Able Team was going to need mobility and speed to survive and get out. The Hondas had 686 cc engines, which could get the 500-pound quad bikes up to 75 miles per hour, more than enough to outrun crowds, and give them the ability to load an unconscious person and get back out. The off-roaders had proved their combat worth with special operations groups in the mountainous regions of Afghanistan, providing them with mobility, as well as the ability to haul serious weaponry like the 40-pound Barret M-85 rifles with their mounted infrared scopes along with more conventional carbines and sidearms.

Schwarz and Blancanales spread out in a reverse V behind Lyons's lead. The Stony Man commandos were clad in leather from neck to the soles of their feet, polycarbonate plates on their joints and high-tensile fiberglass helmets protecting their skulls. The helmets had been fitted with filters that had originally been intended for keeping the team from suffering from the effects of tear gas, but in this instance, they were also going to have to rely on them for protection from whatever airborne contagion was turning an American city into an outskirt of hell.

The helmets had been modified by Schwarz with built-in communications and sound filters that gave them hearing protection in the case of gunfire. In addition they had been reinforced by Stony Man armorer John Kissinger so that the hard shells could deflect all but the most powerful rifle rounds. As they zoomed through the cloying, thick clouds of capsicum solution, none of the powerful pepper extract made it through the filters, which kept their sinuses and mucus membranes safe from the inflammatory effects of the gas that left even the insane rioters twisting and writhing on the ground.

Bursting out of the burning mist, Lyons was glad that they weren't driving full-out, as the streets were clogged with stopped vehicles. The majority were bashed and battered, windshields cracked by bloody fist prints. Other cars were secure and self-contained, but Lyons could see frightened faces within as they had been blocked in by all manner of barricades, both inert machinery and teeming crowds.

"There!" Lyons directed his partners toward an SUV hounded by a howling horde. "Put down the crowd as gently as possible. We can rescue a few people."

Blancanales skidded his ATV to a halt first, bringing up his FN 303 and cutting loose with a trio of oleoresin capsicum shells. The .68-caliber slugs, propelled by 3000 psi, struck two burly men who had been poised to smash in the SUV's windscreen with a torn-up mailbox. The impact trauma of the rounds caused them to drop their improvised weapon, but the fat rounds vomited out clouds of high-intensity inflammatory agent that washed over the rest of the crowd, assaulting the frightened people within.

Their eyes, noses and mouths suddenly filled with searing chemical flame, two-thirds of the attacking mob suddenly broke, scampering away from the SUV. Those who had been shielded from the tear powder bullets whirled in furious reaction to the sudden appearance of the leather-clad warriors.

Blancanales had been tasked as the team's grenadier and area-denial gunner, his long-gun launcher fed with a 15-round magazine full of the oleoresin capsicum shells, while Lyons and Schwarz were relegated to impact rounds for anyone not impressed with the flaming pain in their faces. As such, when the group turned to launch themselves at Able Team, they received a hail of polymer shells that hammered them with merciless force.

The FN 303s were less-lethal, but they were hardly safe, so Lyons and Schwarz made every effort to avoid head and neck shots. At 3000 psi, the FN launchers had the potential to cause skull and vertebral fractures, resulting in permanent injury. Chest and shoulder impacts were sufficient to batter and bruise their opponents, stopping them cold even within midcharge. Half of the remaining dozen collapsed beneath the pounding they received, while the others backed off, dropping their weaponry.

"This is only temporary," Lyons said. "Gadgets…"

Schwarz needed little convincing to zoom in closer to the SUV and wave to the driver, a middle-aged woman whose face was nearly as pale as her platinum-blond hair, giving her directions. The SUV backed away from the capsicum stunned crowd, pulling a one-eighty.

Schwarz slapped the fender and waved her down toward the perimeter.

"Macingham, we're sending out a sand-colored soccer-mom SUV. Uninfected adults and children are inside. Do not fire, and give it a hose down before you let them out," Lyons called back.

He looked to see Blancanales pour more tear gas shells down a street, slowing another sudden surge of rioters. Lyons whipped his FN 303 around and triggered his drum-fed launcher, clear polymer shells smacking hard against the lower bodies and legs of anyone still determined enough to stumble through the burning cloud. Struck in the stomach, groin and thighs, the crazed citizens folded, losing their support and ability to walk further toward them. He noted that Blancanales had emptied his first disk of CS/CN shells and slipped another into place.

"Pol, I've got movement coming from the east," Lyons called out.

"Area denial in progress. Grab some and let's boogie out of here!" Blancanales returned.

"Grabbing sickies," Lyons called back. He left the FN launcher with his quad bike, not only to leave both hands free for picking up infected specimens, but also to increase his maneuverability. Granted, the skeletonized weapon was short at only twenty-nine inches, and relatively light, but eight pounds and two-and-a-half feet of gun were going to be that much more burden on Lyons, especially if he needed to "convince" one of the crazed Gary residents to accompany him for inspection.

Taking off in a quick run, he crossed the twenty-five

yards between him and where the soccer mom and her SUV had been stalled. Men and women were strewed around, some knocked unconscious by polymer impact batons, but most trying to hold their faces on from the searing agony inflicted by capsicum oil extract, which swelled up nasal and eye tissues on contact. This was more than simply tear gas, even though their faces and hands were slicked with tears; this was cause for people even at their most violent to sit still and suck down oxygen as their air passages had been swollen almost to choking.

A woman scurried to her feet at Lyons's approach, her eyes red-rimmed, snot pouring from her nose, but she was not in enough pain to stop her. She would have been pretty if she didn't look as if she were in fright makeup and a shock wig, but her bloody fingers clawed out at Lyons. For a brief glimpse he noticed that her knuckles were split from striking the shell of the SUV, nails splintered by clawing at something. Madness had made her immune to the pain, and only a peripheral whiff of CS/CN had been too little to slow her down.

Lyons whipped out his 303P pistol, triggering a single clear-polymer baton at waist level. The .68-caliber missile hit her in the stomach and she folded over instantly. Lyons took her momentary pause as an opportunity to hook her by the back of her head and shove her hard to the asphalt. He didn't enjoy manhandling a woman, especially one who was likely a citizen, but once her head bounced off the ground, a lot of the fight left her. With practiced dexterity, he plucked off a loop of nylon cable tie and cinched it around her wrists. A second loop bound her ankles, and Lyons shouldered the hogtied woman.

Schwarz rolled up to him on his ATV, swiveling it around so that Lyons could drop her on a wire-cage carriage designed for holding equipment loads. Together, the two Able Team commandos wrapped her with leather restraint straps, securing her to the Honda and limiting her ability to be combative as Schwarz pulled away.

"Ironman, we've got a crowd massing from the north." Blancanales spoke up. "I've emptied two magazines into them, but they keep pushing ahead."

Lyons gave Schwarz's helmet a slap. "Move it. I'm grabbing one more."

"I'm covering you," Schwarz returned.

"Scoot!" Lyons ordered. "We've got one specimen. I don't want to lose her."

Schwarz revved the 686 cc engine and peeled out, knowing that he couldn't change the stubborn Lyons's mind. Once the Ironman had made a decision, he was as hard to bend as the metal he was named for.

Lyons turned and waved for Blancanales to go, as well, but the Politician fed another 15-round disk magazine into his weapon.

"Move your ass, grab your prisoner and we both get out of here!" Blancanales ordered.

Lyons knew he couldn't argue his partner, so he turned toward a male rioter who lay coughing. As he bent toward the man, a rock that the crazed rioter had hidden in his hand flashed up. Madness-fueled strength and rage focused the energy of the stone with more than enough force to shatter Lyons's helmet visor. The blow made the Able Team commander's head swim crazily, and he blinked wildly as wisps of capsicum fog burned his eyes and nostrils.

"Shit!" Lyons growled, lashing out with a forearm smash that rocked the head of his assailant. The assault, backing a hard polycarbonate plate, split the man's skull and left him still with one stroke.

"Carl!" Blancanales shouted.

"I can hear you," Lyons returned. "Get out of here!"

"But…"

"Leave me!" Lyons bellowed.

Blancanales cut loose with an entire magazine, pounding the crowd that lurched forward toward the two Able Team members.

With some shock, Blancanales watched as his friend hefted the unconscious man and strode quickly toward his Honda, strapping him down.

"Carl?"

"Hungry," Lyons answered. "Fucking hungry and I don't like it."

The words came in a furious, subhuman growl, but he threw himself into the ATV's saddle. As an afterthought, Lyons ripped his revolver from its holster and hurled it to the ground with enough force to burst the cylinder from its window.

"Carl?" Blancanales asked.

"Let's go!" Lyons shouted at him. "I don't know what I'm going to do, but I'm going to hold on as long as I can!"

The two Stony Man riders tore off, racing toward

Macingham's roadblock, Blancanales worrying about his cursing and growling partner the whole ride.

BARBARA PRICE WATCHED the War Room's wall monitors, her mouth cast into a grim frown as a dozen smaller screens showed video footage of worldwide mayhem. Twelve cities had been chosen as a display of power for Greenwar and Bezoar, and as far as she could tell, a hundred thousand were already dead. The South African military and police showed zero tolerance for the rioters in Diepsloot, opening fire on the crowds as they lashed out at each other and charged toward the armed men holding the line at the town's perimeter.

Her stomach sank at the sight of men and women of all ages lying out, blood pooling under their corpses.

"Aaron, tell me we've got something," Price said. "Anything?"

"No information about the basis of the hunger plague yet," Kurtzman said. "I've had Hunt and Carmen running air traffic over the outbreak sites. Akira's tapping into the medical emergency agencies of the countries afflicted, trying to see if they've managed to find samples, but there's nothing."

"CDC get anything from the samples that Phoenix captured from the Paris device?" Price asked.

Kurtzman shook his head. "The samples are still in transit from Europe via diplomatic courier. And right now, the FAA is deliberating whether to allow international flights to land."

"We need those samples," Price snarled.

"The FAA doesn't even know if the quarantine will

hold off the spread, but they don't want to take any chances," Brognola said.

"Get that flight permission to land, even if you have to drop it like a lawn dart into the middle of Stony Man Farm," Price ordered.

"That might make analysis difficult if we go that far," Kurtzman said offhandedly, the blurring motion of his fingers belying the joking nature of his words. Price could tell that his brilliant, multifaceted mind was working on a dozen things at once, and the attempt at wry humor was his means of coping with a level of pressure that either broke men or compressed them into shining diamond.

The cybercrew of the Farm had been at the brink of worldwide mayhem before, fighting off nuclear threats, orbital bombardments and more plagues than Egypt suffered in the Old Testament. While not trained gunmen, these computer geniuses had the same strength of will and brilliance necessary to prevent atomic wars and pandemics from arising and wiping out all life on Earth. The kind of resilience to horror that they had developed was something, but Price could see that as the pressure increased, the harder and faster they worked.

It was simple. Humanity had evolved to survive in a world where its skin was too soft, and its natural weapons were too weak to deal with the thick-armored, savage-clawed creatures around them. As such, intellect and skill responded to increases of adrenaline, provided the people could control the fear that triggered those autonomic responses. With men like Lyons and McCarter, that translated into sharper reflexes and increased physical strength. With Kurtzman and his band of electronic wizards, the spurred energy honed their thought processes to laser-keen edges.

Hal Brognola's line blinked to life, and Price took the call instantly with her Bluetooth.

"Sorry to pry, but we need some reassurances here," Brognola said.

"So far, they've picked some of the worst slums on the planet," Price answered. "We've got nothing in terms of where the contagion might have originated. Satellite and radar data show absolutely no aircraft in the vicinity of these cities that might have been able to drop a chemical weapon."

"So, Greenwar has the ability to invisibly turn any city it wants into a battleground," Brognola concluded. "What's the damage so far?"

"Twelve communities of between 100,000 and 150,000 on all six continents," Price said. "The Brazilian Favella was our twelfth outbreak. I'm transferring the exact locations to your smartphone."

"What about loss of life?" Brognola asked.

"It's impossible to tell," Price replied. "Diepsloot has turned into a turkey shoot, though. At least two thousand gunned down at the line between it and Johannesburg."

"Barb!" Kurtzman shouted.

She looked up and saw that one of the cameras had blanked out. The world map suddenly went to atomic alert. "Oh, God..."

"What is it, Barbara?" Brognola asked.

"Qingshuihe disappeared. The seismic and radiation sensors we're watching have registered a nuclear explosion in China, and on-site remote cameras are no longer transmitting," Price said, fighting down the nausea that struck her.

There was silence on Brognola's end.

"There's no word from Beijing," Brognola finally said. "No communications yet."

"You think that China would admit it destroyed one of its own cities?" Price asked.

"I don't know," Brognola answered. "But did they nuke Qingshuihe to contain Greenwar's plague, or did they do it to show Bezoar that they were willing to cull their population?"

Price clenched her fists. "I'll find it out. No one kills a hundred fifty thousand people like that in a vacuum."

"Barb, don't take this personally," Brognola cautioned.

"I've seen two nations willingly exterminate thousands of their own citizens," Price countered. "I'll stay disciplined, but damn it, we're only human. Bezoar, whoever gave the okays for all of these murders…"

"Those nations are trying to save millions more than those already dead," Brognola offered. "Much as I'd like to personally punish those who gave the orders, what we have to do is stop Bezoar."

Carmen Delahunt put her hand to her mouth, green eyes bulging wide, catching Price's attention.

"What now?" Price asked her.

"Able Team has three infected for study," Delahunt said softly. "And one of the infected is Carl."

"Did you hear that?" Price asked Brognola, all emotion drained from her voice.

"I did. Tell David and the others to stay out. We can't afford to lose Phoenix's leadership, too," Brognola said.

Price's jaw tensed, sinews tightened so much that her chin trembled. "I'll get him. Carmen, keep me in the loop about Carl."

Delahunt nodded, a shocked silence falling over the Stony Man War Room.

CHAPTER FIFTEEN

Calvin James clapped David McCarter on the shoulder. "We're not going into Ostbanhof, David. Carl and the boys picked up some specimens to study from the Gary riots."

McCarter looked over his shoulder, easing off the speed. "That's supposed to be good news, so why so grim?"

James looked down. "Carl's under restraints. Someone broke his helmet, and now he's raging and hungry."

"Raging...they have things under control?" McCarter asked.

James grimaced. "What are we going to do, teleport to the Midwest?"

"I'm concerned about him, mate," McCarter replied. "I wish we could be there, but we can't be. He's being treated, right?"

James nodded, his head bobbing jerkily, as if his shoulders were wound too tightly. "I didn't mean to bite your head off. Carl's one of my friends, too."

"We've wasted a trip?" McCarter asked.

"No," Enciso stated. "I've got Hunt on the laptop here."

James looked at his satellite phone. "I just got off the

phone with Barb. She didn't say anything about Hunt contacting us…"

"Because I was trying to keep you guys from becoming extras from *28 Days Later*," Price said, appearing over Huntington Wethers's shoulder in the webcam window. "And Hunt hadn't let me in on his results until a second after I got off with you, Cal."

"We've been looking for commonalities between the different cities that have been affected by the starvation plague," Wethers said, his glasses off as he wiped them with a cleaning cloth. He looked as prim and proper as ever when he was a university professor, but his voice held levels of deep exhaustion. "The first thing we did was to check as much freight movement data as possible."

"What was the big info hit that you made on that?" McCarter asked.

"Lyons might have lost himself gathering samples of the plague, but he's been busy in the time before," Price said. "As soon as there was a global search for shipping information, he'd had Gadgets set up a check that flagged our computers."

"The Chicago smuggling ring he'd busted," McCarter said with a breath of revelation.

"They had some strange shipments of electronic equipment internationally. It had been sent out two weeks ago," Wethers said. "There were a dozen of them…"

"Brazil, South Africa, China…" Encizo offered.

Wethers nodded. "Dead on."

"Any idea what the electronics were?" James asked. "And was it only electronics?"

"So far, that's what we have on the logs, but they had also been used as a clearing house that had transported food storage coolant canisters to about fifty different cities, including, tellingly, a small grocery store in Albion, Iowa," Wethers explained.

"Coolant canisters...the delivery truck that Robespierre talked about," James said excitedly. "Is there any word on him?"

"It's been pretty hectic, so we've been distracted from his situation—" Wethers started to say.

"I've got a CDC contact over at Rush Presbyterian in Chicago, where they took Robespierre," Price interrupted. "She's been monitoring him for signs of infection, metabolic change or dementia, but he hasn't displayed any symptoms."

"So either he wasn't exposed or the effects aren't long lasting," James said. "Or it doesn't hang around in the atmosphere for long...or..."

McCarter didn't like the way his friend's speech trailed off. He'd pulled the vehicle off to the shoulder of the autobahn to avoid distraction while driving. "Cal, you didn't send all of the samples you took in Paris, did you?"

James shook his head, then reached into his rifle case, withdrawing a small sealed canister. "I wanted to make a few tests of my own. So far, all it looks like is colorless air. I've tried different filters of light through it. I even isolated a swab and put it under a microscope, looking for microorganisms."

"Empty?" Encizo asked, looking at the small cylinder as if it were a live grenade.

"Zilch," McCarter said. "Otherwise, you wouldn't still be holding on to it."

James nodded somberly.

"Was the Paris setup a red herring?" Price asked.

"I don't think so," James said. "I haven't been able to have this chemically tested, but I was looking for broader, more dangerous elements like cyanide with the light filtration. This could be a complex protein, but I can tell that it's got nothing on a cellular scale. Proteins are molecular strings, and require far more sophisticated microscopes than we've had access to in the field—"

"Get to the point," McCarter said.

"What if we're not looking at a chemical cause, per se," James asked, "but a simple drug?"

"Guys, according to the shipping records that Able got access to, we only have forty-eight hours before a second set of Greenwar attacks begin," Price said. "There are shipping manifests to fifty cities. The same source as Albion, Diepsloot, Gary, Ostbanhof…"

"That's going by a similar schedule of the shipment preceding this one that spurred the recent mayhem," Wethers added.

"I'm saying that this could be a hallucinogenic chemical, used in combination with technology," James said. "However, since you said these were shipped as coolant, requiring refrigeration of their own, they're fairly fragile and they break down relatively quickly. The right hallucinogen and the right stimulus could combine to create madness."

"Stimulus," Price repeated. "Sonic?"

"Low-frequency sonics were one field of testing by the Soviet Union before the fall of the Berlin Wall," James said. "The right frequency can inspire maddening fear or unreasoning anger."

"Ultra-low-frequency sonics," Price said. "Hunt, what about those iron bomb guidance systems that we assumed were responsible for the destruction of Albion and other small community test sites?"

"You think that they might have some form of sonic broadcast system?" Wethers asked.

"Absolutely," James interjected. "While the bulk of ordnance guidance systems research is directed toward focused laser technology, there's also other means of steering so-called dumb bombs."

Wethers looked over the specifications, calling them up for McCarter and his team to read on their CPDA screens. Five sets of eyes would be far better than scanning lines of text manuals and operational instructions on hand.

"Wait," Encizo noted. "They're referencing a manual EF-1138. There's nothing in there, but the guidance modules for the bombs are keyed in to pick up infrasound tones generated by personal radio sets."

"Anything in the DoD database on EF-1138?" Price asked.

"Checking on it," Wethers responded.

"EF-1138 wouldn't be under the DoD equipment list," McCarter interrupted. "That doesn't fit the designatory protocols regarding new electronic communication equipment. They're generally listed as PRC or GRC."

"That's right," Wethers confirmed. "The designation code is too general for use, but I think that I might have an idea. I'm hacking into the company that did the majority of electronic work on the guidance systems."

"And see who else that they have done work with," Price said. "Our military might not have wanted to use ultra-low-frequency sonic beacons to draw in artillery and upgraded iron bombs, but someone else would have been interested."

"Akira! I'm going to need you to help me here," Wethers called out. "Check for broadcast signals that share a common radio or television frequency for the cities that have come under siege."

"What are we looking for?" Tokaido answered.

"A baseline that is simple. It'll pump out a low-frequency sonic tone," Wethers said. "Carmen, another idea…"

"You want me to correlate the radius of the outbreaks, and look for central broadcast points or towers," Delahunt offered. "That's why we're only getting small communities for now. They're working through local, small-market transmitters that have a reach of 150,000 potential listeners."

"It's not a limit of the system," Encizo said. "It's a test parameter and a way of ensuring a blanket of sound. Even if only one in five televisions or radios picked up the signal, we're talking about ultra-low-frequency sonics, which can permeate an area, even without being audible to a conscious mind."

"I'm not picking up any anomalies," Tokaido said as his image appeared on the laptop screen in a separate window from Wethers and Price. "Even if there were a broadcast, where would the chemical or protein be distributed?"

"This is happening in proximity to major transport hubs," McCarter said. "Look at this. Johannesburg, Berlin, Chicago…"

"Chinese Inner Mongolia?" James asked.

"The Huehatote Export Processing Zone," Wethers interjected. "They export tons of coal and natural gas, as well as wheat."

"Wheat?" James pressed. "Oh, my God. I think I know what the trigger is!"

James typed quickly on the laptop. "Food growth regions have been the initial targets, as far as we can tell, as well as centers of commerce and transportation. Robespierre saw a grocery delivery truck, and yet, we don't know exactly what was being delivered, since we don't have his testimony, but what if we were looking at ergoline?"

"Ergoline?" Encizo inquired.

"It's an alkaloid that is found in a wheat and grass parasitic fungus called ergot," James said. "The Great Fear in France and the Salem witch trials have been suspected as being spurred on by mass breakouts of the hallucinogenic effects of the fungus on food stores."

"Wait a second, Cal, Dr. Caporael's theory has been disputed by Spanos and Gottlieb in historical studies," Wethers countered.

"Hunt, look at the situations we have here. We're seeing several growing seasons resulting in late harvest and overly moist conditions, the perfect breeding ground for ergot," James said. "We throw in situations like Albion suffering a similar self-destruction as the Pont-Saint-Esprit mass poisoning as late as 1951, which resulted in seven deaths and dozens restricted to asylums due to madness."

"There's some dispute about that, too, but only minor, as it was still a mycotoxin produced by aspergillus fumigatus," Wethers told him.

"Either way, we're dealing with a hallucinogenic mycotoxin that has been enhanced by the use of a sonic trigger device," James said. "Can I look at something?"

"Shoot," Wethers and Tokaido answered.

"Check for underproduction in the areas we know that there have been outbreaks," James said. "Especially check Albion. This might not have necessarily been sprayed on crops, but the fungi could have gestated in silos, then vented. Put those numbers against high-mold-content pollution warnings in the days preceding the outbreaks, as well."

"Akira?" Wethers asked.

"Fingers are flying as Cal asked for it," Tokaido answered. "Going in fast and nasty. As I'm collating the data, I do have to say, I spent a summer in the Chicago suburbs, and damned if there wasn't a corn processing plant that would belch out a cloud of starch that could be smelled thirty miles away."

"Yeah, it's a ways down Route 171, right where it turns onto Archer Avenue," James said. "I passed it on the way to a funeral for one of my classmates before my own parents died."

"Not saying the corn plant is responsible. For one

thing, ergot apparently isn't interested in corn—it's easier to hide among barley and dark ryes," Tokaido said. "Had an incident in 2002, Ethiopia, where tainted barley caused an outbreak."

"That's another problem going with ergot," Wethers said. "In its spore form, it's a reddish color which makes it easier to spot among various cereals."

"True," James said. "But it doesn't take much to alter the coloration of fungal species, especially if we're looking at the creation of a brand-new form of mycotoxin, custom developed as a weapon by Bezoar."

"He's an enzyme specialist," Price said. "I've been looking into mycotoxin prevention techniques, and one of them is enzyme treatment."

"Esterase, epoxidase, even yeast and a breed of bacterium called Eubacterium BBSH 797," James answered.

"I am so glad you've been doing continual education on this," Price said.

"Striker had a problem with a customized form of rycin a while back, so looking at naturally produced toxins was added to my list of stuff I gotta know to protect my team," James said. "I might not be a biochemist, or a fungus genius, but I've got plenty of study on what can be done."

"Got it, gang," Tokaido reported. "All twelve locations currently under siege have had silo ventings that increased the mold-spore counts greatly for areas out to fifty miles in radius on average. In fact, the situation in Gary and Albion produced a cloud that stretched from Milwaukee to Nashville… Sweet Jesus."

"Those are transport destinations that Lyons and

Gadgets got for us from Chicago," Wethers said. "Refrigeration trucks and coolant canisters factor into this somehow. That's what you found in the Paris device."

"Fucking bell," McCarter grumbled. He opened the sample of air from Paris and took a deep breath. The others in the van waited.

"Nothing," James said. "We should have thought of it. The resonance produced by a bell can cover a broad band of frequencies, and be heard for miles through the sonic spectrum that human ears can consciously pick up."

"So the triggers on the devices were to activate... what's inside the tanks?" Price asked.

"Speakers, a tonpilz projector," Encizo suggested. "That's generally what most active sonar devices utilize to produce the sound waves that hydrophones pick up in response. Built inside of a tank, you've got a system called a tonpilz, or a singing mushroom."

"The coolant tanks can project omnidirectionally," McCarter said. "They wouldn't need electronic receivers, as people can barely hear the kind of sound waves we're talking about."

"Seventeen hertz," James said. "That's the exact tone the brain responds to. Mix in a proper hallucinogen, and you've got the making of mass terror."

"Barb, if the test subjects are right, then we're going to need to find the source of the sonics," Encizo observed. "Can we get a pinpoint to see if there's a projector in use in Berlin?"

"That would take some sensitive microphones. Since most of the stuff we look at is gathered through electronic surveillance and cable intercepts, not emplaced mikes, we're at a loss for detecting the infrasound projectors," Price answered.

"Not necessarily," James offered. "Check with seismic institutes in the areas we're looking at. Infrasound will show up as it causes vibrations in the air and the ground alike. Seismographs can pick them up as if they were marked with neon signs."

"Great," Price said. "That'll give Aaron something to do. I'm going to call the medics treating Lyons to see if the countermold treatments work on him," Price said. "We'll tap seismic institute data and triangulate the closest source of infrasound in your area. Guys, you're going to need to stop the tone. If knocking out the sound works, then we're golden to stop the riots."

"And if we blow it, the American Midwest becomes a wasteland of hallucinating madmen," McCarter growled. "Lord knows what will happen across other countries and continents."

GARY MANNING'S Remington Modular Combat Shotgun bellowed once more, its 12-gauge payload striking the last of Grozna's bodyguards in the jaw. The pellets spread out to gouge one eye into a spurting well of blood, while his mandible was no more than splintered bone held together by perforated and shredded skin, muscle and connective tissue. If the guy wasn't immediately dead from the impact of a full load of buckshot, he was completely paralyzed by the neck-breaking impact that shoved his skull off its vertebrae, shearing the spinal cord.

Whatever the man's final fate, he crashed through the door to Grozna's office, not even uttering a grunt of escaping breath, rubbery arms and legs spilling all around him as he flopped onto the carpet. The Russian's eyes were wide as he immediately dropped his Makarov PM from his beefy hand.

"Wait! Don't shoot!" Grozna pleaded.

"Give me a reason!" Hawkins bellowed, rushing through the door and bowling the agent back onto his desk, the four-inch barrel of his .45 revolver shoved into his cheek so hard, skin tore under the pressure.

"T.J.!" Manning shouted, bursting in and reaching to restrain his partner.

"Back off, meathead!" Hawkins snarled. "I'll blow your kneecap off!"

Manning paused, eyes widening at the sudden rage displayed by his partner. Grozna felt his bladder release as a seething, twang-accented madman ground the muzzle of a big gun into his face hard enough that Grozna could hear the crunching of his cheekbone under Hawkins's weight.

"You'll get nothing from me if you kill me," Grozna scoffed, his voice raspy from the fear that tightened his throat.

"Don't even speak to me, bastard," Hawkins said. "Cities around the world are killing themselves because of you and Bezoar. Where the fuck is he?"

"You said—"

Hawkins drew back the big Smith & Wesson and whipped it hard across Grozna's forehead. Blood sprayed from the sudden laceration, pouring down into the Russian's eyes and stinging them. "I asked you a question! Not to tell me what I asked you. Shut the fuck up!"

Grozna started to wriggle, twisting beneath Hawkins, but suddenly the muzzle was jammed right behind the Russian's ear. The hot metal, warmed by a dozen gunshots that had torn his protectors to pieces, was a chillingly new experience. "India…"

"I said fucking shut it!" Hawkins snapped, his face looming in Grozna's vision as the blood cleared from his eyes.

"No…" the Russian rasped as suddenly Hawkins was grabbed by Manning and hurled to one side. The Remington MCS clacked as the Canadian chambered another round, leveling its fat business end at the American Southerner.

"Stand down, T.J.!"

"Shut up," Hawkins growled with a sneer. "You're not even an American!"

"Stand down or I will end you!" Manning ordered.

"I dare you," Hawkins returned, his mouth twisted into a cruel arch.

Suddenly, the sound of a 12-gauge going off shook the office. Grozna flinched, eyes clenched tight, when a gentle hand grabbed his shoulder.

"You're bleeding," Manning told him. His voice was soft, and he helped the Russian to sit up.

"You…you killed your own man," Grozna said.

"We're working together, but hardly friends," Manning answered. "He was a loose cannon for too long on this team. I don't even know why I was told to cooperate with a hothead like him."

"He'd have killed me," Grozna croaked with a sob. "He'd have taken my head off without even giving me a chance."

"Well, you've got it," Manning said. "Make the paperwork for covering up this idiot's death worth it and tell me where Bezoar is working from."

"He's in India," Grozna said. "That's where he and the rest of his allies have been working on the mycotoxin production."

"Mycotoxin?" Manning asked. "This is fungus based?"

Grozna nodded, trembling. He couldn't bring himself to look at Hawkins, afraid he'd spring to life once more, lunging at him in vengeful fury. Even so, the man's right foot twitched, dead nerves misfiring. "Please, I'll come quietly. Your man is insane...was insane."

"Still am, sucker," Hawkins stated.

Cold terror gripped Grozna's heart in an icy fist. The American had sat up, hardly a mark on him.

"I knew a survivor like you wouldn't break under interrogation, but the prospect of a brutal, messy death at the hands of a madman..." Manning revealed.

"Insanely talented," Hawkins added. "Insanely talented madman."

Grozna trembled.

"You already gave us a little bit," Manning told him. "Even that much will put us on Bezoar's track, but if you want your remaining years spent with even a hope of sunlight peeking through your window, then you'd better spill the rest."

Grozna looked between the two men. "Bezoar isn't

crazy. He's got an anarchistic streak in him, but you have to realize, he's been feeding a lot of people the means to finish up their grudges."

"Like something in Chinese Inner Mongolia?" Hawkins asked. "Let me guess that Outer Mongolia wanted a chance to bite deep into China's profiteering from their captive countryside."

Grozna nodded. "Yeah. And the situation here in Paris, or in Germany. There's a lot of people who would pay to see major urban disruption occurring across Europe. Bezoar has local anarchist groups, political rivals, war profiteers, all eating out of his hand."

"If you've got a list of names, cough it up," Hawkins said.

"Just for Western Europe," Grozna said. "He kept us compartmentalized."

"We'll take what you've got," Manning said, pulling his Combat PDA. "I'm recording now."

The Russian sang.

CARL LYONS GRIMACED as they gave him another shot.

"What was that?" Lyons asked.

"Just support treatment for the aflatoxin in your system," Blancanales told him. "How do you feel?"

Lyons ran his fingers over his cleanly shaved head, grimacing. "Like I've been pulled through an asshole made of sandpaper."

"We had to make sure that you were properly decontaminated," Schwarz said. "Are you feeling cooler now?"

"Yeah. Aflatoxin?" Lyons asked. "That doesn't sound like a hallucinogen."

"Cal's been burning up the research since we first learned of Bezoar's weapon, trying to find out what it was. He finally coordinated with the CDC and we've run tests. It's a blend of aflatoxin, which can affect digestive enzymes, and the alkaloid ergoline," Schwarz answered. "The ergoline was what made you highly susceptible to rage and fear, and the aflatoxin went to work on focusing it on your digestive system. It can make it possible for people to starve to death, but with the right enzyme treatment, we shut down the toxin and neutralized the alkaloid in your system."

"I remember hearing about the fungal poison. There's no antidote for aflatoxin," Lyons murmured. "That came out during the dog-food poisoning outbreak."

"You can be treated, and your system bolstered to minimize the effects and heal the damage dealt," Blancanales said. "The aflatoxin was the spur that the alkaloid was attached to. Two separate fungi were blended to make this mixture, and a powerful low-frequency sonic transmission took care of driving you nuts."

"Or nuttier," Schwarz added. "You showed a hell of a lot of control."

"It helped that I knew there was a chance that this wasn't going to be either permanent or fatal," Lyons said. "Believed rather than knew. Aflatoxin causes liver cancer and a loss of liver enzymes, right?"

Schwarz nodded. "You're asymptomatic, according to the CDC crew. They're also crop-dusting the city of Gary with bacterium necessary to deal with ergot."

"That will kill whatever molds are present and they won't release more toxin," Lyons said. "What about the people afflicted with Greenwar's weapon?"

"There's going to be a booming market for specialists in northern Indiana for a long time, keeping an eye out for aftereffects of poisoning," Blancanales told him. "We're going to keep an eye on your liver functions every checkup, too."

"Yeah, I'll lay off the hard liquor," Lyons growled. "What about getting back to work? I can stand up, I can pull a trigger and I hate being sidelined."

"You check out." Schwarz sighed. "You sure you're up to it?"

Lyons heaved himself out of bed and onto the floor. "Where's my boots? Greenwar's not dead yet, and I aim to fix that."

CHAPTER SIXTEEN

The President looked at the reports that Stony Man had assembled. So far, they knew that the components of Bezoar's concoction were several molds with complementary mycotoxins that produced digestive incapacitation and hallucinatory effects. The one that attacked the digestive system had no antidote and the potential for long-range health effects, making it a juggernaut of a weapon. So far, the violence that had erupted in Gary, Indiana, had died down, thanks to knowing what to look for as both the sources of the mold contagion and the ultra-low frequency that triggered the hallucinogenic rages that incited madness and chaos across the globe in a dozen locations.

They had also managed to track the next fifty strike targets, the European cities confirmed by a captive Russian who was working alongside Greenwar. The fifty cities were enormous, and the potential for mass illness and contamination would affect over 120 million people worldwide. It wasn't the billions that Bezoar threatened, but so far, China had shown the brutal efficiency with which they would quell riots. The sight of a mushroom cloud expanding on an orbital-mounted camera was chilling, as the President knew that 150,000 human lives had been snuffed out. Another thirty thousand had been confirmed dead in South Africa, both from clashes with the Johannesburg police and from mycotoxin-induced rage that pit madman against madman. Greasy black clouds of smoke rose from the shanty town, indicating that more were dying in the slum.

He turned to Hal Brognola, sighing. "We have a means of decontaminating areas, but we're not able to reverse the effects of the weapon?"

"Aflatoxin is something that can only be ridden out, and then you have to watch for continuing health effects," Brognola said. "One of our people breathed in the air in Gary, however, and he seemed only to be affected by the alkaloid hallucinogen produced by the mold, and that quickly subsided."

"We can rebuild the city, right?" the President asked.

Brognola nodded. "And remove mold contamination." He took a deep breath. "Right now CDC and Department of Agriculture are trying to locate enough materials to neutralize the mold introduced in the upcoming targets, but it's not looking good."

"So we have to prevent a release?" the President asked.

"Which is going to prove difficult, because we're looking globally. There's also the danger that once these major cities are infected, the potential for spread simply through interstate and international commerce is exponential," Brognola explained. "We're on a deadline that ends thirty-four hours from now."

"A day and ten hours," the Man repeated. "Which

could be less, because the mold has to be vented to spread, right?"

"No, we've managed to pinpoint the timetable, so we're on a thirty-four-hour countdown," Brognola said. "One option that the Air Force is thinking of is that it takes temperatures of over 900 degrees Fahrenheit at a few minutes to deactivate the mold spores."

"We fire missiles at the release sites, and if they're in populated areas," the President asked, "how many citizens do we incinerate?"

"It's not something the Farm likes, either, but we're working on a plan that can shut off the countdown," Brognola said.

"Find the people who will release the contagion and kill them," the President concluded.

Brognola nodded.

"That's my order for you, then," he told the head Fed of Stony Man Farm. "I'm not trading noncombatants for the lives of others. You told me, when I first came into office, that there was one particular credo that your people followed. There are no acceptable losses."

"Except in one case," Brognola added.

The President frowned before saying anything more. "The ones responsible for threatening or ending lives. Frankly, these jackasses have murdered at least two hundred thousand people worldwide, and the numbers aren't going to stop. They've earned their punishment. Kill them."

"We're already acting on that contingency, anticipating your response," Brognola answered.

The Man nodded, standing and tossing the files onto the coffee table. "The pundits love raking me over the coals, but if they knew the kind of shit that has been threatening the world on my watch, on my predecessors' watches, they'd agree that they need to take a long drink of 'shut the fuck up.' Hell, I'm sitting in that chair now, remembering what I used to say, and thinking that I was an idiot for being so ignorant."

"Sir, in Stony Man's case, ignorance *is* an excuse," Brognola told him. "We're the guard dogs who stand at the door, waiting for threats so that our families don't have to know fear or suffering. I know one day we'll be found out, gnawing on the thigh bone of someone who tried to break in, and when that day comes, we'll face calls to be put down like mad dogs, but until then, we do our job."

The President grimaced at the thought. "I'm so glad no one has ever caught wind of the Farm. Just imagine what the release of your information would do."

"We've had that sword over our head a few times," Brognola said. "It's not easy, but we've gutted it out."

"If we can stop Bezoar from setting the vents in motion, that will put an end to the threat?" the President asked him.

"It'll give us more leisure to send in containment teams to deactivate the molds and decontaminate any spillover," Brognola said. "Luckily, the Department of Agriculture has a dedicated division tasked toward potential mycotoxic outbreaks."

"They've identified the mold," the President began,

nodding at the files. "What's to keep someone else from using it?"

"We've been watching this, and it's a multilayered combination," Brognola said. "They needed to process tons of mold, store it up in silos in several countries and then find a means of controlling it so that it seemed even worse than it already was. This took years for Bezoar and his cohorts in Greenwar to put together, working under the radar, and only the infrasonic nature of the bomb guidance system gave them the means to orchestrate things."

"Ultra-low-frequency sound," the President mused. "Infrasound has some powerful psychological effects on people, doesn't it?"

"At subthreshold acoustic levels, specific tones, specifically in the seventeen-hertz range, can cause unease and discomfort. Infrasound has been used extensively in entertainment to enhance the 'creepy' feeling that audiences experience, but there have been experiments in how to weaponize it," Brognola said. "Now, with the use of hallucinogenic mycotoxins, it becomes a perfect storm—a complex but thoroughly effective way to snap the wills of entire cities."

"So, I repeat, what keeps someone else from using this technology against us again?" the President inquired.

Brognola smirked. "We know about it now. It won't be a surprise next time."

The Fed's phone chirped, and he pulled it out. There was a quick, hushed conference between him and the person on the other end, taking no more than fifteen seconds. When it was over, Brognola turned to the President.

"Phoenix Force is in position to deal with one of the infrasound projectors operating in Berlin," he told the President. "Hopefully, this will sedate and control the violence in Ostbanhof."

"Trial run," the President said.

Brognola opened his laptop. "We'll be able to keep an eye on things from here. The Farm will send us a secure feed."

The President sat back down, leaning toward the screen, his face set in a mask of concern as three men prepared to throw themselves at a segment of a global crisis.

IT WAS AN ABANDONED church, complete with a tall spire that housed an old, rusting church bell, long since stilled by the loss of parishioners and the money needed to maintain it. The church had been revived with the fall of the Berlin Wall, the Iron Curtain torn and allowing a wave of religious freedom to wash over what had been East Germany, but the global economic crisis of 2007 had silenced the sermons within.

Rafael Encizo, still a practicing Catholic, made a sign of the cross, sending a silent prayer for forgiveness for spilling blood in such a consecrated place. It was a quiet, quick gesture, and he turned his focus back to what needed to be done—stopping the sonic broadcast originating in this building and the influence it held over more than one hundred thousand victims of a double dose of fungal poisons.

If there was one thing that the Cuban commando was able to reconcile, it was the use of violence in the defense of innocent noncombatants. He had little concern for the fate of his foes, whether they surrendered and allowed themselves to be taken to jail or if they chose to fight and fall beneath the bullets and blades he wielded against them. The men he battled had made their choice, and there would be no quarter granted. He, McCarter and James had scanned the building with thermal vision scopes, and had picked up a dozen men working the churchyard's perimeter for security, each of them packing a compact assault rifle and a sidearm. The Farm had picked up several pinpoints where radio communication could be detected, giving the numbers to be closer to twenty with inside staff working on the broadcast beam.

Encizo did a quick touch check, making certain he had a half dozen spare magazines for the Heckler & Koch MP-7 machine pistol, and another half dozen for the P-30 9 mm autopistol by the same maker. The HK P-30 was a slick, easy-to-use little weapon holding 15 rounds in its magazine, and an extra shot up the pipe. He'd gone for a standard double-action/single-action model with a decocking lever just under the hammer and the heavy double-action trigger as the only things preventing an inadvertent discharge.

McCarter was similarly equipped, except he had brought along his Browning Hi-Power 9 mm pistol, a

tool he'd used since he'd first joined the fabled British
Special Air Service. James broke the team's mold, carrying an M-4 carbine with an underbarrel-mounted grenade launcher to help equalize the punch of the small,
three-man team against a group that out numbered them
eight to one.

With the thermal camera recon, and the additional
real-time data received from Stony Man Farm thanks
to satellite surveillance, the members of Phoenix Force
had a formulated game plan. Even so, going into combat was a crapshoot every time they moved. Prepara-
tion, marksmanship, reflexes were all factors in making
things more survivable, but victory was by no means a
given. However, even if they failed in the assault, Price,
back at the Farm, was working to mobilize local German
special forces. That, unfortunately, would take time,
something that Berlin and its besieged suburb could not
afford.

"When you're ready, Rafe," McCarter whispered over
his hands-free communicator.

Encizo had positioned himself at the back door of
the church complex, where the offices would have been
had the building still been an active center of worship.
This was one of the few entrances to the churchyard
that wasn't topped with belly-impaling wrought-iron
spikes. The doors were thick and heavy, but there was
a transom at the top that he'd been able to line with a
puttylike low-velocity explosive detonation cord. He
keyed the explosive, and the outline of the transom
sizzled in a flare, the shutter dropping free as grav-

ity plucked it from where it had been severed from the transom window.

With lightning speed, Encizo rushed the door, leaping and using the friction of his combat boot against the door and its knob to boost him to the lip of the transom. Thick, powerful swimmer's arms hauled him up through the hole he'd cut in relative silence as in the distance, the sudden chatter of a dozen gunshotlike pops occurred, attracting attention at the same moment his much softer detonation went off.

It was a DEF-Tec distraction device, miniature charges set to fire at random like a string of firecrackers, but even more staggered, meant to sound like a gunfight had suddenly started. While Germany had strict gun control laws, it was not strange for criminals to have firearms while the law abiding had been disarmed. The nearby gunfire could have easily been part of a spillover of violence from the nearby rioting suburb.

Sure enough, as Encizo dropped to the floor inside, he swept the hallway with his night-vision goggles, spying men retreating toward the sound of the ruckus. They had been at the extreme range of his IR illuminator beam that the NVDs picked up on, which was even more good news. He turned and waited for David McCarter to drop down beside him.

"I hope Cal can keep them busy without getting hurt," Encizo mentioned. James had used his underbarrel grenade launcher to pop off the distraction device, but he still needed to be closer to the main cathedral, giving his partners a clear avenue of entrance.

James's purpose was to buy them time to locate and disable the broadcast center.

McCarter pulled out a small, compact microphone that looked like a tiny radar dish attached to the handle of a ray gun. He swept the phone, looking at an LED monitor hooked to it by a slender black wire. There was little doubt that the church grounds were ground zero for the infrasonic signal that spurred the rioters further.

Encizo was filled with dread, and had he not learned to focus in reaction to fear, he would have sworn that he was being tormented by an unseen force, a chilling hand reaching from the church's graveyard to clutch his heart from his chest. Shadowy figures seemed to hover in his peripheral vision, ghostly haunts that sought to stay just out of sight, but the Cuban was aware what was making him see these "spirits." The infrasound waves permeating the air vibrated on a frequency that resonated within the vitreal humors of the human eye, and in the presence of those sound waves, apparitions could seemingly appear due to ripples that showed up on the optic nerve. Another thing that helped Encizo cope with the ghostly figures he noticed was the fact that his peripheral vision was blocked by the rubber eyecups of his NVDs. Even if there were such things as ghosts, he wouldn't have been able to see them simply because they would have been hidden.

"This is the joint, and sure as hell, we've got a climb ahead of us," McCarter said, putting away the infrasound-sensitive microphone and its display. "The noise is coming from the bell tower in the cathedral."

Encizo grimaced, tugging off his goggles to restore his true peripheral vision and regain his head's mobility. He'd mapped out the course, and the night-vision device had shown their way was clear. "How're you handling the effects of the infrasound?"

"I'm annoyed and edgy," McCarter said. "We're supposed to make the assault quietly, but damn if I wouldn't mind a row or two on the way to the tower."

"Fight-or-flight instincts," Encizo answered. "You like the fight option."

McCarter nodded. "Time to move."

Encizo unlimbered his MP-7 machine pistol, a foot-long suppressor screwed onto its threaded barrel to capture the escaping gasses of its bullets without retarding the velocity of the slender 4.6 mm rounds to hinder their lightweight impacts any further. If they ran into trouble, the MP-7 would take at least five solid hits to bring down a man-size foe, and despite a rate of fire of 950 rounds a minute, the brief milliseconds it would take to make all of those shots would feel uncomfortably long.

Avoiding close-range, silent combat all lay on Calvin James's shoulders.

ON THE OTHER END of the churchyard, on a roof across the street from the abandoned cathedral and its tall bell tower, the Chicago-born Phoenix Force veteran was nestled in shadow. His dark skin and the broken pattern of blacks and grays on his BDUs made him difficult to see as he sat in an overwatch position for his partners. He looked down at the shielded LED screen of his Combat

PDA, following the progress of Encizo and McCarter, as well as the positions of the security force in the run-down Berlin chapel.

The gunmen that they had located were massed close by, listening to the snap and crack of the distraction devices last petering charges go off. James launched a second of the distraction shells from the grenade launcher beneath his rifle's barrel, depositing the advanced noise-maker in the bushes just across from the twenty-foot-tall wood-and-iron-trimmed cathedral doors. The semblance of a full-blown gunfight rocked to life, and through his thermal scope, James could see the guards in the church spin immediately toward the sound of gunfire.

These men were well trained, immediately able to focus on the sound of trouble while maintaining the discipline necessary to not inadvertently fire a shot.

"They're pros," James whispered into the throat mike of his hands-free radio. "Careful."

"Can you figure out how they're able to keep a bloody focus?" McCarter rasped into James's earbud. "This in-frasound is making me daft."

"Earplugs, maybe even something that produces its own low-volume sonic countervibrations," James offered. "Hold on, there's a guy who looks like he's in charge. He's waving in a squad of men and pointing toward the corridor linking the offices to the cathedral proper."

"The distraction devices only bought us half a minute," McCarter returned. "These bastards caught on quick. We'll handle it."

"Want me to deal with them? Let them know it's a real fight coming to their doorstep?" James asked.

"Hold off," McCarter returned. "It looks like we're sneaking in just ahead of them."

James remained silent, knowing that if McCarter made any sound to acknowledge him, the other two Phoenix warriors would come under enemy fire.

That's when the African-American Phoenix medic noticed movement in the courtyard. Someone had pulled himself into position at a broken window, and would have been unseen except for the active thermal optics attached to James's M-4, something that could be carried all the time without loss of peripheral vision or limitation of head movement as it rode as a scope on a rifle. There was a gunman there, aiming right at him in the darkness, and suddenly the Chicago badass found himself lurching to the rooftop, tarpaper rough against his cheek as he heard the thumps of suppressed rounds strike the cornice of the roof. Other bullets made a zip sound as they sliced through the air above him.

"David, they spotted me!" James breathed into his radio.

"Go hot!" McCarter snarled in a loud voice.

Things had turned around and were going to hell for the infiltrating Phoenix Force.

McCarter and Encizo were on their way up the stairs into the bell tower, stopping and remaining still as they heard the approach of the Greenwar sentries hurrying toward the posts they had been drawn from. There was a moment of silence as a couple of the gunmen paused at the base of steps.

"Get to the hostages. On my signal, drag them out to be human shields," one of them grumbled in German, a language that McCarter understood. He tossed a quick glance at Encizo, who only knew enough to order a meal or ask for directions, but the look on the Phoenix commander's face was more than sufficient to inform the Cuban of what was going on.

Suddenly, McCarter winced at the harsh warning that came over his earbud. "David, they spotted me!"

James had come under fire, which meant that things were breaking down. The moment their sniper opened up, the threat to whatever hostages were present would increase exponentially. "Go hot!"

The shout was loud, sudden, and as he spoke, he snapped up the MP-7, aligning the sights on one of the trio at the base of the stairs. The shadows were no longer any form of concealment for him and Encizo because of the cry, but that didn't matter as much now. Imagery had told them that the bell tower had people within it, but right now, even if there were guards above with whatever hostages there were, the risk to their lives was right below them—the gunmen who intended to use innocents as living bullet sponges to protect themselves.

The tritium front sight of McCarter's machine pistol locked on the upper chest of the lead gunner, a dozen rounds snarled from the end of his suppressor and cut through ribs and chest muscle to tear the man's heart to pieces. The Greenwar terrorist tumbled backward, blood erupting from his lifeless lips even as the other two sentries swung their weapons to bear. McCarter had chosen his first target well, however, as the weight of the man's corpse toppled into the arms of one of the shooters, ruining his aim as Encizo's HK ripped off a half dozen rounds through the face and throat of the unimpeded gunman.

With two burned to the ground, the last of the trio struggled hard to get away from the entanglement of his dead partner, but twin streams of 4.6 mm high-velocity rounds disintegrated upon impact with bone and muscle, and his upper body was turned into hamburger under the two Phoenix fighters' assault.

"Cal, there's at least one guard on hostages in the bell tower," Encizo said into his mike. "Do you have a shot?"

"I'm dealing with incoming fire right now," James answered. "Let me handle this—"

There was a thunderous boom that erupted, echoing through the depths of the chapel and reverberating down the hall. "No, no shot on any hostage takers...it's up to you."

"We've got it," McCarter called. "When I say, you nuke the damn bell."

"Getting the hostages out of the way?" Encizo asked, following on McCarter's heels.

"Yeah," the Phoenix commander returned. He let the MP-7 drop on its sling, drawing his Browning Hi-Power with one sleek, smooth movement. While it might have been counterintuitive for many to transition to a handgun, the Cockney commando was a master surgeon with the World War II-era pistol. Encizo stayed with his MP-7, only pausing for a heartbeat to feed the chatterbox a full magazine and flipping the selector switch to single-shot. With the shoulder stock and the excellent sights, the Cuban could thread needles with the 4.6 mm projectiles it fired.

"Me high, you low," McCarter growled.

"Got it!" Encizo returned.

The Briton didn't even pause as he leaped from the ground, aiming a kick at the door where they figured the hostages would be. Wood splintered on the jamb, the door slamming almost off its hinges with explosive force. McCarter landed inside the room, out of Encizo's way as the Cuban dropped to one knee.

Again, the Greenwar terrorists had been cheap with manpower, but considering four hostages were bound at the wrists, waists and ankles and on their knees, one man was capable of overseeing them with economical ability. The guard, however, was suddenly torn in his reactions between the tall, fox-faced commando and the stocky, swarthy warrior in their two spots.

The brief instant of indecision was rendered moot as McCarter put a single 9 mm parabellum round through the bridge of his nose while Encizo's 4.6 mm rapid-fire salvo punched through his chin and throat, severing his spinal cord on the third shot.

Doubly dead, the gunman collapsed, leaving the hostages safe. The two women wore nun-style headdresses, while the other two with them were bruised burly men wearing coveralls. Their shoes had been taken off, and they were bound and gagged, so it was obvious that these people had been hostages of opportunity, a couple of nuns working with local workmen to refurbish the church in the hope of getting it back on its feet and tending to its flock. McCarter's heart went out to them, he could see the terror in their eyes, right now leavened with a spot of relief due to the fact that the two Phoenix Force commandos were not there to harm them.

Unfortunately, freed hostages in a crisis situation were the most vulnerable hostages, often finding themselves caught in a cross fire. He had to leave them bound and gagged, for their protection. On the ground and quiet, they would be safe until the Greenwarriors had been cleared out.

"Rafe, grab a couple, umbrella move," McCarter grumbled. "Cal!"

"Boom," James said over the earbud.

McCarter scooped the two women hostages in his arms and shoved them to the floor, shielding them as a thunderbolt shook the ceiling, dust and chunks of plaster dropping on them.

As soon as the grenade detonated, McCarter's feeling of unease and need to bolt from the building disappeared. The infrasound blanket that resonated through the building disappeared, meaning that the signal from above was dead.

Encizo lurched to his feet, moving away from the bound handymen, plucking a grenade from his harness. "We're going to get some attention up here soon enough."

"That's why I had Cal pump a grenade into the tower," McCarter said. "They wouldn't think we'd blow the hell out of that if we were concerned about the hostages."

"He's right," James said over the radio. "They're heading to reinforce the rear entrance."

"Weapons free, Cal. Rafe, hold the line here to keep them from running up to grab the hostages. I'm going out to get bloody," McCarter said.

He fed his machine pistol and went out to finish the night's butcher's work.

CHAPTER SEVENTEEN

Hal Brognola strode into the Stony Man Farm War Room, pouring himself a cup of Aaron Kurtzman's high-test coffee to gain a shot of energy after the surveillance of the Greenwar conflict in Berlin.

"What's the latest?" he asked Barbara Price, who stood overlooking the cybercrew's workstations.

"The riots dropped in intensity almost immediately after the bell tower was taken down," Price said. "Right now, the German government has troops assisting in Ostbanhof, utilizing fire departments, paramedics and police from Berlin and the other suburbs. There's a lot of damage, a lot of wounded, and more than three thousand dead so far as we've discovered."

"Any signs of people not succumbing to the toxins and infrasound combination?" Brognola prompted.

"Actually, we're picking up quite a bit from different locations," Price said. "The Brazilian police have discovered pockets of people who have been hiding from the rioters, made immune to the stomach-churning effects of aflatoxin thanks to antifungal medications. It's pretty rare, since the Favela is a huge slum, but Ostbanhof came through much better with a slightly higher rate of medical care."

"Any indications that there were deaf people affected by the infrasound?" Brognola asked.

Price shook her head. "The ultra-low frequency of the tone is felt more than heard. It causes sympathetic resonation within the human body, fluids, bone structure. However, we're looking at a way of neutralizing the sonics."

"The hallucinogen alone is not effective?" Brognola wondered.

Price pursed her lips, looking over her readout. "There are thousands of people still at risk due to the inhaled alkaloid, but without the infrasound to trigger fear and anxiety, the incidents of mass violence are far smaller. We're also seeing a lot of different reactions from populations that have adequate housing, like windows with weather seals."

"The fungal poisons can't get through the weather seal," Brognola concluded.

"Correct," Price answered. "Granted, when stuff goes bad in places such as South Africa or Brazil, where the toxins were released into literal shanty towns, everyone was at risk."

"So what happened in China?" Brognola asked.

"Qingshuihe was in the unfortunate situation of being a town where the infrastructure was stressed beyond the breaking point," Price returned. "There were thousands of extra immigrants and migrant workers in the city, and with an overcrowded flophouse..."

"Windows would be cracked to let in the air even in the coldest weather," Brognola finished. He sighed. "So we're going with a trio of factors combined to turn people into maniacs who believe they're starving to death and driven to terror and fury. If we isolate the factors, things get a little better."

"There's no way to deal with aflatoxin via instant antidote, so we're looking at a million and a half people who could end up as victims of digestive problems and liver or intestinal cancer," Price said. "We've also got them, with the cessation of the infrasound trigger, still in a vulnerable, fragile mental state where they are dealing with confusion and less violent hallucinations for the most part."

"For the most part," Brognola repeated. "But there's still a percentage of these populations who can have very bad reactions, bad acid trips, so to speak."

"You're dating yourself, Hal," Price responded. "But you're right. Luckily, the body can metabolize and eliminate the alkaloid within a week with very little leftover effects."

"Still have to keep an eye on them. Then we're looking at fifty major cities worldwide, aren't we?" Brognola asked.

Price nodded. "We can look at half a billion victims off aflatoxin, even if we're somehow able to intercept the infrasound release. Half a billion people stricken by heavy-duty carcinogens isn't cities going down in flames, but it's still a monstrous crisis."

"Even worse, since the communities hit weren't the extent of the toxin's airborne spread," Brognola said. "Given wind and weather patterns, we could be looking at a solid billion humans potentially stricken by cancer. That's not counting livestock, too."

Price grimaced. "Yeah, Hunt ran the numbers. We could be looking at a severe meat shortage for a release of that magnitude, not to mention that the mold spores would seek out areas to propagate, which means even more flour, rye or other bread products become worthless and dangerous to eat."

"Tell me that we have something to deal with all of this," Brognola said.

"Currently, the Department of Agriculture is working in concert with similar agencies in neighboring countries. The one thing we have on our side now is finally determining Greenwar's weapon. The DoA and the CDC are operating in concert, doing what they can to send out squads to deal with possible fungal storage sites in the areas of the cities that we have listed," Price said. "Those squads are operating under escort from FBI and Department of Energy NEST teams."

"The DoE Nuclear Emergency Strike Teams?" Brognola asked. "Well, they are highly trained in nuclear, biological and chemical hazard conditions."

"If Greenwar has guards on duty, we're speculating that they're not going to be like the force that was in Berlin—a trained group. A dozen cities and a dozen squads is one thing, but fifty cities around the globe is a whole different matter," Price said.

Brognola's jowled face creased into a deep frown. "That's all dependent on knocking the infrasound projectors out of action. Then that relatively bad-off half-billion cancer victims becomes a half-billion-strong riot."

"Beijing already showed how far it was willing to go

to quarantine and contain Bezoar's madness. Just imagine them tossing nukes across borders to keep themselves isolated," Price said.

Brognola nodded. "That's where my frown came from. Russia isn't one to suffer such madness, either. They'd definitely drop hell on anything that compounded Greenwar's attack. Any word from Moscow after we exposed Grozna?"

"They're saying that Grozna was a complete rogue. He had no official sanction to operate within Europe. Whether that's ass covering or solid truth, it really doesn't matter because the State Department and their foreign service are gabbing like gossiping neighbors over Bezoar's threats," Price explained. "So far, we've managed to map out all of the chatter and 'to the vest' operations like the Syrians that Phoenix encountered in Paris. Akira, could you throw it up on my monitor?"

Tokaido nodded, tapping a few keys. There was a flattened globe map on Price's widescreen, high-def monitor, with lines of communication and pinpoints of operational activity occurring planet-wide.

"India looks awful quiet," Brognola said. "That's where the victim in the video hailed from. He was an operative for their government."

Price nodded. "India's quiet, and Pakistan is lit up. That tells me everything I need to know that there's at least a faction in the government or the military who are working on using this as a distraction to clean out Pakistan and make the whole subcontinent theirs."

"But there's no overt military mobilization, is there?" Brognola asked.

"Just one bit that fits the rest of Greenwar's efforts. Wagah, the only road-border town between India and Pakistan, had an outbreak on the Pakistani side," Price said. "Indian troops and law enforcement were assembled, but their purpose was more to provide assistance to their counterparts on the other side of the gate."

"I've seen video of the nightly border closing ceremony. It's hardly Checkpoint Charlie. They puff and preen, but they end things with a handshake," Brognola said.

Price pointed at the screen. "I can't see the soldiers in the city being a part of an armed assault on their neighbors. But look down the Grand Trunk road...Lahore. A ten-million-strong population, counting the rest of the population in the Cantonment, er, state. There are twenty-first-century-level roads connecting it to all of the major cities in Pakistan, especially Islamabad. While the infrasound and hallucinogenic alkaloid might not travel well, the aflatoxin producing spores can and will."

Brognola rubbed his stubble-covered chin. "But something like that could look like an actual attack on Pakistan. It'd take very little effort to convince Islamabad to throw down and hit India back hard.

"So, where's the list of people in the subcontinent, or nearby, who'd profit the most from a shooting war between Pakistan and India?" Brognola asked.

Price tapped a key icon on her portable tablet's screen, and the LCD monitor displayed a list of names.

"We've got players on both sides of the cold war over the Kashmir province, but nothing major has blown up since the 1999 Kargil War. Back then, Pakistan had sent in professional troops under the guise of refugees, and the violence in Kargil was intense. Pakistan has plenty of reason to spark a war, and the radical Islamist factions are not afraid to sacrifice ten million citizens to do it. We've been tracking money, and noticed that one man in particular, Bahkt Mhaanluk, has been moving a lot of cash around, receiving money from elements of Kashmiri insurgent groups, a front company that has alleged ties to the Chinese Special Action Department and the Pakistani military," Price said.

Brognola looked at Mhaanluk's records and his eyes narrowed. "There's also one particular group that really pops on that list of contributors."

Price nodded slowly. "The Lebanese Teachers Struggle Bloc."

Brognola grimaced. "Which is a front company for the Popular Front of Liberation, a Syrian-backed organization working in the fuzzy, porous border between Lebanon and Syria. Mhaanluk is the center of all of this?"

"Not the heart. I'm sure that Bezoar has been working with foreign fighter corps operating and training on Syrian territory to give him the kind of manpower and money needed for all of this."

"Killing or sickening a billion people for what?" Brognola asked.

"Mhaanluk has laid claims to some large tracts of India, what his family owned before the end of the British Raj and the partition of the subcontinent," Price answered. "There's a lot of scholastic dispute with

Mhaanluk's claims, but in the end, the truth doesn't matter to someone who's making a deal with Bezoar."

"Power and land. I suppose the SAD wants northeastern India," Brognola said.

"If it happens, then they'd be happy. The involvement of the Maoist Liberation Organization of Arunchal Pradesh gives them a 'hands-free' approach to the region," Price said.

Brognola looked at Mhaanluk's photograph. "So he's the one funding this. I can see where he's invested a lot in agriculture, specifically growing cereal grasses, which would give him more than sufficient access to spawn the amounts of mycotoxins necessary for this. Bezoar, he might be working officially for Syria, or he might be operating with a rogue element of their Inter-Services Intelligence to retaliate against the U.S. and Israel."

"We're going with the latter theory. Information from the Syrian contact that Phoenix Force worked with has pointed out that they are in no way interested in seeing Bezoar get away with anything. The scientist has gathered a fanatical core of ecoterrorists around himself," Price said.

"Which is why he's using mycotoxins," Brognola concluded. "A natural occurrence in nature."

Price nodded. "But Bezoar also wanted something to put the fear of God into international leaders. Hence the tests, making it seem as if he could infect the whole world."

"Mhaanluk wants to break down India, and he wants to do that with the help of Bezoar's plague. Bezoar sure as hell doesn't want the rest of his efforts to be a distraction, so where is he going from there?" Brognola asked.

"I think I can help with that!" Carmen Delahunt spoke up from her terminal. "I've been researching Bezoar's past, and there's very little data on him before he popped up in the joint KGB-Syrian bioweapons production program in the Mediterranean. The Satan Virus was a holdover from the Cold War, but it wasn't originally a KGB project. I've been going through records from the U.S. Army Medical Research Institute for infectious diseases and found a similar project utilizing weaponized fungal toxins to destroy the food supplies behind the Iron and Bamboo curtains. It never achieved funding, thank God, but the project was still there before Bezoar appeared to be working with hardline old school Communists and eventually Syria."

"We've been operating under the assumption that he was a native Syrian, but he's not?" Brognola asked.

"Ethnically Syrian, but I've been sifting for more about him," Delahunt said. "He appears to be a Charles al-Mahklouf, born in Chicago, Illinois."

Brognola's jaw set. "American. But the name sounds familiar."

"His grand-uncle was the foreign minister under Husni al-Zai'im, and was executed alongside him during the 1949 coup of Syria," Delahunt told him. "Doesn't sound like he'd do a lot to work with the Syrian government, does it?"

"Which is why Damascus is saying he's gone rogue," Price said. She turned to Brognola. "He tried to get revenge, which is why he'd ended up on the watch list and drew the attention of the Syrian hit squad."

"Revenge on who? We haven't heard of any attempts to get at the government," Brognola said. "Unless... who's the director of Amn al-Dawla?"

Huntington Wethers spoke up. "Their state security was headed up by Nur Fakhri. And he was the son of one of the lead generals in the coup in 1949. There's a litany of disputes between the two families that goes back centuries."

"So, a family grudge against one man set Bezoar to destroy the world?" Brognola asked.

Wethers shook his head. "No. He killed Fakhri. His stomach wall disintegrated...presumably the Satan Virus."

Brognola frowned. "Then why...damn it. I should have seen it."

"What?" Price asked.

"Bezoar's voice and attitude. He seemed cold, aloof, distant, but...can you run it again?" Brognola asked. "Do we have any behavioral analysis experts on the Farm?"

"Two FBI BAU experts were rolled in via the black-suit program," Price said.

"Get them, but I think Bezoar may have learned the one lesson about revenge that everyone learns sooner or later," Brognola said.

Price tilted her head, quizzically. "What's that?"

"Be careful what you wish for."

CHARLES AL-MAHKLOUF, aka Bezoar, held up his glass, watching the sunset gleam through the amber liquor within. Only a few minutes ago he'd received word from several sources, specifically his Greenwar operatives in the field across Europe and the operation here in Chicago, that somehow they had located the infrasound beacons responsible for the "warning cities" and shut them down, creating a dramatic decrease in violence in the city of Gary, a stone's throw away along the southern shores of Lake Michigan.

"Sir?" the Greenwar officer queried. "Are you all right?"

"Why would I not be?" Bezoar asked, setting down the tumbler, still admiring the fluid motion of the whiskey within.

"Will this change any of our plans?" the officer asked.

Bezoar hadn't bothered to learn the names of his minions. They didn't know his name, and he didn't care enough to remember them as anything more than pawns who stood between him and whoever would put an end to his apocalyptic goals. Personifying them would only make things more difficult for him emotionally, something he'd learned long ago.

People in the great, seething herds that smothered the Earth were nothing more than a parasitic drain on what could have been a utopian world. Yes, humankind had the potential for greatness, but his years after his expulsion from Rush University Medical Center had been but a single step on the road that led him to the revelation of the worth of the useless apes.

He remembered a night, holding the hand of a little girl who had been shot in a drive-by. He'd worked with the rest of the E.R. crew as they tried to save what was left of her brain from the catastrophic damage that turned its cells to gelatinous slush.

He'd followed the trial; it had been one of those rare instances where the drive-by shooter was a gang member who was aiming at another target altogether. Bezoar watched as every bit of evidence, everything that would have made it a lock for conviction, for the idea of bringing that creature that dared to call itself a man to justice…all of it was crushed and swept aside by the so-called justice system. Bezoar took his name from the very situation he had witnessed.

America needed something to counteract the callous, inhuman poison coursing through her veins. He would do what was necessary, and if America couldn't digest what was necessary, then he would become a true bezoar, the indigestible clot in an animal's gut that absorbed ingested poisons. He used his medical skills to kill the man responsible for the girl's death, and found that he was treated as far worse of a villain than the murderer of a child.

Al-Mahklouf protested. He railed against the American judicial system with his bully pulpit in the press, becoming the darling of a few far-right-wing radio personalities until he condemned the writers of the Constitution. That's when he was sprung from his pretrial confinement by a group of men.

They offered him the ability to strike against the nation that had tried to crucify him for his belief of what had to be done. They were believers in the good old ways of the KGB, tired of seeing justice usurped in their home country, looking for the means of gaining power that could vault them into a position of true power. He had been taken to Syria, and there, Bezoar worked on the Satan Virus, a modification of the enzyme that had subjected a child murderer to such writhing agony that he chewed his own tongue off before his death.

They tested it in Greece, and the hardliners would have succeeded had it not been for the interference of a team of commandos who struck without mercy. Bezoar had watched the events unfold from the joint Soviet-Syrian command center, and knew that there had been a chance for something good in the world. The hardliners had been convinced that these were American agents who'd stopped the harvest hell, men who worked outside and beyond the confines of their hobbling legal system.

Bezoar refused to accompany his hardline masters when they wanted to return to Russia. Syria had been his family's ancestral home, and he felt a bond with the country. When they insisted, they found themselves victims of the same deadly enzyme they'd had him develop. Their corpses were shipped out of Syria with the stern warning that Bezoar would no longer be anyone's tool. As he worked for the whims of Damascus, making materials to wage war on the racists in Israel, he saw courage on the other side, but any positive was quickly pissed away as he watched neighborhoods full of women and children blown to shreds by assault helicopters and fighter-bombers.

Humanity would take one step forward, then slide clumsily a dozen steps back, as if collapsing under the weight of its own ungainly mass. Too many people, too many problems, and there seemed to be no end in sight. Be they massive tidal waves, environmentally catastrophic oil spills, hurricanes or even man-made disasters like epic terrorist attacks, only the worst of situations would draw people together, unifying them to help others. But once the emergency was shown to have ended, they would be back at each others' throats.

Bezoar knew what the solution was. There had to be a unifying threat with no accompanying positive side. It was with cold irony that he realized that the world would have to take a poisonous pill to soothe itself. The mycotoxic cocktail of fungi he'd created, both hallucinogenic and carcinogenic, would be an oppressive, deadly weight that couldn't be shrugged off, that couldn't be personified as it was now a force of nature.

Already, at least three hundred thousand were dead around the world, another one-and-a-half million doomed to a lifetime of health struggles as they battled the aflatoxins working within their bodies. On the other side of the world, Mhaanluk had set up his base in India, allied with Chinese-backed Communists and Pakistani-funded religious fanatics, all of whom were drooling at the thought of carving up the subcontinent to regain lost, ancient territories and enact vengeance for perceived slights. Bezoar hadn't cared what would happen one way or another. The fifty stress points that had been assembled globally by Greenwar were situated in hubs of transportation and agriculture.

Bezoar's fungal biotroph wouldn't be released and affect a mere half billion humans worldwide. It would become an ever-present sword of Damocles for the planet. That was what he'd called the fungal hybrid…Damocles.

"The value of the sword is not that it falls, but that it hangs," Bezoar said out loud.

"Sir?" the Greenwar officer asked.

"The mainstream media isn't reporting that this problem will be over soon," Bezoar told him. "But you see, even if they do somehow kill all of us, it's too late for them. Unless they somehow all band together to purge the world of my little mycotoxic friends, the threat shall always be there. Twelve cities in the hearts of agricultural communities on six continents have been infested, and the mold spores will find a way to survive, to escape. They could shoot me in the head in the next second, and nothing would be stopped, especially with that fool Mhaanluk working in India."

"He has a weapon that he doesn't realize the power of," the Greenwar lieutenant mused. "Of course, we've got the medications to stay alive, to help guide the few survivors of the spreading fungal plague to a better, more peaceful communion with our mother Earth."

Bezoar fought hard to restrain the smirk such a blindly faithful comment inspired in him. It was almost comical how these ecological maniacs were ill-informed about how nature *truly* worked. The spores would eventually mutate to survive antifungal countermeasures. Aflatoxin itself was a persistent threat, engendering constant vigil by farmers and agricultural specialists, and even then, outbreaks still popped up every now and then. Kenya had been one of those instances, and it had been fortunate that only a few died.

Aflatoxin working in concert with the alkaloid hal-lucinogen ergoline would create a pall of madness and starvation. Those with the ability to cure the deadly intestinal cancers produced by the mycotoxin would have their wits hampered by the mind-twisting aspects of lysergic acid. The Greenwar eco-fanatics beneath him were simply delusional enough that anything that warped their minds would go unnoticed. They actually believed that Gaia was a living, thinking goddess that was made up by the totality of Earth's biosphere and that she would end the plague once balance had been restored by Damocles.

The discovery of the infrasonic projectors had refined the effects of Damocles so that its sufferers would be-lieve that they were damned to starvation. Even if the mold didn't destroy billions of tons of cereals, it would still find its way into human bodies because that was what fungus did. It found a way; it adapted and contin-ued to attack.

"Get the vent protocols ready. The silos will release my spores, and Gaia will soon be in balance again," Be-zoar said.

The officer nodded, leaving the scientist in his lounge to take another sip of his drink.

He smiled. "To the men who stopped me the first time, if you can stop the apocalypse I've set in motion, then you will have proven that mankind is worth sav-ing, not exterminating."

Bezoar threw back the final dregs of his liquor, gri-macing at its bitter taste. "Now we enter endgame."

CHAPTER EIGHTEEN

Hal Brognola was back in the Oval Office, his laptop filled with updates from the Farm regarding the on-the-ground efforts by Able Team and Phoenix Force to deal with the violence, what the cyberteam had learned about Bezoar and who he had been working alongside to make such a global effort possible.

The President looked at Mhaanluk's and Bezoar's networks of aides, multiple small radical organizations that had been held together by the separate strands of either religious or political mania, supported by either Syrian or Chinese intelligence networks for the purposes of destabilizing enemies. Bezoar's own contacts within the United States were also an eclectic assemblage of disenfranchised hardcore nihilists who masqueraded as Christian identity or anarchist organizations. Based on the total count of each of the groups involved, Greenwar's membership numbers were obscene, reaching into the tens of thousands, but the truth was that probably fewer than one thousand people were actively in on Bezoar's big plan.

"Chicago doctor," the President said somberly, looking at the screen. "In another world, Bezoar might actually have been something good for the world."

"He started killing out of grief," Brognola countered.

"While you and I both know one man in particular who exemplifies what grief can turn someone into, Bezoar's jump onto that slippery slope threw him down into a gutter."

"Maybe," the President answered. He plugged his internet-enabled phone into the laptop and pressed Play on a recent video mail.

"Mr. President, you have chosen to ignore my demands to make changes in the world. For that, I salute you, and I also salute your teams working against me," Bezoar said, silhouetted, voice distorted. "I don't believe that you will have much more time to wait to know my true identity, but I won't make things any easier for you. All I have to say right now is that my weapon, Damocles, is going to be a test for all of mankind.

"You've figured out what it can do, and how it can turn the world upside down. You also have to know that the fifty cities I intend to strike are just the tip of the iceberg. Damocles is a self-sustaining, highly capable organism that will breed unchecked. You know that fungus is also rapidly evolving and can adapt itself to any environment within a few generations. The USDA is mobilized, so I know that you will try to do your best to minimize the effects of Damocles, but your vigilance will have to be eternal. There are already twelve zones on this planet that are in need of massive decontamination, and millions of people infected and doomed to a lifetime of health problems.

"I will admit one thing to you. If you can stop me before the protocols I've put in motion have counted down, the sword will not fall. But the value of the sword is not that it falls, but that it hangs. It is my lesson to mankind, as I know that I am not the first, nor the last, with the ability to destroy the fragile house of cards you've built. In the end, your idiocracies will have to become smarter and do what is important, or join the dinosaurs in extinction."

The video ended.

"Please tell me that you can sheathe that sword," the President said.

Brognola nodded. "Phoenix Force is currently scrambling to India, and Able Team is back in Chicago."

"Where Bezoar's journey started," the President concluded.

"We're tightening the cyberleash around the necks of Greenwar, and the crew at the Farm is coordinating the efforts of a dozen governments in locating and destroying the silos where the fungi are being stored," Brognola said. "Thanks to the shipping manifests captured from the black market smuggling operation that Able Team hit in Chicago, we've managed to confirm sixty percent of the targets."

"Sixty percent. So instead of half a billion initial victims, only two hundred million will suffer from aflatoxin," the President answered.

"That's why we're still having the Farm work on coordinating the other agencies. Price is soothing egos as fast as she can, and trying to do it without compromising the Sensitive Operations Group's existence," Brognola explained. "Thankfully, we've been able to tap our contacts in the CDC and USAMRIID to be the main spokespeople. We've also got friends inside the World Health

Organization, and we've been spending favors as fast as we can remember them."

"With WHO, we've got something that can actually push through to Beijing and other potentially hostile powers," the President said. "Good idea. But what if WHO can't open the doors fast enough to save the other two hundred million? And hell, two hundred million is an underestimation, given how infectious and insidious Bezoar says the fungus is. He's saying that with the release of this Damocles, the whole world's going to suffer."

"We've run the numbers on the damage done to livestock and grain crops should this spread, and global food resources would be cut by up to sixty percent. Even those without aflatoxic-induced liver cancer or intestinal breakdowns will be left starving," Brognola said. "And the three-fifths of the locations we've covered to be taken out, they only delay the inevitable spread to the outcome of over half the world suddenly without food."

"So we've found out what the weapon is and we've learned how to shut off the hallucinogenic riots, but it's still going to be the springboard to a worldwide starvation epidemic," the President answered. He squeezed his eyebrows, groaning at the thought. "Able Team is certain they have Bezoar targeted in Chicago?"

Brognola nodded.

"And what is Phoenix Force doing?"

Brognola brought up a map of India. "They're being taken in a B-2 Bomber-mounted infiltration HALO pod to Mhaanluk's mountain fortress."

"Mountain fortress," the President repeated. "Well,

according to the reports you have, Mhaanluk can certainly afford to live like a James Bond villain. Why not a mountain fortress? Where did he get it from?"

Brognola tapped a few keys on the laptop. "Mhaanluk is one of the remaining Pakistani infiltrators who entered India in the Kargil war, and he's been working since 1999 to put together everything necessary to bring India's control over the Kargil district to an end. If you look at the map…"

The President's eyes widened. "It's equidistant between Pakistan and China. A line of demarcation for both countries to reach. Hit from the southwest and northeast, India wouldn't stand much of a chance of holding on to that territory."

"The perfect spot to lob the opening shots of a big damned war," Brognola said. "China has already proven that it's willing to detonate a fuel-air explosion to destroy an infected city."

"It wasn't nuclear?" the President asked.

Brognola shook his head. "No. The radiation surge we picked up was solar-flare activity. That doesn't mean 150,000 people aren't dead, though. It was several MOAB-level bombs that incinerated Qingshuihe, maddened victims, spores and all."

Sadness twisted the President's features. "Dead is dead. And let me guess, the forty percent of targets that we haven't gotten a handle on…"

"All along the Chinese and Pakistani borders," Brognola said. "Mhaanluk has been building up a supply of SCUD-class missiles with warheads designed for spreading the mycotoxic spores. India wouldn't have a solid excuse for where the SCUDs were fired from, and no international recourse to help when Pakistan and China move in to attack."

"Of course they wouldn't," the Man returned. "Especially with rogue elements in Islamabad and Beijing cooperating to frame India. And it's not as if the U.S. or any other nation would have room to deal with that problem when we're already trying to contain outbreaks of Damocles in our own borders. Mhaanluk just doesn't know that the firepower he has will backfire on him. The mold spores will spread back to India ahead of even the fastest of armies from either the Aksai Chin or the Kashmir. Three big nations, all pissed off over territory they feel they want to own…"

"A pool of gasoline, and Mhaanluk has the match lit," Brognola said. "That's why we're air-dropping Phoenix Force. They're the only small unit we've got with the firepower and maneuverability to slip in, destroy Mhaanluk and his base of operations and keep all three governments in the dark about what's really happening."

"We've been trying to talk to them, though," the President replied. "I've had the Secretary of State trying to keep heads level over there since you told me about the Pakistani-Chinese rogue elements. She's about ready to pull out her hair over this, but they're talking."

"And we have allies in back channels hunting down the rogue elements. Trouble is, the minute Mhaanluk pops off…"

"World War III," the President concluded. "Three nuclear-armed states with giant armies. This would be a damned nightmare even without Bezoar's bioweapon."

Brognola nodded.

"You'll keep me apprised?" the President asked.

Brognola sighed. "Of course. But if Phoenix blows it… I have a feeling that you'll know the results when northern India explodes."

The President looked at the map on the laptop screen. "Godspeed, Phoenix."

The Oval Office was deathly silent as Brognola closed the laptop.

MHAANLUK PACED back and forth, pausing only to look at the monitor, waiting for it to show Bezoar's features so the stalling damned fool could release the protocol locks that would make the bristling SCUD missiles emplaced in the mountainside something more than decorative gunmetal-gray phallic symbols and paperweights. His dark eyes flared with increasing anger with each circuit of the control room. This was something that no one in the Harkat ul-Mujahideen had seen before.

Mhaanluk was normally a patient man, cunning and manipulative when it came to the assembly and growth of nearly twenty of the fifty-odd insurgent and terrorist groups operating in northern India. With the backing of the Pakistani intelligence and millions in illicit funds sent over the border, Mhaanluk had created a literal subempire that continued to fan the fires of ethnic conflict and international turmoil.

The Kargil operation had allowed Mhaanluk to infiltrate the hated nation of India, the false territories built up and artificially defined by the idiot British upon their abandonment of the subcontinent. Working alongside the Chinese, who'd provided an even greater influx of funds and materiels, Mhaanluk had been able to propel the region into a heightened state of madness and mass murder. Northern India made nearly every other section of the globe seem as if it were a pacifist utopia, as tens of thousands had died in the decade since Mhaanluk's arrival.

That calm and patience was gone now. He was waiting for the keys to the kingdom. Without Bezoar's codes, everything was for naught. Fifty SCUD missiles waited, each holding more than enough fungal spores in its warhead to cover vast tracts of territory with mycotoxins.

Mhaanluk had been chosen for the job of destabilizing northern India for one reason. He was an utter sociopath who only felt one thing in life, the satisfied rush of crushing and destroying lives by the trainload. Pakistani intelligence had done psychiatric evaluations on him and determined that if there was someone who could destroy a nation's ability to control thousands of square miles of its territory, it was Mhaanluk. They gave him money, weapons, ammunition, and with that, Mhaanluk lived dreams of malice and avarice, pitting brother against brother, neighbor against neighbor, pulling the puppet strings of religion and political ideology with the skilled touch of a harpist.

The one thing that Pakistani intelligence hadn't counted on was Mhaanluk discovering the organization known as Greenwar. The meeting between a nihilist intent on reforging humanity through the fires of extinction and a soulless madman who lived for the prospect of planetary extermination had created a perfect storm as the elements of Damocles had come together to create a world-smashing biological weapon.

If Mhaanluk could feel something like love, then he would have professed it for the Syrian-American scientist. He pitied Bezoar in only one way...that the biochemist didn't realize Mhaanluk's complete understanding of the power he now held in his hand.

Certainly the assault of SCUD missiles would incite a shooting war between three on-edge nuclear powers, but even if the Chinese and Pakistanis held their atomic bombs in reserve for the sake of survival, it wouldn't matter. Damocles would destroy human digestive systems, infect and ruin crops, leave vast herds of livestock as rotten meat where they fell. Bezoar had figured Mhaanluk's motivations to be political, when they were as universally destructive as the scientist's. Cold, emotionless logic ruled the sociopath's intellect, and he understood the ability for mold spores to spread, adapt and survive, especially since they were in weaponized format. Mhaanluk didn't even mind that it was possible that he could die in the starvation plague he released. If he lived, whatever survived in the world would be prey for him to stalk and destroy personally. If he died, then he died along with the billions of humans and other creatures on the Eurasian continent, perhaps even around the globe thanks to the vast storehouse of lethal mycotoxic spores at his disposal.

"Sir." Jahbi, one of his communications officers, spoke up. "We've picked up on the wire that China is currently beginning an extensive campaign of dealing with a fungus that has destroyed crops around the city of Qingshuihe."

Mhaanluk turned at the sound of that statement. He'd personally observed the release of Bezoar's Damocles against the Mongolian Chinese settlement, staying in communication with the dispersal team via encrypted radio. He'd told them that their contribution would be vital to the goal of China's regaining the lands they'd lost to the British, and then to the Indians.

As soon as they were in place, Mhaanluk watched them through a web camera, spores unleashed, infrasound humming through the computer speakers, as they clawed at each other, struggling for food to fill their bellies. One man finally had killed all the others for a crumb of cake, then set about tearing the flesh from his dead partners' limbs, gorging until he suffocated himself.

It was the greatest thrill Mhaanluk had ever experienced.

Now, with the news of China actually doing something about the fungus he'd sent to that city, he knew that the jig might be up. The chance of sparking a war with China over northeastern India was going to fade, and quickly.

"Jahbi, call Bezoar," Mhaanluk growled. "We've fallen behind."

"As soon as I got the news, I went to work raising him. Texts, emails, nothing's been answered," Jahbi returned.

Mhaanluk glared at the communications officer. "Anything from the Chicago news?"

"No information about a state of emergency, other than dealing with the sudden riots in Gary dying down," Jahbi said. "It looks like other nations are getting their problems under control, as well."

"They've found a way to counteract the hallucinogenic effects of Damocles, but that doesn't mean they can deal with the aflatoxin," Mhaanluk muttered. "Rowan!"

Mhaanluk's personal computer hacker, a disenfranchised Indian tired of his country being the whipping dog of America's outsourcing critics, jerked his head up from the monitor. "Bezoar set up his protocols tight, but I'm sure I can get this thing cracked. Right now, I'm only about twenty minutes from breaking the code."

"Twenty," Mhaanluk muttered to himself. "Anyone have a hook on mobilization by the Indian military?"

"Jaguar Force is busy with the Maoist guerrillas operating in Khardung, as you've arranged," Bardam, his military intelligence commander, answered. "NDRF, the National Disaster Reaction Force, is mobilized, looking at Pakistan after the Lahore Cantoment had an outbreak. They're bracing for refugees. Basically, India has a lot of fires, and the military is not looking at us. You've got everyone running around, chasing distractions, all according to plan."

"Keep me apprised. Twenty more minutes, and we'll be golden," Mhaanluk said. There was very little satisfaction in his voice. The taste of mass killing was in the air, and like a shark, his instincts were humming. He wanted blood, and he wanted it in waves that only the arsenal of mycotoxin-loaded SCUDs could provide.

Mhaanluk fixed Rowan with a glare, fists clenching and relaxing fitfully. "Twenty minutes."

The computer expert nodded, sweat glistening on his brow.

Rowan had the scent of prey upon him. Mhaanluk could see the terror in his eyes, the discomfort, the knowledge that his existence was utterly contingent. Mhaanluk wondered if he would ever feel the same satisfaction out of an individual, face-to-face kill that he would receive from causing the death of millions, perhaps even billions.

In twenty-one minutes, Mhaanluk intended to find out as he crushed Rowan's throat mercilessly.

INSIDE THE B-2 bomber's bay, David McCarter and the men of Phoenix Force were huddled within the pressurized HALO deployment pod. He'd already noticed the sudden decrease in atmospheric pressure, and he and his team slid into their helmets and High Altitude, Low Opening breathing gear.

Deployment was only moments away. At just under the speed of sound, the B-2 had taken them from Europe to forty-five thousand feet above the Ladakh mountain range. It had taken a few in-flight corrections for the stealth bomber to get them this close as Stony Man Farm and NORAD had continued to narrow down the location of Greenwar's northern India commander, Mhaanluk. The mountain fortress he maintained had once been Namgyal Castle, a ruin that was only ten kilometers from the famous Chemrey Monastery.

Namgyal Castle was nestled against the granite cliffs

of the Ladakh mountain range, and according to the satellite reconnaissance photos he'd observed on his Combat PDA, it was nine stories tall, with thick walls that had withstood the elements for centuries. Thermal readings were difficult because Mhaanluk and his allies had added shielding and scramblers, but McCarter had little doubt that nothing less than an army was going to be present to defend a madman's bid to hurl China, India and Pakistan into a three-way war that would compound the mycotoxic plague unleashed by his arsenal of SCUD-class missiles.

McCarter didn't need to work the slide or bolt on any of his weapons. The Browning Hi-Power in his thigh holster was loaded with a 17-round extended magazine, one extra in the pipe, hammer cocked back with only a swipe of his thumb to bring the pistol to action. He'd battled for years with the Browning in his hand, and it was an extension of his being.

He was only slightly less familiar with the SAF Carbine, better known in Britain as the Sterling Submachine Gun. The SAF was license built in India, and while it was going to be phased out for a newer design, it was still an effective, efficient old warhorse with a 34-round, side-mounted curved magazine, and a sedate rate of fire at 550 rounds per minute.

The rest of the team had gone with SIG-Sauer P-226 9 mm pistols and the Indian version of the 7.62 mm AKMS rifle. Gary Manning, however, who went with the Indian 1A SLR, a locally produced variant of his favored FN-FAL in 7.62 mm NATO. Backup pistols and knives accompanied loadouts of 300 rounds of ammunition for the main weapons and 120 rounds for their sidearms. Manning maintained a kit of plastic explosives and various timers, James had his medical kit and a bandolier of grenades for his 40 mm grenade launcher and everyone had three Indian-army-issue 36 mm hand grenades. With body armor, communications and other assorted gear, each Phoenix commando was burdened beneath the weight of seventy pounds, not including their HALO jump kits.

"Now or never. T.J., count us down," McCarter said.

Hawkins nodded. This was the Texan's milieu now. After joining the Airborne Rangers, he'd trained hard and constantly, giving himself a level of expertise to the point where he became the jumpmaster for his unit.

The deployment pod's doors opened, and below, the world streamed past as a black, slurry blur. The B-2 had noticeably decelerated, so as not to tear apart the men leaping from its belly by ejecting them into a wall of air moving at close to the speed of sound.

"David, go!" Hawkins ordered, his voice audible over speakers in the helmet that McCarter wore.

The Briton launched himself, gravity taking hold of him and sucking him into the inky black night. Even as he fell, there was little way for McCarter to determine which way was up, so he spread his arms and legs to catch the air. Once the small altimeter gauge visible on his visor gave him his bearings, he pulled his limbs in tight, forming a human arrow that raced toward the focus of an infrared laser beacon marking the target, Namgyal Castle.

Somewhere behind him, he heard Hawkins call out

James's name, meaning that only the Texan was left to deploy. Each of the team had a small illuminator visible only through his goggles, infrared beams allowing Hawkins to track the course of Phoenix Force.

"In formation. Keep on target, David," Hawkins said over the comm.

McCarter didn't answer. He didn't have to.

All he had to do for the next several minutes was to plummet to the earth at terminal velocity.

Next stop, Namgyal Castle and their final battle with Greenwar.

CHAPTER NINETEEN

Bezoar wasn't in Chicago's metropolitan area. He wasn't even in Cook County, but to say that he was more than thirty minutes from the Loop would be exaggerating. The building he and Greenwar owned was a fifteen-story mirror-surfaced tower of glass and steel in a suburban industrial park, tall enough that the Willis and Hancock towers were easily visible from even the first floor, and the horizon curved surface of Lake Michigan was noticeable from the top floors.

Carl Lyons sat in the Able Team van, his traditionally dour mood not made any better with his recent brush with rage thrust upon him by a mixture of hallucinogens and infrasound. He'd seen images in his mind, bloody thoughts that showed what would happen if his self-control was ever taken apart by a foe.

His wrists bound, held secure by multiple pairs of handcuffs, he was immobilized by sights of demons wafting through the air, visions brought on by infrasound resonance in the fluids of his eyeballs, and his adrenaline glands were firing at full force. The doubled cuffs and chains had been a necessity, since Lyons had been able to shatter the chain on a pair, albeit nonstandard counterfeit, long ago when he'd gone on his first mission with Able. Fueled by fury, the stocky, powerful

Stony Man warrior would have torn loose from normal restraints. He was glad that he was with Schwarz and Blancanales, men who were not only partners in the field, but literal brothers in blood, even if it was spilled blood.

The anger remained, subdued, no longer spurred by a vibratory frequency designed to drive people mad. They'd neutralized the alkaloid in his system, and had taken liver function tests. By all rights, he should have been free, clean. But someone had violated Lyons, usurped his will and nearly turned him into a monstrous killing machine that would have turned on people undeserving of the kind of rampage he could inflict.

Or worse, he could have attacked his friends before they could restrain him.

He'd have the blood of Schwarz and Blancanales on his hands, all thanks to the bastard whose operation was housed inside the glass tower in front of him. His jaw ground angrily when he felt a calming hand on his shoulder.

"You control the anger," Blancanales said softly.

Lyons nodded, but he was pissed enough to be unable to speak. Too much fury, and he wouldn't be able to focus his firepower or his fighting skills. He wanted to cut loose, and he would, but he had to keep himself on a leash.

Still, the mental image of his fists full of the torn throats of his brothers haunted him.

"Heigh-ho!" Schwarz said, opening the door of the van, dropping to the ground and picking up his toolbox. "It's off to work we go."

Lyons looked Schwarz over. He was dressed in a denim coverall that concealed the armored, load-bearing vest and body-hugging blacksuit beneath. Inside Schwarz's toolbox was one of the three KRISS Vector .45 ACP submachine guns that the trio had brought with them. To have magazine and ammunition commonality between the SMGs and their sidearms, Able Team also carried with them Glock 21 SF handguns, the .45 ACP Glock magazines the basis for the 17- and 30-shot extended magazines that the Vector utilized. Suppressors were ready for both sets of weapons, since they didn't want to alert Bezoar that he'd been discovered until the last moment.

Schwarz hauled his toolbox along with him, with Blancanales bringing up the rear. They had plastered an air-conditioning company logo on the side of their van, the same logo adorning their coveralls and baseball caps. It was the perfect camouflage for the men to enter the building without attracting a second glance.

Schwarz went to the security desk and signed in for them, secure in the knowledge that Aaron Kurtzman had generated a request for maintenance and clearance for the members of Able Team to walk into the building. The bored security guard looked at the signature, glanced to the air-conditioner repairmen, then waved them through. There were no metal detectors that they had to go through; there wouldn't need to be.

The guard himself, Lyons noted, was a simple rent-a-cop, not some mercenary hired to be the wall between infiltration and the building he protected.

That didn't mean Bezoar wasn't surrounded by gun-wielding troops. He owned the top five floors of the office building, and there was a listing of seventy people on the staff of his front company. Lyons wondered how many of them were office workers hired as cover, and how many were Greenwar fanatics who had been assigned to repel the final push by Stony Man against his plans of worldwide apocalypse.

"Control the anger," he repeated under his breath.

Lyons was not a thug. He was a protector, a defender against the monsters of the world. If there were noncombatants surrounding Bezoar, he would hold his fire until he got a clear shot at a threat. As much as he wanted the scientist's death, he fought against the giddy memory of the Damocles fury that showed him promises of spilled blood.

They walked to a service elevator and got on in silence, waiting for the doors to close before the coveralls unzipped. With a powerful shrug, Lyons tore himself out of the concealing garment, letting shredded denim pool on the floor of the elevator car. He bent and immediately went to work drawing out the Vector, affixing its suppressor and slinging it over his neck. Right now, he had a .45 ACP submachine gun that could spit out its 30-round payload at 900 rounds per minute, and bring down targets with ridiculous ease at out to 300 feet. The close quarters of an office building wouldn't provide the need for that kind of stretch, but it also meant he had the marksmanship on hand to thread the needle in taking out a hostage taker cowering behind an innocent human shield.

"Stay cool, bro," Schwarz whispered.

Lyons looked at his friend. "Keep saying that, and you'll piss me off."

Schwarz smiled. "I know. We need Ironman here, not a gelded caveman."

Lyons returned the grin, little humor showing in his eyes. "I grok you."

Schwarz winced. "Wow…you'd almost sound cool… thirty years ago."

Lyons rolled his eyes, focusing on the door.

"Perfectly leavened," Blancanales complimented.

Schwarz smiled. "Hey, I've been cooking Lyons for so many years, the Food Network wants to give me my own show."

"The Irony Chef?" Lyons asked.

Schwarz gave him a mock slap on the shoulder. "Back to grumpy, asshole!"

Lyons bared his teeth. "Thanks."

Schwarz's answer was almost too soft to hear. "Anytime."

THERE WAS A KNOCK at Bezoar's door, and he saw his chief of security, DeMarco, standing there.

"Sir, I think you might want to see this."

Bezoar pursed his lips. "No. If it is what I think it is, have men stationed and ready to shoot."

DeMarco seemed surprised. "Sir?"

"Are they ready? This can't be a coincidence," Bezoar said.

DeMarco nodded. "Yes. Everyone's primed and ready. You've got a literal army between you and the outside world."

"Good. Nothing can stop today. Things are going to remain on schedule," Bezoar said.

DeMarco took a deep breath. "We shouldn't accelerate the countdown?"

Bezoar glared.

"Right. My apologies," DeMarco said. He backed out of the door.

Bezoar opened his drawer, pulling out the pistol that he'd taken off the murderous bastard who'd launched him on a career away from being a healer and toward sitting in the position he was in today. It wasn't anything special, just a 9 mm pistol, fully loaded. It was a Hungarian gun, an FEG something or other, but it worked, and Bezoar had gotten used to it over the years.

Just in case he'd ever run into someone that he couldn't poison.

A bullet was as good as anything else in fixing the world.

Bezoar doubted that if anyone could fight his way through the bodyguards, he could take them down with a handgun, but it was a point of pride. They had to stop him before he unleashed Damocles, the sword that would hang over humanity's head until it got its act together or died out.

If the men who made DeMarco anxious were that good, and that diligent as to fight through an army to save humankind, then mankind truly was worth fighting for. He set his notebook on the desk, open to the page that would give anyone access to the protocols and disarm them, preventing the release of hell upon the surface of the earth. He even had the foresight to have the page laminated, in case his blood sprayed all over it.

There were forty gunmen, though, and all of them were armed to the toenails with Heckler & Koch SMGs and Remington shotguns. Fighting through a gauntlet that thick, unless they somehow tossed an entire army at the building, would be next to impossible.

"What will destiny bring?" Bezoar asked, idly spinning the FEG pistol on the top of his desk. His computer monitor showed video of the men who'd aroused DeMarco's suspicion. They were fit-looking, but uncommonly bulky around their chests and shoulders, as if they were hiding body armor. Each carried a large metal toolbox, as well.

They behaved like bored, quiet workmen, but Bezoar knew that the air-conditioning in this building was flawless. He'd set it up himself, and there were filters within that would stop fungal spores from entering the ventilation system. This tower would be Bezoar's observatory, watching the fall of humankind, so he'd wanted it ready.

He flicked the monitor over to look at the cameras overlooking the service elevator.

"Who's come visiting?" Bezoar asked.

JUDD APONE KNELT behind his shield bearer, Willie Garfield, barely showing anything of his body as he rested the muzzle of his Remington 870 against the side of the tall fiberglass-and-armor tower shield. There was a window through the top that was reinforced, transparent plastic, giving Garfield the ability to see through the slot, giving him something to aim his laser-equipped MP-5 around. The elevator doors were silent, though the floor indicator built into the burnished-steel frame above showed that the car was quietly relentless in reaching their floor.

Apone had his 870 loaded with three rounds of saboted slugs, each one more than capable of punching a three-quarter-inch hole through the metal and shred anything on the other side of it. The follow-up rounds were standard 12-gauge buckshot, for when the doors finally did open. If the invaders were wearing body armor and somehow hadn't been floored by the heavy-duty armor-piercing slugs, then Apone would simply aim low, grinding their legs to chowder while Garfield and his MP-5 directed a stream of tungsten-cored 9 mm slugs into their chests.

Apone and Garfield weren't the only pair who were covering this elevator. Three other teams, all hidden behind thick tower shields, were ready to open fire while repelling enemy bullets. On top of the inch-thick, reinforced-steel shields, they all wore ballistic helmets and Kevlar armor with ceramic trauma plates. Whoever was coming up would need a nuclear bomb just to knock them on their asses before they were yanked to pieces by swarms of projectiles.

Even so, an errant bead of sweat tickled its way down Apone's forehead.

"Stop shaking," he whispered harshly to Garfield.

"Only if you stop, too," the shield man said. "What the fuck is keeping them so long?"

"Keep it down, you idiots," called Chester, standing at the corner. "They want us to get nervous."

"One more floor," Apone stated.

The car paused. It seemed to sit on the floor below them for an eternity, but a quick glance at his watch told Apone that it was only three seconds. Then the elevator dinged.

The doors jerked and started to open.

"Fire!" Chester bellowed.

Apone's 870 bucked violently against his shoulder, and he got off two slugs, accompanied by another six and a blistering forty armor-piercing rounds before the doors bumped open, showing only the torn and tattered interior of an empty car.

"What?" Garfield muttered.

"Reload!" Apone yelled, thumbing new shells into the tube magazine of his shotgun.

Garfield let his MP-5's clip drop to the floor, and he jacked a new stick into place. The others were only moments behind in following their lead.

"Sweep team!" Chester called out.

Four men released a barely audible groan in unison, advancing toward the open doors. Two held it open, while the others edged inward, looking at the ceiling of the elevator car. As soon as they had an angle on the roof, they cut loose with their HK chatterguns, emptying their magazines in short bursts, punching into the elevator shaft above to slaughter anyone perched there.

When the submachine guns were emptied, the gunners held their ground and a fifth man, armed with a hook, entered, pushing at the trapdoor that exited the elevator car and into the shaft. The trapdoor clattered, a sixth using the fifth man as a living stepladder to climb up into the shaft, his SMG tracking up into the darkness.

Apone ground his teeth as the sixth member of the investigation squad disappeared into the elevator shaft. Something was wrong. If someone had been hiding up there, the gunner would have seen him, opened fire, even yelled something as a warning to his comrades in the hallway.

Nothing, which was the word that came down through the trapdoor.

"What the fuck, man?" Garfield asked.

"Focus!" Chester snapped.

Apone chewed his lower lip. "It's a trick. It has to be—"

Suddenly the elevator car disappeared with the sound of two sharp bangs. The three gunners inside of it let out screams that trailed off into the darkness of the shaft below.

"Shit!" Garfield shouted. His finger tightened on the trigger, and luckily he had enough presence of mind to put the contents of his SMG through the open doors of the elevator shaft, avoiding any harm to the men bracketing the entrance.

"Stand down! Stand down!" Chester bellowed.

"Will you can it?" Apone asked. "Yelling doesn't—"

The world suddenly flashed bright white, spiked hammers striking Apone in the ears despite the steel-reinforced Kevlar pot on his head. He staggered backward, losing contact with Garfield in an instant. His eyes saw only an all-consuming yellow fireball that dominated his vision, his head swimming under a high-decibel overpressure assault. Blind and deaf, he wasn't even certain his hand was still wrapped around the stock of the shotgun.

At least if Chester was shouting, he couldn't hear the dumb bastard.

Suddenly, Apone regained his sense of touch as he found himself slammed against the floor, a massive weight riding his back and pinning him down. The mercenary thrashed, but all his fingers could clutch at were smooth, finely fitted tile. He stretched, fighting to get a handhold, and he found a limb and clenched it in a death grip.

Apone's wrist exploded in agony, and he hauled his arm back in, wondering if he even had a hand left at the end of it. His vision started to clear, and he noticed that he had a black claw dangling out of his sleeve, an incongruous thing until he remembered the cool black tactical gloves he'd worn. Curved fingers arched inward, but the hand they were attached to was at a totally wrong angle.

Suddenly, Apone felt himself flipped over onto his back, and through the haze of exploding stars that filled his visual field, he spotted a beastly creature in a black gas mask, blond hair poking out the top of it, cold blue eyes glaring through the lenses.

CARL LYONS RESTRAINED himself as he bounced the mercenary's head off the floor, satisfied that the man's eyes rolled back into his skull into unconscious slumber. Four corpses were at the bottom of the elevator shaft, ten stories below, and the other seven gunmen up here were either out cold or in the process of expiring quickly, heads filled with .45 ACP slugs.

Schwarz and Blancanales had joined him as he swung down the elevator cable, hot on the heels of the exploding flash-bang grenades, attacking swiftly and mercilessly, knocking helmets off the stunned and helpless gunmen after their Vectors tore through the unarmored legs and arms of the three gunmen who had been able to avoid blindness from the trio of high-volume, high-candlepower detonations.

Lyons reloaded his machine pistol, jaw set in the realization that any hope of stealth was gone, but he had expected to have to fight his way through Greenwar's high command. The odds had dropped significantly, thanks to the blazing element of surprise that they'd taken, not only exiting the elevator car, but scaling ten feet above the roof, using the dismantled metal toolboxes as plate armor to further slow whatever gunfire had been put through the roof.

The empty elevator car trick was the oldest one in the book, but Able Team knew it worked well, and knew its weaknesses, preparing for them readily. The metal toolboxes were designed to open into flat shields that would absorb bullet impacts, thanks to a polymer layer sandwiched between two layers of lightweight, high-tensile titanium. The car's ceiling might have been no match for AP slugs, but the multilayered boxes could soak up gunfire, robbing even the most powerful bullets of killing energy. A quick detonation of the pulley system holding the car into place, and Able Team was free to make their move.

"At least a dozen down," Schwarz announced. "How many to go?"

Lyons sneered. "Not enough. Let's move!"

CHAPTER TWENTY

The roof of Namgyal Castle was relatively empty. Indeed, the upper floors were a treacherous patchwork to land on, with large holes leading between the roof to the floor below. McCarter had to steer quickly and tuck in his legs to keep his limbs from being shattered by an off-balance landing on the edge of one hole. He tore away his parachute, releasing the quick clamps on his rig, looking up to see how the others were doing. He'd already called out the sorry state of their landing pad, but felt glad for the relative wreckage on the top of the old castle.

In an effort to minimize the appearance of habitation, Mhaanluk had been smart enough to only inhabit the lower floors of the structure, leaving the higher levels empty and in disrepair, providing a barrier of stone and darkness between satellite observation and whatever headquarters he'd installed. McCarter peered over the lip of another hole between the ninth floor and the eighth, seeing equal amounts of decay below.

"All down," Hawkins announced as he alighted on the roof of the castle.

"Bloody marvelous," McCarter answered. "The top three floors are Swiss fucking cheese, which doesn't bode well for what's below."

"Nervous, David?" Gary Manning asked, repositioning the pouches on his load-bearing vest now that he was no longer burdened by oxygen tanks and parachute harnesses.

The look on the Phoenix Force commander's face was all the indication that the Briton didn't find his Canadian friend's taunt funny at all. "I'm point. You next. You lot with the noisy guns hold back so we don't blow the element of surprise."

With that, McCarter tucked his feet together and hopped, falling to the eighth floor, landing in a crouch to absorb the impact of his weight. He scurried to another hole and grabbed the lip, swinging himself down again. He flipped down his night-vision goggles, scanning the floor and seeing that while there were gaps in the stone, there was an unbroken ceiling beneath them. Manning dropped to his side, seeing everything that McCarter illuminated with his IR light.

"Get the can opener," McCarter told Manning.

With that, the burly Canadian pulled a roll of detonation cord from his demolitions pack, creating a ring on the reinforced floor panel. The process went swiftly for the demo expert, and Manning backed off after plugging a pencil detonator into the putty-like explosive rope.

"Come on down, lads," McCarter invited, but Encizo was already at the pair's back.

"We pop the roof, we're going to attract a lot of attention," Encizo noted.

McCarter shrugged. "There didn't seem to be any missiles in position to fire, and if they do light up, we've got satellites and ABM systems ready to intercept."

"Boom goes the dynamite," Manning whispered.

With that, Mhaanluk's hidden fortress suddenly had a brand-new entrance blown through its ceiling. Hurling concussion grenades through the hole, Phoenix Force followed hot on the heels of their detonations.

ROWAN'S HEAD JERKED up once again, looking away from his monitor as the command center shook with a nearby rumble of explosions. At first, the computer hacker wondered if it was thunder, but he remembered that Mhaanluk had spent a decade insulating the Namgyal fortress to be immune to the elements, as well as invisible to outside detection. He hadn't heard even the worst thunderstorms outside in the years he'd been working directly under the Pakistani terror master.

"Oh, God…" Rowan whispered. He looked at Mhaanluk, who stood immobile, frowning at the sound.

"God's busy. So should you be," Mhaanluk growled. Alarm klaxons blared. "If they reach this control center before I get control of my SCUDs, I'm going to use you as my personal shield, dumb ass!"

Rowan nodded and he turned back to his workstation, fingers flying madly on the keyboard. Bezoar's encryption had built a nigh impenetrable wall around the activation codes for the flight of missiles that Mhaanluk wanted, and he was banging away at it so that gradually he could see more and more of the Pakistani's most precious prize.

One thing niggled at Rowan's mind. In penetrating the walls of protection between the outside and the protocol codes, he'd discovered a small document directed at anyone who penetrated this deeply. Its message was short and simple.

"If you've gotten this far, Mhaanluk has grown impatient. If you release the missiles into his control, you're opening Pandora's Box, except once open, nothing can close it. The weapon inside the missiles is indiscriminate and insidious. Cut loose and launched over the area Mhaanluk wants it to go, you will doom the entire world to extermination.

"Written in truth, Bezoar."

He'd seen it only a moment before the thunderous rumblings shook Namgyal Castle, and now Rowan wondered what he should do. The Pakistani's threat was all too real, but Bezoar promised global extermination if the missiles were released. Now, especially with Mhaanluk's fortress breached, firing the SCUDS would do as much to kill Rowan as the terror master himself.

At least a bullet would prove quick, wouldn't it? Rowan asked himself, even as he continued to gnaw away at the protection that Bezoar put into place. Or maybe it was just a bluff, an empty threat to make certain Mhaanluk behaved.

Whatever the case, Rowan was certain that not giving Mhaanluk at least the semblance of what he wanted would result in something very brutal and painful for him.

There was no choice, and if he did become infested with a plague, as lead he'd have the opportunity to kill himself before the suffering became too great.

He hacked at the encryption more, fighting for the

launch codes byte by byte, remembering an English phrase.

"Damned if you do, and damned if you don't."

THREE HUNDRED ROUNDS might sound like a lot for going into combat, but even the most powerful assault rifle wasn't a homing laser. Gary Manning, a marksman and Phoenix Force's designated sniper, was fully aware of that as he opened up with the SLR-1, 7.62 mm NATO slugs spitting out one at a time, punching into a wooden door that a Greenwar terrorist had taken cover behind. Thick wood had either deflected or minimized the effects of the first two rounds he'd tossed at the enemy gunman who'd thrown himself behind cover the moment his allies began falling like tenpins.

The Canadian fired twice more when finally he noticed the terrorist's leg spasm, kicking out and splashing through a puddle of blood, finally put out of the fight thanks to the powerful penetration of his rifle. Manning discarded the empty magazine and plucked another twenty-rounder from his harness, slapping it home. He'd been tempted to use a hand grenade to root out the guard, but his purpose was a search-and-destroy mission. A fragger would have drawn attention to him as he broke off from the rest of Phoenix Force and sought out where the missiles had been stored. The suppressed FAL-copy, on the other hand, wouldn't attract that kind of heat while rifles and grenades thundered on the other side of the castle.

Mhaanluk and Bezoar would have been savvy enough to store the SCUDs away from the fortress, but there would be a covert access tunnel to allow access for maintenance. Programming and targeting a flight of missiles was one thing, and Manning suspected that now that Bezoar's deadline loomed ever closer, Mhaanluk would have people on hand and ready to send out the deadly salvo on its mission of damnation.

Sure enough, on the first floor of the castle, Manning saw that there was a position where nervous guards stood at the ready, torn between maintaining their posts at a door that was obviously rated to contain contagion, and to join their fellow warriors in the defense of Namgyal. The Canadian lurched back out of sight the moment he saw the pair, but they were in such a heightened state of anxiety that they spotted him. Their rifles were already in their hands, and chattering streams of full-auto bullets raked the corner that Manning had taken cover behind.

The Greenwar sentries were galvanized into standing their ground, and the swarm of 7.62 mm lead ate away chunks of stone. Manning pulled out his metal SWAT mirror and swung it toward the pair. One of them had run out of ammo and was busy trying to quickly reload the weapon, ignoring the radio on his hip. Once he figured out that things would go easier with backup running to his aid, the guard would grab that walkie-talkie and summon help.

That was something that Manning couldn't afford, so he had to act, no matter how dire the consequences. Exposing a piece of himself to take a shot at them would end in serious injury. He plucked the pin from the anti-personnel grenade and hurled it, bouncing it off a wall on an angle that would drop the minibomb between the pair. There was a yelp of terror as the terrorists spotted the ugly black egg hurtling toward them, but it was cut short by the instantaneous detonation of the powerful blaster. Manning took a moment and pulled out a tripwire, hooking a second grenade to it and providing himself with some cover from behind.

Anyone rushing down the hall wouldn't see the fine length of transparent fishing line that was hooked to the grenade's cotter pin. With a kick, the cooked grenade would prime and detonate instantly, blowing reinforcements to ribbons in a crash of high explosive and metal shrapnel fragments.

Booby trap set up, Manning rushed toward the airlock that the two Greenwarriors had been guarding. One of them shuddered, an arm still capable of movement, despite the fact that he was missing his three other limbs. The Canadian barely paused, taking only a moment to level his SLR and punch a mercy round through the man's forehead.

He looked to see if an access card was necessary, but the threat of a spore release on the other side of the door seemed to be all the security necessary to supplement two gunmen covering it.

Manning paused long enough to pull on a MOPP mask, sealing himself off from respiratory contact with errant mold spores. Maybe the SCUDs were airtight, and maybe they weren't. It wasn't a risk he was willing to take as he pried open the airlock door and shut it behind him. He could decontaminate himself later, after exiting the launch bay.

All that mattered right now was that he do the one task that he was sent to do.

Kill Damocles, and kill it with fire. The rocket fuel necessary to hurl the SCUDs hundreds of miles would be more than sufficient to destroy the spores.

As he locked the other airlock door and then jammed one of the dead men's rifles into the handle to secure it, he heard the unmistakable thump of his tripwire going off. Through the glass, he saw severed limbs bouncing on the floor.

It was a grisly sight, but far less guilt-inducing than allowing millions to starve and die thanks to Bezoar's deadly weapon.

CALVIN JAMES GRIMACED as the enemy's AKs chattered, homing in on Encizo and him. Using the grenade launcher on his AKMS, James was drawing the bulk of the enemy force away from McCarter and Hawkins as they worked their way to the command center. Sure enough, the detonations of 40 mm shells in the hallways of the castle were not only attention-getting, but they had also proved once more that having an underbarrel launcher was a great way of evening heavy odds.

Encizo played mop-up alongside his friend, raking dazzled and injured Greenwar troops with his AKM's deathsong in pulsing bursts that seemed as if it would be a sustained stream of automatic fire, but was really only short strings that followed each other swiftly as he let up the trigger, acquired a new sight picture and cut loose once more. Having the advantage of cover thanks to a low wall, the two Phoenix Force commandos had more than enough room to maneuver and fire while being relatively safe behind a foot of stone that ate up the COMBLOC rounds Greenwar was sending their way.

When Encizo didn't have enough ammunition or a good angle on the opposition, and James was between reloading his AKM and its launcher, the Cuban plucked one of the 35 mm antipersonnel hand grenades he'd brought along and hurled it. Sheets of notched steel wire were launched when the explosive core detonated, the sharpened, inflexible metal bouncing off hard surfaces and cutting like butter through anything softer that got in its way. Unfortunately for Mhaanluk's sentries, their bodies and uniforms were that softer surface.

"Any idea how much we've cut through this bunch?" James asked as he rattled off a short burst with his rifle.

Encizo shrugged, feeding his hungry AKM another magazine. "Why, you have somewhere to go after this?"

James ducked as gunfire slashed at the thick stone he used for cover. "Nah, I'm just getting a headache from all this racket."

"Then take an aspirin and keep shooting," Encizo retorted.

James rolled his eyes, forsaking the pain pills and going with the second half of his friend's advice.

McCarter needed them to keep pouring on the pressure and bullets so that he could work his way toward decapitating Greenwar in northern India.

DAVID MCCARTER MONITORED the conversation of his partners over the radio, and suppressed a grin, knowing that they were egging him on. A few hundred rounds of ammunition and a bunch of grenades was quite a lot of firepower for two men to lug, but it wasn't going to last them forever. He paused, looking at T. J. Hawkins, who had spotted a group of men running toward the intersection that James and Encizo had controlled.

"What?" he asked the Texan.

Hawkins nodded. "Empty hallway after those boys passed. I think they've committed as much as they can to rooting out our buddies."

"It's still going to be a lot for them to deal with," McCarter noted.

"Not unless someone puts a boot to their ass," Hawkins said.

"Go for it. I've got the command center and whatever's left there," McCarter said.

With a grin, the Southerner slipped down the corridor that the squad had just entered. McCarter waited for a moment, then was rewarded by a cowboy hoot, accompanied by the sudden crash and rattle of an AKM opening up on full auto.

If that didn't provide Hawkins with the element of surprise in his flanking maneuver, nothing would. The Greenwar troops holding the Namgyal fortress were sewn up neatly. The command center only had a trio of guards at its entrance, and they were smart, not exposing more than an inch of themselves to McCarter as he edged toward them, staying out of sight himself.

The command center backlit the trio of gunmen, making it obvious that there were banks of computers and monitors, all set to the job of directing Mhaanluk's deadly missile salvo.

He set his Sterling across his lap and pulled a pair of flash-bangs, popping the pins on them with his thumbs. One after the other, he skidded them across the floor toward the doorway, one skittering through the door and entering the room they guarded, and one rolling up short, braking to a halt right in front of the command center entrance. McCarter's aim was dead-on, as sandwiched between the twin grenade detonations, the three sentries were left momentarily insensate.

McCarter launched himself, leaping into the open, having shielded himself from the instant of blinding and deafening he'd unleashed. He had his full senses, while the riflemen down the hallway were struck dumb and helpless. One of them had staggered into full view, and the Briton triggered his SAF-1, ripping a line of heavyweight, flat-nosed slugs through the stunned gunner's chest. He flopped noisily and bloodily backward, weapon clattering to the floor with unceremonious quickness.

By the time he toppled, McCarter was in the doorway, lashing his knee into the neck of one of the remaining sentries to his left while jamming the muzzle of his submachine gun against the head of the other rifleman. Slugs burst out of the second's skull as McCarter's full weight shattered the first's collarbone and dislocated neckbones with spine-scissoring force.

A half-blinded soldier, handgun clenched tightly in hand, staggered into view, but even though he was in uniform, he wasn't a trained fighter. McCarter ripped off a short burst that caught Jahbi in the sternum, chopping his heart to ribbons. With a hole blown through his chest, the communications officer collapsed, vomiting blood on his way to the floor.

McCarter scanned the room, looking for any other opposition. There was a slender young man, clutching himself into a fetal position, crying and gibbering as he rocked beneath a keyboard-laden desk. Rowan had been certain that the detonation of the stun grenade was the end of his world, and his mind retreated from the cold logic of breaking encryption to the shelter of madness as he continued to blabber helplessly.

Still, the sight was more than enough to hold McCarter's attention long enough for Bardam to recover his senses and take a shot, punching a single pistol round between the Briton's shoulder blades. The bullet's impact was jarring, but thanks to the layer of Kevlar and the trauma plate in his load-bearing vest, the Phoenix Force commander had another few seconds to turn the sudden ambush around. With a lightning-quick pivot, he brought up the Sterling and emptied the last six rounds in the magazine, parabellum tumblers ripping through the military intelligence officer's guts at 550 rounds per minute. Internal organs rendered useless hash, Bardam sprawled across his workstation, knocking monitors to the floor, where they landed in sprays of sparks and broken LED panels.

McCarter let the Sterling drop on its sling the moment it clacked empty, and he swiftly pulled his Browning Hi-Power from its holster, safety off, fourteen rounds ready to fly at a moment's notice. The transition was so quick that there was a grunt of surprise from behind the Phoenix Force commander.

McCarter pivoted and brought up the Browning, but Mhaanluk's forearm crashed against his wrist, preventing the Briton from aiming at the terror master's head.

A powerful uppercut sliced under McCarter's jaw and knocked him away. Mhaanluk pressed his attack with a slashing spin kick that broke McCarter's middle finger and sent the Browning hurtling across the command center. The Briton bit back a cry of pain over the shattered digit, catching a glimmer of a knife blade in Mhaanluk's hand.

"Bugger," he swore as he leaped backward, feeling the razor-sharp tip of the dagger pluck at the pockets of his load-bearing vest.

"Fucking British! Figures you'd try to shit on my parade!" Mhaanluk growled, lunging again, McCarter only preventing his own disembowelment by using the frame of his empty submachine gun to deflect the keen point.

"Still mad over the damned line of control?" McCarter asked, shrugging out of the sling and holding the SMG like a club. His other hand reached behind his back, but the grab for his Glock 26 was interrupted by a wicked slice that was half an inch short of opening up his forearm like a gutted fish.

"No," Mhaanluk answered. "I just happen to think that you white people just like getting in the way of things that don't matter to you."

"Mankind's extinction matters to everyone, you dumb berk!"

"More to me than you'll ever know, British," Mhaanluk snarled back. McCarter noticed that the Pakistani was circling toward Jahbi and his fallen pistol.

The Briton went for his backup Glock again, but Mhaanluk scooped up a chair with his free hand and hurled it at McCarter. This time, the piece of furniture was enough to disarm the Phoenix Force commander, the empty SMG wrenched from his grip and opening up the cut on his forearm even further.

Still, McCarter had his fingers wrapped around the Glock, and straightened his arm. Mhaanluk charged, pushing the gun hand aside. The gleaming knife flashed again, but McCarter brought up his bloody forearm, blocking the falling point from spearing his heart. The impact against his lacerated limb elicited a pained grunt from the Briton and the two men toppled over a table, crashing to the floor.

The fall separated the two, and McCarter scurried backward, putting his feet between himself and the Pakistani, catching the angry terror master in the shoulders. Mhaanluk grimaced as he felt his collarbone fracture under the impact, but he drove the dagger into McCarter's thigh. Only the presence of his Browning's holster had kept the razor-sharp edge from reaching his femoral artery.

Even so, it was more than enough to cause the Briton to cry out in pain.

"You're dead, British!" Mhaanluk brayed.

The command center suddenly shook, any furniture that still stood suddenly heaving with the flex of the mountain beneath them. The blast could only be one thing: dozens of SCUDs being blown up by thousands of gallons of flammable fuel.

"Damocles…" the Pakistani whispered, distracted by the ground-shaking, mountain-rocking explosion.

"No, damn you, Mhaanluk!" McCarter snarled. Mhaanluk turned at the sound of his name, saw the muzzle of the 9 mm baby Glock, then saw nothing after a brilliant flash of light.

McCarter stuffed the pistol into a pocket to free his hand to take care of his badly wounded right arm and leg. "Cal, you free?"

"David, what's going on?" James asked.

"I'm cut into bloody bread slices. Literally! Why do you think I'm calling you?" McCarter asked. "I'm leaking all over the place."

"On my way," James said. "Our resident Texan did a great job playing the cavalry. We were running out of bullets for these bastards."

"Any word from Gary?" McCarter asked.

"What, a granite cliff imploding from a fuel-air explosion wasn't enough?" Manning's voice said.

"How the hell are you doing?" McCarter asked nonchalantly.

"I banged my knee when the ground decided to jump three feet," Manning answered. "But I can still walk."

"The spores are dead, right?" McCarter continued.

There was a sigh on the other end. "A few thousand gallons of military-grade rocket fuel. If angry mushrooms can live through that going up, then they can have the damned planet."

McCarter nodded, smirking. "That'll do. Thanks for saving my arse with that big boomer."

"Don't mention it," Manning returned.

McCarter closed his eyes. "That's a deal."

CHAPTER TWENTY-ONE

DeMarco clutched his shoulder, clamping his fingers so tight over the torn muscle that he could feel the ugly, mushroom-shaped clot of copper and lead squeezed between the tissues inside. The whole arm was numb, blood pouring down the limb after he tried to sneak up on one of the three commandos who'd raided the office building. The man had emptied his submachine gun, and was in the process of reloading it when DeMarco tried to make his ambush.

The whole thing was shot to hell when the Able Team attacker, Hermann Schwarz, seemed to exhibit a sixth sense at the security commander's approach. With the speed of a cobra, Schwarz drew his Glock 21-SF and fired blindly. He hit DeMarco twice in the body armor, but one round embedded itself deep in his shoulder joint. More than muscle was damaged by the passage of the bullet, not with the bright red, arterial blood pouring down his sleeve and the complete lack of sensation in the whole ruined arm. He scurried along, retreating from the battle before he became another victim of the brutal trio who had stormed Greenwar's headquarters.

He had no clue as to how many of his troops were left, but he'd lost contact with more than a third of his force the moment they announced they'd made contact with the elevator they were supposedly on. DeMarco dispatched reinforcements to help them out, following quickly on their heels, but the Greenwar guards had run into a wall of blazing gunfire.

DeMarco couldn't be certain, but he thought that he recognized the machine guns he'd issued to his men being used against them while the trio had other, science-fiction-looking weapons slung over their shoulders. Closing in on Schwarz, DeMarco recognized that the Able Team commando was carrying a Vector SMG.

It made sense to DeMarco. Greenwar's guards had been packing armor-piercing ammo in their MP-5s, and he was hard-pressed to imagine a .45-caliber AP round. They were being screwed by their own guns.

DeMarco stopped in a doorway, panting. He clamped his blood-soaked hand on the jamb to keep from slipping, noticing the dead, dangling thing that hung from what used to be a shoulder. If he made it out of this, he was going to be crippled for life. He grimaced at the sight of his useless limb, then stiffened at the sound of footsteps behind him.

DeMarco whirled, and saw Schwarz, the Able Team commando he'd tried to flank while reloading. He lifted one bloody hand in surrender.

"Wait! Wait! Don't shoot!" DeMarco shouted.

Schwarz had the Glock leveled at his face, unwavering. "Kneel and put your hands behind your head."

"I've only got one hand that I can move," DeMarco answered as he dropped to his knees. "I'm done."

Schwarz eyed him warily. There was no way to fake the huge, ugly cavity and the odd dangling motion of a dead arm, at least nothing that could have been accomplished in less than a minute and a half. Keeping his distance, he gripped DeMarco's wrist, twisted his good arm, and cuffed his wrist to a doorknob, cinching the other end tightly and behind the security chief's back. "Don't move, and you'll live."

DeMarco eyed the Able Team commando warily. "You guys aren't SWAT."

Schwarz jammed a pressure bandage into the wound, applying force to the artery that was quickly squirting out DeMarco's lifeblood. "No. We don't care about making arrests. I'm not even sure why I'm working so hard to keep you from bleeding to death."

"Because I quit. Soldiers don't murder helpless people. Not good ones," DeMarco said.

Schwarz frowned, tying down the pressure dressing with a stretch of tape. "You're a good soldier?"

DeMarco looked at his bloody, tourniqueted limb. He'd live, but he'd be maimed, probably even have the arm amputated. "I'm just following orders. Bezoar's orders."

Schwarz stepped away from DeMarco. "Don't remind me that you work for him. You know how many helpless people are dead because of him? In China? In South Africa? Just across the state line in Indiana?"

DeMarco looked at the ire in the Able Team commando's eyes. "He hired me to protect this place. That's all."

Schwarz sneered. "No. A good soldier doesn't kill helpless targets. But you'd better hope I'm a good enough field medic that your tourniquet doesn't come loose and you bleed to death anyway."

DeMarco winced as his other shoulder began to cramp behind his back. "Are you going to loosen these cuffs? I'm not going to be going anywhere."

"No, you're not. But the more you stay still, the more likely you are to keep that tourniquet tight," Schwarz said. "I made sure your life is safe, comfort be damned. You fidget enough, try to make your other shoulder comfortable, who knows what's going to come loose. That's all the orders I need to follow, and my order for you is to sit your murderous little ass still."

DeMarco swallowed hard, grimacing as Schwarz turned and left him behind. His tourniquet still hadn't loosened by the time Blancanales arrived to make sure he wouldn't bleed to death.

CARL LYONS KICKED down the door to Bezoar's office. He'd expended so much ammunition in the battle through the mad scientist's security force, both MP-5 and Vector magazines, that all he had left was the Smith & Wesson .357 Magnum he carried for backup. Bezoar didn't flinch as the broken door crunched beneath the Able Team leader's boots, nor did he cower from the long-barreled cannon aimed at him. Lyons frowned, noting that Bezoar had a pistol in one hand, a notebook in the other.

"Drop the weapon," Lyons ordered.

Bezoar raised an eyebrow. The 9 mm FEG wasn't aimed anywhere in particular, but it was still a weapon in an enemy's hand. Lyons didn't like the look of this.

"Are you a computer expert, sir?" Bezoar asked.

Lyons shook his head. "He should be along shortly, though. Why do you ask?"

Bezoar set the notebook on the desk in front of him, tapping the laminated top page. "These are the instructions necessary to defang the Damocles network I've set up. You've been pretty quick, I must admit."

"Does that go for the bastard and his army in northern India, too?" Lyons asked.

"Mhaanluk? He wouldn't be able to fire off any of those missiles without the proper access. There're layers of black ice that it would take a genius to bust through, and even if they did, they'd come across a warning about what would really happen if he continued," Bezoar said.

Lyons lowered the .357, but he didn't put it away. He'd spent his time around enough criminals and terrorists to know that dead, calm voice that accompanied the decision to commit suicide by cop. The pistol in Bezoar's hand was all the trigger necessary for anyone to recognize as a threat. "So, why don't you put down the pistol?"

"I've made some shrewd decisions based on one single fact, that the world itself is a rotten, hopeless place where no good remains. Nations will squabble, fully willing to throw away sanity for the sake of petty arguments. Laws will be perverted not for the sake of justice, but to allow murderers to go free," Bezoar said.

"Dr. al-Mahklouf, you didn't allow a murderer to go free," Lyons said. "You may have broken the law…"

"Because I did one good thing doesn't mean shit. Not with the people I've sacrificed for my little social experiment. I expected the governments to keep to themselves, to scramble to make deals with me. Instead, I've been listening to the news. It seems that even the Chinese and United States governments are working together to fight a new form of ergot that has cost lives in an outbreak," Bezoar said. "No... I'd had a psychotic break, trying to punish everyone for a crime that had gone unanswered."

"Put the gun down. You'll go to prison, and you'll pay your debt to the world. Especially if you do something to help the people you've sickened with aflatoxin," Lyons said.

"I've run a tally of the people who died. Is a lifetime in prison worth 324,876 lives?" Bezoar asked.

Lyons felt rage welling inside of him, but he wasn't going to let his emotions override his intellect, nor his morality. "No. But how about the 1.4 million who will need to deal with the cancer you've condemned them to? Fair enough trade."

"You don't have to barter with me for a cure," Bezoar said. "The formula that will counteract Damocles's long-term health effects and to neutralize what pockets have survived have been written down with the protocol cancellation codes."

Lyons looked at the laminated sheet of paper. "I'm not like you, Doctor—"

"Bezoar. No doctor. Hippocrates would spit on me if he knew what I had done."

"I can't kill someone who won't fight back. And I know you're going to take a pot shot at me to get me to shoot you. The armor I'm wearing is way too good for that pop gun you're carrying."

Bezoar sighed. "So you'll let me live, and a mass murderer gets to live, free from punishment? Where's the justice in that?"

Lyons took a deep breath. "Fill your hand, you son of a bitch."

Bezoar smiled, turning the FEG's muzzle toward the Able Team leader. "Thank you."

Lyons's Magnum bellowed.

"Don't thank me, bastard," Lyons snarled back.

He knew that the bitter taste in his mouth wouldn't be washed away with a million drinks.

He picked up the notebook with the neatly typed formulae necessary to undo whatever liver and intestinal damage had been inflicted upon a million and a half people.

No, the bitter truth that Bezoar was right about what was justice and what wasn't couldn't be washed away through drinking. But maybe, with dozens of nations working together to heal the effects of the horrors Bezoar had unleashed, the betterment of a whole world, the tiny steps taken toward international cooperation and global sanity, would make Earth a sweeter place.

"It'd be pretty to think so," Lyons answered himself. He turned and went to find Schwarz, ignoring the corpse sprawled on the office floor behind him.

Extinction had been derailed again.

* * * * *

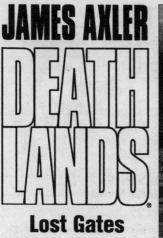
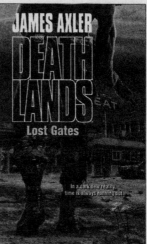

TAKE 'EM FREE

2 action-packed novels plus a mystery bonus

NO RISK
NO OBLIGATION TO BUY

James Axler
Outlanders®

INFESTATION CUBED

**Earth's saviors are on the run as
more nightmares descend upon Earth…**

Ullikummis, the would-be cruel master of Earth, has captured
Brigid Baptiste, luring Kane and Grant on a dangerous pursuit. All
while pan-terrestrial scientists conduct a horrifying experiment
in parasitic mind control. But true evil has yet to reveal itself, as
the alliance scrambles to regroup—before humankind loses its
last and only hope.

Available November wherever books are sold.